THE DAY OF DOOM

A Toal came striding through the shattered gate, a dark tower against the light. Someone hurled a boar spear. It missed. The Toal gestured. A bolt of power blasted a gap in the furniture wall. Ventimiglian soldiers sprang forward. Blades darted and clashed. Men cried out. The Toal came on like something out of a nightmare. . . .

The Toal flung an arm around in a hard horizontal arc. People toppled like wheat at the stroke of a scythe. A black mailed fist smote Gathrid's chest . . . and a darkness closed in . . . got to hide, he thought. . . .

THE SWORDBEARER
GLEN COOK

A TOM DOHERTY ASSOCIATES BOOK
NEW YORK

THE SWORDBEARER

Copyright © 1982 by Glen Cook

A Tor Book
Published by Tom Doherty Associates, Inc.
49 West 24th Street
New York, N.Y. 10010

Cover art by Keith Berdak

ISBN: 0-812-50307-4

First edition: June 1990

Printed in the United States of America

0 9 8 7 6 5 4 3 2 1

Chapter One
Kacalief

Summer dessicated the earth and made the horizons waver behind air heavy with dust and pollen. There was no breeze to gentle the gnawing heat.

Hooves thundered across hard earth. A war cry slapped the morning's face. A crack hit the still air as a rider's blade bit an oaken post standing in the center of a field where only the most determined grasses survived. A woodchip arced away.

The rider's sword flew from his hand. It spun across the powdery earth.

A fifteen year old sat watching his brothers rehearse the skills of war. He had his behind nestled in a grassy hummock. His arms were around his shins. His chin rested on his knees. His face was grim. He smiled only weakly when Belthar gave his brother hell.

Fabric rustled behind him. He did not turn. His sister came round his shade bush and settled beside him. She was a year older, blonde and striking. She would become a beautiful woman.

Anger flashed in her pale gray eyes. "Gathrid?"

"Uhm?"

"I heard you had another argument with Father."

"Uh-huh. Same old fight. He won't let me train with Mitar and Haghen. Don't let the poor cripple get hurt. . . ."

"He'll never let you, either. Not if you keep pushing him. You've got to get around sideways and make him think it's his idea. I don't have any trouble."

"I'm not a girl, Anyeck. I can't do all that bounce and soft eyes and 'Oh, please, Daddy.' "

Anyeck laughed. "You make me sound like a courtesan."

"Sometimes you act like one."

"You're looking for lumps from everybody, aren't you?"

"I . . ."

A horrendous thump interrupted them. They sprang up. Their brother Haghen had fallen off his horse. Belthar and his men rushed him. Belthar started cursing.

"He's all right," Anyeck said. "Belthar wouldn't yell if he wasn't. That's really what you want to go through, huh?"

Haghen rose and beat dust off himself. Gathrid did not reply.

Anyeck continued, "There was a messenger from the Dolvin. Father has to go to Hartog. I'm going to get him to let me go, too. He said he'll leave as soon as Symen gets back from Rigdon."

Gathrid became worried. His father was just an unimportant knight in one small corner of Gudermuth. His liege, the Dolvin, was responsible for Gudermuth's entire frontier with the kingdom of Grevening. "You think it's because Father hanged those raiders?"

"Franaker Huthsing sent them over, but even he wouldn't have the gall to complain if they got caught and hanged. I don't know what it is. He just said he has to go."

Gathrid's family and its retainers lived in a small fortress called Kacalief. Their father was Safire, or knight protector. The Dolvin's Savard March, guarding the kingdom of Gudermuth's easternmost frontier, had been in dispute between the Kings of Gudermuth and Grevening for decades. The Sheriff of Rigdon, a town on the Grevening side of the border, had a habit of sending small bands of bravos over to cause trouble. The latest bunch had gotten out of hand and killed some sheep. The Safire had hanged them. He had sent his oldest son to return the bodies.

"Maybe Huthsing won't be so pushy now," Gathrid said. He watched his brother Mitar gallop around. Mitar was clumsier than Haghen.

"Maybe." Anyeck seemed unconvinced. Or just not interested. "Really, why do you want to go out there and get yourself knocked around? What do you want to prove, anyway?"

Gathrid scowled at her, turned his attention to the field. He didn't have to answer that.

He had had a brief bout with polio. It had affected one arm and one leg. The corner of one eye drooped. The disease hadn't crippled him, but his father considered his slight handicap sufficient to prevent his ever becoming a knight.

"They're turning me into a jester, Anyeck. All they let me do is study. I'm bored stiff with Plauen's lectures about the Golden Age and Anderle. I'm up to here with learning numbers and languages."

"Somebody has to do those things, Gathrid."

"Somebody who gets paid. I don't see you going into ecstasy over Plauen's lessons. It's not manly, scribbling in books, playing with numbers, studying old stories about the Immortal Twins and Tureck Aarant. Who cares about them anymore, anyway? They've been dead for a thousand years."

Anyeck laid a gentle hand on his arm. "Don't get upset. Maybe while Father and I are gone . . ."

"You're kidding. Can you see Belthar doing anything without Father's okay?"

"No. I guess not. Maybe I'll talk to him."

They sat there a while, watching their brothers build themselves cases of sore muscles and bruises. The shadow of the bush began to dwindle. Gathrid drifted off on a reverie. In daydreams he could be the most dreaded warrior ever to have lived. Men would pale at the naming of his name. No weakness hampered him in daydreams.

Anyeck nudged him. "Symen is coming."

Gathrid opened his eyes. Symen and his men-at-arms were approaching at a canter. Something about them portended bad news. The men on the practice field racked their weapons and dismounted. They formed a clump and waited. They reacted like herd animals sensing danger.

Gathrid stood, helped Anyeck rise. Hand in hand, they went to join the others. They were close. She was the only one who understood him. He was her only confidant.

Gathrid limped slightly. It was barely noticeable. There had been champions more handicapped than he. By Heaven, he thought, Cashion was blind.

It was an old, old world. Its inhabitants were a worn and weary people fallen into long rhythms of empire and dark age. Its unremitting feudalism remained eternally static.

Symen stopped his animal and swung down. He handed his reins to a soldier. His homely face was drawn and pale. "You look like you've seen a ghost," Haghen observed.

Symen shuddered. "No. But I did see the shape of tomorrow."

Gathrid glanced at his sister and frowned. "What happened?" Anyeck asked. "Did Huthsing? . . ."

"It wasn't Franaker Huthsing. He's a toy devil compared to this."

"What, then?"

"Ventimiglia invaded Grevening. From the Tower in Rigdon you can see the smoke of the burning villages. The whole eastern horizon looks like there's a big bank of fog coming in." Symen's eyes seemed haunted as he exchanged glances with each of his siblings.

Every year the eastern darkness had crept a little closer. Now it was devouring Grevening. There would be no more buffers. There would be no more illusions about Ventimiglia being satisfied with what it had taken. The Grevening border was so close Kacalief's people would be looking tomorrow in the eye.

The world's last great empire, Anderle, had torn itself apart ages ago. Only now, after centuries, had the cycle turned. The Mindak Ahlert of Ventimiglia, with his wizardries and exhumations of ancient sorceries, was riding a rising wave.

Gathrid shuddered. How long before that wave crashed upon tiny Gudermuth? This summer? Or would Ahlert wait a year? "I think I know why the Dolvin wants Father," he said.

Anyeck nodded, squeezed his hand. Her fingers were cool and moist. She didn't say anything.

She was seldom at a loss for words. Usually she was full of chatter and scatterbrained plans for fleeing Kacalief to make herself a great lady. She wanted to take back what her mother had given up by becoming Safirina.

In a soft, frightened voice, Symen said, "They say the stories aren't exaggerated. They say Nieroda and the Toal are killing everybody."

"They're real?" Mitar asked. "Did you see them?"

"No. I didn't want to. Seeing some of their victims was enough."

The Toal, often called the Dead Captains, and their commander, Nevenka Nieroda, were the most terrible horrors the eastern sorcery had dredged from the past. They commanded a merciless sorcery uniquely their own.

They could not be killed, for they had died already, in battles ages past.

"I have to tell Father." There was no relish in Symen's voice, just a sad resignation.

He thinks we're living on borrowed time, Gathrid thought.

His vision of himself as a great champion dispersed before this dread new wind. It seemed silly. The Dead Captains. Who could stand against them? Maybe a Magister of the Brotherhood. Not a gimp boy from Kacalief. You're a fool, Gathrid, he told himself.

The whole crowd walked slowly up to the castle. They remained very quiet. Anyeck murmured, "I don't think I want to go to Hartog now. It would be too depressing."

"Uhm." Depression had arrived already. Symen's news was a thunderclap declaring the end of an era. Borrowed time, Gathrid thought again. He glanced toward the border.

The day seemed normal enough. No evidence of war rode Grevening's western winds.

The Safire met them at the gate. He was an almost laughably tall, lean, craggy man. He proclaimed himself the ugliest man alive. With the exception of Symen, his children took their looks from their mother. In her youth the Safirina had been one of the great beauties of the royal court at Katich. Twenty-five years after the fact, Gudermuth's nobility remained bemused because the Safire had wooed and wed the woman.

The Safire was a dour and quiet man. The occasions of his smiles were historical reference points. Today he appeared more gloomy than ever. "Huthsing get a little too melodramatic, Symen?"

"Didn't say a word about them, Father. He had other things on his mind," he explained.

"That explains why the Dolvin summoned me. We'll be next. I suppose there's no time to waste. Though Heaven knows what rush there is when you face the invincible."

Gudermuth had no realistic hope should the Mindak choose to take her. She was another of dozens of tiny, feeble states filling the continental hinterland. Ventimiglia was, reputedly, already as vast as the Anderlean Imperium at its greatest extent. Ahlert would swat Gudermuth down like a rude puppy. His weapons would be Nevenka Nieroda, the Toal and his sorcerer generals. And an army so vast no one could count the number of men in it.

The world was old. Its historics were layered and deep. There were living sorceries, and memories and shadows and ghosts of sorceries, dense upon every land. A man of power could stand anywhere and touch some echoed wizardry of the past. He need but have the confidence and strength to reach out and seize it.

The Mindak of Ventimiglia had the confidence, strength and will. He was hammering out an empire built of the bones of little kingdoms like Grevening and Gudermuth.

"Is it really all so hopeless?" Mitar asked. "They're men the same as us."

"It's probably worse," the Safire grumbled. "What are you doing here? Take them back to the practice field, Belthar. Gathrid. Anyeck. Why aren't you at your studies? Mhirken. Saddle me a horse."

Fifteen minutes later the Safire and his esquire departed, bound for the Dolvin's castle. Gathrid and Anyeck watched them go. "What're you going to do?" the youth asked.

"Do?" His sister seemed puzzled.

"Sure. You always figure an angle." In his sourer moments Gathrid thought Anyeck a greedy, ill-tempered, conniving little witch. Totally self-centered. And half-crazy with her silly schemes for getting their father to send her to Gudermuth's capital, Katich. Or to one of the great cities in Malmberget or Bilgoraj, the bellwether kingdoms of the west. Or, better still, to Sartain, the vast island city constituting the heart of today's diminuated Imperium.

She was determined to profit from an outstanding marriage.

"Don't be so bitter. Yes. Maybe there is an angle in this. Maybe he'll listen now. For my safety." She became thoughtful. After a while she began unrolling an implausible plot.

He loved her anyway. They were best friends. She listened to his dreams, too. And she did not laugh.

"We'd better find Plauen. Father will check." The Safire was a methodical man.

"Wow. I'm overwhelmed." She was no more excited about education than he.

Their instructor, Mikas Plauen, was doing his Brotherhood Novitiate. The Safire had contracted his services with his Order, the Yellow.

The Brotherhood was an anomaly of the times, a nonsectarian organization which, nevertheless, displayed characteristics of a religious mystery cult. Its avowed purpose was to preserve, conserve and transmit knowledge. The lower ranks everywhere appeared as court scribes, secretaries and, as here, as instructors of the nobly-born.

At its highest levels, though, the Brotherhood formed the aristocracy of wizardry. All the great western sorcerers belonged, and at the very top stood several men possibly the equal of the Mindak of Ventimiglia.

There were two major Orders, the Red and the Blue, and three minor, the White, the Yellow and the Green. The minor Orders remained devoted to the Brotherhood's founding purpose.

The Red and Blue, though, had become worldly, political and contentious, always striving for control of the Brotherhood and the temporal power that mastery represented. Many an intrigue had been played between the two. The Blue Order was dominant at the moment, but the Red was making a comeback under a cunning, vicious, unscrupulous Magister named Gerdes Mulenex. Rumor said this Mulenex was a western would-be Mindak.

Gathrid did not care. He couldn't untangle the political and philosophical differences between the Orders. He saw only naked power lust. For him it was enough to know that the Orders existed and that, though they supposedly shared a common purpose, sometimes contended to the point of armed confrontation.

The lesson of the day was another of Plauen's dull monologs on the Fall of Anderle. Plauen was not a skilled teacher. He could make anything boring.

"Why are we studying this stuff about the Tempter and the Twins?" Gathrid asked. "They've been dead a thousand years."

"I notice you don't complain when we study Tureck Aarant, Chrismer or one of those."

"They were heroes."

"You're interested in them. That's all. Except for Aarant, they don't have many lessons for us. The Immortal Twins, and Grellner and Aarant, and to a secondary extent, Theis Rogala, are the ones who left a significant legacy. They made the mistakes from which we should learn."

Gathrid shook his head. Same old thing. Over and over and over again. Learn from the mistakes of the past. That was stupid. Only fools lived in the past. His father had said so.

"Pay attention, Gathrid. It's important that you two learn. Nudge Anyeck, please. She's sleeping with her eyes open. Heavens. What am I going to do? They're cretins, and I'm supposed to have them ready in time for . . ."

A chill crept down Gathrid's spine. There was something grim about Plauen's muttering. "In time for what, Brother?" he demanded.

"Nothing. Adulthood, I suppose. I'm sorry. You're

exasperating me. I've never dealt with such stubborn students.''

Gathrid became mildly embarrassed. That surprised him. Plauen's tactics usually irritated him. Maybe it was the implication of deliberate ignorance colliding with his knowledge that he *had* been sabotaging the sessions.

''We don't *know* what Aarant, Grellner and their contemporaries were really like,'' Plauen said, resuming his lesson. ''The stories we have now were shaped by a thousand retellings, and it's in those retellings that they've acquired their significance for us today. The characters we associate with the Brothers' War have become archetypes. Grellner brought Temptation into the Paradise of Anderle. The Immortal Twins lost Innocence. . . .''

Gathrid had heard the line of reasoning before. He knew it by heart. Yet Plauen kept returning, as if there were a point he and Anyeck kept missing.

''The real ambiguities of the age surround Tureck Aarant and Theis Rogala. Was Aarant a hero? Not by the usual standards. Was Rogala his servant or master? Did Aarant's weapon, the Great Sword, control him instead of the reverse? Think about those questions. You'll be facing similar, though less symbolic, situations all your lives. We'll be examining them all next week.''

The session ended. Gathrid and Anyeck climbed to the parapet of the tower at Kacalief's southeast corner.

''I don't see anything,'' Anyeck said. ''Can you? Your eyes are better.''

Gathrid searched the east. ''I don't see anything, either.'' His gaze followed the road that looped round the marsh and headed south toward Hartog and the Dolvin. Their father had long since disappeared. He turned slowly, scanning the marsh itself, the vineyards, the wild rolling hills to the north. They were the Savards, from which the March took its name. He and his brothers hunted there occasionally. He said, ''The hills look dry. Be dangerous if there's a fire.''

"Everything is dry. We need rain. They say the marsh is drying up."

They passed an hour speaking of nothing, afraid to talk about what was on their minds.

Ventimiglia seemed to weigh on their brothers, too. Their efforts on the practice field were decidedly feeble.

The Safire was gone a week. When he returned, he announced, "The King himself was there. Things may not be as bad as we feared. The Brotherhood knows about Grevening. The Fray Magister, the Emperor and Kimach, King of Bilgoraj, have called for a conference at Torun."

Bilgoraj, one of the west's leading kingdoms, was Gudermuth's neighbor to the west. Its capital, Torun, was one of the great cities of the day, and Kimach Faulstich was sometimes called one of the great Kings.

The Safire continued, "They're going to form an Alliance of all the western states and Brotherhood Orders. The King says the Alliance's protection will include Gudermuth, so we won't stand alone. Ahlert won't dare attack. Not unless he wants to fight the whole west at once."

Gathrid had never heard his father make a longer speech. He hoped it was all true.

"He sounds like he's whistling in the dark," Anyeck whispered.

"What? Why?"

"He doesn't believe in this Alliance. He's just trying to make us feel safer."

The fighting in Grevening washed against the border next day. Gathrid woke to alarms. The Safire's men-at-arms had exchanged arrows with Ventimiglians who had strayed over the line. He rushed to the east wall.

Smoke obscured the dawn, catching bloody fire from the rising sun. Below, just across the frontier, one of the Mindak's patrols was passing. He watched for a few minutes. His father came up, stood beside him. After a time, he said, "Gathrid, go have your breakfast, then start your lesson."

"Yes, Sir." He had given up arguing.

He tried to keep his mind on his studies. He could not. There was skirmishing going on across the border. The noise of the watchers on the walls kept distracting him. Anyeck had run out earlier.

Plauen slammed his book back into its protective case. He snapped, "Very well. Go ahead. Go applaud the Mindak's barbarism."

Gathrid gathered his study materials. His heart began to flutter.

"Gathrid," Plauen called after him. "Don't fall into the trap that's caught Anyeck. Don't start thinking there's something romantic and wonderful about this. It's war. It's an ugly business."

The youth could not conceal his disagreement.

"I wasn't always a Brother, Gathrid. I saw a few battles in my time. I saw my comrades lying on muddy fields, their guts spilled, stinking of their own ordure, the terror of death filling their eyes. . . ."

Gathrid shuddered and ran. He did not want to hear that part. He wanted romances and lays. Blood and pain were not real. The economics, politics and psychology of warfare just made the old stories dull.

He wanted adventures grim with dread perils overcome, but with the clear certainty of a strong hero standing victorious in the end. Plauen kept trying to kill the shine. He insisted that it was all hogwash. He wanted you to believe that heroes didn't always win, that putting your money on evil was usually the better bet.

He reached the wall in time to witness the passing of a large company of eastern troops. Sunlight twinkled off their wildly varied armor. Their equipment rattled and clanked in a steady, grim beat.

His gaze locked on the black figure at their head. "One of the Dead Captains," he murmured. His stomach did a flip.

As if hearing him, the Toal halted, faced Kacalief. It stared at the fortress a long time, as if quietly amused by its audience. Its gaze swept across Gathrid. He felt as though an icicle had been driven into his brain. He shuddered. For a long moment he was frightened.

"Aren't they gorgeous!" Anyeck bubbled. These easterners were richly and colorfully clad. Gathrid understood most brigades dressed more somberly.

He turned to his sister, his upper lip rising in a half sneer. Her greed blazed through her common sense. He wished she would outgrow having been spoiled. "They're dreadful," he said. "Look at the Dead Captain. Tell me he's glamorous."

She gave him a nasty look.

"He does fit the particulars of the husband you want."

"Gathrid, don't take out your frustrations on me."

"And you'll get a chance to meet one soon enough, I think."

Their mother stepped between them. "They won't, Gathrid," she said. "The Alliance will stop them. Ahlert won't risk the united wrath of the western kingdoms and the Brotherhood."

Then Plauen was behind them, smiling a distant smile. "Don't blind yourself, My Lady. Ventimiglia is a dragon with one head. It speaks with one voice. It strikes with one sword. It marches to one will. This Alliance will be a beast of a hundred heads, every one trying to drag the body in a different direction. The Mindak will sneer at it. He'll spit on it. And he'll trample it into the dust."

Gathrid stared at the Brother in disbelief. Never had he heard the man speak with such despair. "Plauen!"

"I'm sorry. I forget myself. The rage of frustration seethes within me. I'm afraid it's too late. The Mindak has the scent of fell artifacts of which only a few Magisters are aware. Had he been stopped farther east, he might never have learned that they had survived the Fall."

The Safirina asked, "What *are* you talking about, Mikas?"

The redness left the teacher's face. He seemed to fold into himself. "Nothing, My Lady. Unfounded speculations I shouldn't be discussing. Pay me no mind. I'm a long-winded fool."

Gathrid stared. There was a look in Plauen's eyes, when the man glanced at himself or Anyeck, which turned his heart cold. And behind the look was a poorly controlled fear.

It was a puzzle, the youth thought.

Chapter Two
Ultimatum

The armies of Ventimiglia halted just east of the Grevening border. Their encampments covered the countryside. Gathrid tried counting tents. He would get into the thousands and lose track. He gave up.

Refugees poured into Gudermuth. They carried tales so cruel nobody believed them. They featured Nieroda and the Toal in such monstrous roles that Kacalief's people rejected the accusations. Nobody could be that bloody and black.

The Easterners erected semipermanent fortifications and barracks throughout autumn. Their numbers diminished. Spies reported that many of the Mindak's soldiers had returned to their families for the winter.

It was a small thing, but a human touch which offset the alleged brutality of that somber army.

Gathrid's father continued to hope weakly for the Alliance. His mother was convinced the Mindak would not defy it.

The battles with his father became more heated. The

youth thought the threat justified his being trained. His father refused with increasing vehemence.

Anyeck, too, knew her disappointments. The Safire refused to let anyone run to safety. "We're responsible for this corner of the March," he insisted. "Neither I nor any of mine will shirk. We have our duty. We stand here. We set no cowardly examples, come peace or come war." And that was the final word.

Gathrid could not help but admire his father's stubbornness. It was the stubbornness of the heroes he worshiped.

Winter came with its snows. The Ventimiglians remained out there, their nearest works just a mile away. Their presence became ever more grating, more fraying to the nerves. Each day one of the black-clad Toal would ride to the border and sit, sometimes for hours, staring at the fortress. Plauen named it a clear declaration of intent.

"Where are those armies the Alliance was going to raise?" the Safire growled. "Why aren't there any tents on our side of the border?" He sent messengers to the Dolvin. The Dolvin queried the King. The King could not answer the questions. He had heard nothing from Torun.

The snows ceased. The white melted away, leaving the ground soggy and the marsh full. The first wildflowers appeared. The birds returned from warmer climes.

The tension in Kacalief grew daily.

One morning Anyeck came flying down from her place of worship on the wall. "One of them is coming!" she shrieked. She sounded half terrified, half delighted. "One of the black riders. He's over the border now."

The Safire growled at his sergeants. Alarms sounded. Men-at-arms rushed to the walls. Someone shouted down, "He's alone, Sir. White flag."

The Safire stopped his people before they started the fires to boil water and emptied the arsenals of their sparse store of arrows and shafts for the ballistae. "They want to parlay. I'll stall them all summer long."

Gathrid scampered to the wall. He looked down at the rider. The rider looked up. Gathrid suddenly felt very cold, very small, very vulnerable. In that instant of eye contact he believed all the dark tales.

"This is a new one," Anyeck said. "I thought we'd seen them all."

"This one is Nieroda. The Dark Champion. Their commander."

"How do you know?"

"Logic. The Toal don't talk. Nieroda looks pretty much like them, but isn't a Toal himself. Since this one means to parlay, it follows it must be Nieroda."

Anyeck stuck out her tongue.

Kacalief's massive oaken gate creaked open. The dark rider approached.

Gathrid surveyed his home and felt more vulnerable. Kacalief was old and small and weak. It did not stand on much of a hill. It had no moat, just a stake-filled ditch round the foot of its wall. It had no drawbridge and no barbican. Its walls were solid, but not that tall. If one were breached there was nowhere to retreat but into a small central tower which served as his family's quarters. Everyone else lived in huts and sheds against the inner face of the wall.

They probably laughed at the place, the planners out there.

The dark rider passed under the wall, halted just inside. He did not look around. He seemed indifferent to the castle's defenses.

The Safire strode into the court. He had donned his rusty old war gear. He did not look impressive, though the sword he bore was in keeping with his size. "Nevenka Nieroda?" he asked.

The rider inclined its head slightly. "I speak for the Emperor of All Men. He commands you to put aside all manner of excuse and delay, and yield up the sword named Daubendiek, also called the Great Sword, and the Sword of Suchara."

The Safire exchanged a look with Symen, then with Belthar. He was baffled.

As were Gathrid and everyone else within hearing.

"What's he talking about?" Anyeck asked. "What Great Sword?"

"Maybe he means the one Tureck Aarant carried." There was a local legend about Aarant's dwarfish companion, Theis Rogala, having buried the mystic blade in the Savards, but not even peasant storytellers took it seriously.

The Safire regained his equilibrium. "The Great Sword? That's a child's tale. The thing isn't here. It never was. I couldn't give it to you if I wanted. And I don't want. I wouldn't give your Emperor a bucket of water if he were burning."

The rider inclined his head slightly. "As you wish. You'll regret that attitude." He departed.

"Hey! Hold on." The Safire started to chase the horseman, remembered his dignity. He stopped, looked at his master-at-arms and sons. He wore an expression of bewilderment deeper than any Gathrid had ever seen.

The youth caught a glimpse of Plauen. The Brother was farther along the wall, observing Nieroda's departure. His face was the gray of death.

"What the hell?" the Safire finally roared. "Are they trying to confuse us to death? Plauen! Get down here. Transcribe a message to the Dolvin. Word for word, what Nieroda said. And tell him to get some people up here. They're going to take a crack at us."

The Dolvin's contribution arrived four days later. A company of two hundred men. A laughable force, considering the countless thousands loafing beyond the border.

And loafing was all the Ventimiglians were doing. They spent a while each day practicing marching to their battle signals, then just sat around. Their very indolence irritated Gathrid. It shouted their contempt of Kacalief's defenses.

A month passed. The Dolvin sent carping messages.

He wanted to know how long the Safire meant to tie up his men. Nothing was happening.

Nieroda returned. He made the same demand in the same words and tone. Gathrid's father gave the same reply. And it was true. He could not surrender something not in his possession, something which probably did not exist at all.

"The Emperor of All Men has bid me say this much more. In his mercy he gives you two days grace. You may yet save your people."

"Tell him he can go to Hell."

Gathrid was not fond of his father. He was at that age where the man could do no right, but he did find himself admiring the man's stand.

Nieroda returned to Grevening. Gathrid watched the eastern armies shed their somnolence and become astonishingly agile and coordinated during a day-long exercise. Anyeck was impressed, Gathrid frightened, and everyone else intimidated. At that evening's council of war, Symen asked, "Will we meet them in the field?"

"Don't be stupid," the Safire snapped. "With six horsemen? That's not enough to match the Toal."

"There'd be seven if . . ." Gathrid said.

"You shut up. No. If they come, we make them come over the wall. We make them pay for every square foot they take, and we hold till the Alliance relieves us."

He had sent a message to the Dolvin saying the Mindak planned to attack two days hence. He did not, honestly, expect either a reply or help. Even the Safirina's faith in the Alliance was growing strained. It hadn't bothered making a token showing.

Haghen, having been put up to it by Gathrid, at Anyeck's suggestion, asked, "Father, shouldn't we send the women and children to Katich? The capital can stand a siege better than we can."

The Safire's face became taut. The color drained away. The ugliness vanished too. He became just a tired, frightened man. "No. I meant what I said before." His voice was barely audible. "We have our duty. We won't shirk it. None of us."

In that moment Gathrid both loved and hated him. He met Anyeck's eye and shrugged.

Plauen tried to pursue the argument. The Safire cut him short. "We won't discuss it. We're here to talk about how to keep them from taking Kacalief. What can we do?"

"Nothing," Plauen replied. "Unless you conjure up the Great Sword."

"I don't find your attitude acceptable, Brother. Can you contribute something more than yak? I know a few small spells. What about you?"

"I can create pretty colored lights. I can make a few useful chemicals. I can concoct poisons. It's up to you to get the easterners to drink them."

"Hunh! Just what I expected. Useless as nipples on a boar hog. Why'd I let them talk me into hiring you?"

Gathrid's eyes widened. He exchanged looks with Anyeck. The presumption had been that their father had gone looking for the teacher, not the reverse. Neither she nor Gathrid contributed to the discussion after that. Their mother and brothers said nothing either. The Safire and Belthar did most of the talking. Plauen inserted the occasional suggestion.

"Summing it up: We have to stall," the Safire grumbled. "We have to grab hold of our courage and delay them as long as we can. If the gods be with us, the Alliance will arrive in time."

Later, on the wall, under stars that sparkled mockingly, Anyeck said, "Father is whistling in the dark. There won't be any help from the Alliance. And we won't stall the Mindak. He'll tear Kacalief open like we open clams."

"Don't be so negative. He's a stubborn man."

"I'm scared, Gathrid." She took his hand. Her palm was cold and sweaty. "I'm scared to death."

Softly, "So am I. I wish his pride would let him send you and Mother to Katich."

Nothing got said for several minutes. Then, "Gathrid,

look!'' Her free hand indicated the sky a short way above the eastern horizon.

''A comet! There hasn't been one since before Father was born. These are evil times for sure.''

Anyeck shook her head. Her hand was trembling now. ''You paid more attention than me. Didn't Plauen say a comet forecast the Brothers' War?''

''Yes. Look at the villagers.''

Several peasant villages surrounded Kacalief, lying at varying distances. Theirs were the people the Safire was supposed to protect. Tonight those villages were bright with torches and fires.

''They're moving into the hills.'' A procession of torches departed a village. It snaked toward the Savards.

''They've seen the comet, too.''

''Look. They're burning their homes.'' Flames spread through the first village abandoned. ''You think the men will report like they're supposed to?''

Gathrid watched another procession begin, another village start to burn. ''No. Well, maybe a few. But they know there's no hope for Kacalief. Why should they get caught in the death trap, too?'' Though the feudal bond created obligations both ways, and the Safire was meeting his commitment, Gathrid felt no resentment toward the peasants. They were doing the smart thing.

''Gathrid? Would you hate me if I ran away?''

''No. But I wouldn't be very proud of you, either.''

''We could go together. If we started tonight . . .''

''No.''

''I'm scared.''

''I know.'' For the first time in her life, he thought, she faced a situation she could not somehow control. It had to be cruel, to have the world suddenly turn around, to stop being the golden one everybody spoiled, to find all the exits locked and nobody listening to your pleas.

She released his hand. In a small voice, she said, ''Good night, Gathrid.'' Her shoulders slouched as she walked away.

He stayed a while, watching the villages burn, the comet carve its silver slice from the sky, and the Mindak's men pursue their nocturnal duties amongst the galaxy of their campfires. The Great Sword, he thought. Why would Ahlert pick such a bizarre *casus belli*? Just to establish a demand impossible to meet?

He gave it up after a while. Nothing made sense anymore.

The Dark Brigades marched and countermarched all the following day. Their execution was flawless. Gathrid heard Belthar mutter, ''If they're trying to intimidate me with skill, they're doing it. They're damned well trained.''

The youth surveyed his father's fief. His brothers and the Safire were out gathering stores, and having little luck. The peasants had taken everything with them.

Belthar's men and the Dolvin's company were trying to make the approaches to Kacalief less hospitable. Gathrid suspected the trap-building was makework. Belthar wanted the men too busy to brood about the coming battle.

The day passed. There was no word from the Dolvin. There was no sign of help from King or Alliance. Faces grew longer and longer. Gathrid did not hear a word from his mother all day.

The next day was worse. Hardly anyone spoke except to growl or snarl. And still there was no word from outside, nor any sign of help.

Gathrid slept only in snatches that night. Several times he went to the wall and stared at the ominous comet. The sentries passed him silently. Usually they had a word or two for the youth they considered a sort of mascot. Now they pursued their rounds in a dark dream. Once Gathrid found his father on the wall, watching the Ventimiglian camp. He stood beside the tall man for a few minutes. Neither spoke.

For a while battle morn looked like just another day. The easterners did nothing threatening immediately. The Safire took time to feed his garrison a good breakfast, then had the arsenals opened. Fires crackled under the big water kettles. Women and children moved to the central keep. Gathrid had a terrible argument with his father. The Safire cut it short by snarling, "Belthar, take the pup to his mother."

The master-at-arms seized Gathrid's collar and escorted him to the Safirina, where he received another vigorous tongue-lashing. It left him feeling shamed by his handicaps.

Anyeck sat with him, holding his hand. She was pale. Her hands shook. He started to brush her off, then realized she had to do this for her own sake.

Seconds dragged on into minutes. Finally, one of the guards left to the keep descended from its parapet, said, "It looks like they're coming."

Wearily, Gathrid rose. Leading Anyeck, he climbed to the tower's top.

He was surprised to find that it was barely midmorning. Hours seemed to have passed. . . .

The Ventimiglians were drawn up in their brigades, facing the border. Directly opposite Kaçalief were Nieroda, the Toal and a man who could only be the Mindak himself. Two hundred soldiers waited in loose formation behind them. The Mindak surveyed his host. Apparently satisfied, he spoke to a bugler.

A horn squealed. The brigades surged. Drums struck a marching beat. Behind the attackers, camp followers began torching the army's winter quarters.

"They're not even coming at us!" Gathrid said. "They're heading toward Hartog and Katich. . . ."

Every brigade headed for Gudermuth's interior. Only the one small group remained facing the fortress.

That much contempt irked Gathrid. Two hundred men to attack a fortress held by nearly four hundred! His father's men were not professionals, but they had to be better than that.

"Oh!"

Gathrid spun. His mother had fainted. She could no

longer convince herself that the Mindak would not defy the Alliance. The truth was too much for her nerve.

"Take her to her bedchamber," Gathrid told the guards. "Tell the women to look after her."

Anyeck grabbed his arm. "They're coming, Gathrid." Her grip was painful.

Nieroda and the Twelve Dead Captains crossed the border, walking their horses. Their soldiers picked up their arms and loafed along behind them.

A nervous arrow arced out, fell short. The Safire cursed the bowman. Gathrid saw his father turn to Plauen, heard him tell the Brother that now was the time to do something. If he could.

The Dead Captains spread out, encircling the fortress. Fifteen to twenty soldiers accompanied each, remaining just out of bowshot. Nieroda remained near the Mindak.

Ahlert produced a white scarf and rode forward. He halted below the Safire's post. He shouted, "Will you yield Daubendiek now?"

Gathrid could not hear his father's reply. He supposed it was suitably defiant. The Mindak stiffened, turned his horse, rode back to Nieroda.

The Toal swept forward. Arrows whistled from the wall. Even the best-sped ricocheted off the Dead Captains' armor.

"They're ensorcled!" Gathrid snarled. "We can't touch them."

Nieroda galloped toward the fortress. A shower of arrows did him no harm. The Dark Champion bore a javelin in one hand. He hurled it at Kacalief's wall.

There was a tremendous flash. The Ventimiglian soldiers sent up a chorus of battle cries. When Gathrid's sight returned, he saw easterners rushing the fortress. The Toal were at the wall. They swarmed up its naked stone face with the ease of flies. Several fell off, washed away by kettles of boiling water. They got up and came back for more. The heat did not bother them.

"Look!" Anyeck said. "There!"

Not far from where their father had established his command post, where Nieroda had hurled the javelin, the wall was breached. A Toal was through and slaughtering everyone within reach. It wielded a huge black blade which sliced armor and swords the way a sharp knife cut soft Savard cheese.

Plauen and the Safire attacked the Toal with the puny spells at their command. It ignored them.

Nieroda stepped through the gap. The courtyard tableau froze. Then a second black blade joined the slaughter.

Now there were Toal atop the wall. Ventimiglian soldiers tossed up grapnels and joined them. Attackers poured through the gap opened by Nieroda. Here, there, a hard-pressed Toal simply pointed a finger and men fell, torn apart from within.

Anyeck whimpered, "Gathrid, we've got to get out of here."

He had never been this frightened. He thought the end was near. But he snapped, "Control yourself!" He turned and started downstairs.

She followed. "Where are you going? Don't leave me."

"To find myself a sword. Father can't stop me now." Brave words, he thought. He hoped his voice hadn't trembled too much. He turned away and limped down into the cool inwards of the tower that had been his home.

The keep gate exploded inward. Oak beams flung about like straws in a gale. A woman screamed. Gathrid's palms were cold and wet on the leather-wrapped hilt of his great-grandfather's sword.

Men flung through the broken gate. His father's men, fleeing, dragging their wounded with them . . .

"Here they come!" Gathrid shouted. The keep guards crouched behind a barrier of overturned furniture. Ventimiglian soldiers popped inside, keeping low behind their shields. The retreating Gudermuthers scrambled over the furniture.

An old man dropped beside Gathrid. "Belthar! I thought . . ."

"I'm a tough old buzzard. You did all right here, boy. Your mother and sister upstairs?"

"Next level. Father? . . ."

"I don't know. Hang on here. I'll get the women. We'll break out and run for the hills." The old soldier darted away.

A Toal came striding through the shattered gate, a dark tower against the light. Someone hurled a boar spear. It missed. The Toal gestured. A bolt of power blasted a gap in the furniture wall. Ventimiglian soldiers sprang forward. Blades darted and clashed. Men cried out. The Toal came on like something out of nightmare.

Belthar thundered orders. A boar spear smashed against the Toal's breastplate. The Dead Captain staggered. "Go!" Belthar roared. He slapped Gathrid's shoulder as he passed. The youth threw a clumsy stroke at the nearest Ventimiglian, joined the rush. His mother and sister were beside him, eyes huge with terror.

The Toal flung an arm around in a hard horizontal arc. People toppled like wheat at the stroke of a scythe. A black mailed fist smote Gathrid's chest . . . and a darkness closed in. And then it went away, he knew not how much later. But enough later that he was left alone with the dead. He wept for his mother, who lay within his narrow field of vision.

It wasn't over yet. He could hear it going on still, elsewhere in the castle. He tried to move. His limbs responded shakily.

Got to hide, he thought. Got to hide till I can get out and run to the peasants in the hills. . . .

Chapter Three
The Savard

The smoke no longer rose from the ruins. The Mindak Ahlert had gone on to enjoy the rape of Gudermuth. But the Dark Champion and the Twelve Dead Captains remained at Kacalief. They searched tirelessly, their dead eyes burning angrily. If Gudermuth would die before surrendering Daubendiek, so be it. The Sword's pommel would rest beneath the Mindak's palm even so.

Gathrid crept through the ruins like a frightened rat. The Twelve were everywhere. How long before they flung him onto the mound of dead and tortured flesh growing in the main court?

Those who had fallen, sliced like sausages by the witchblades of Nieroda and the Toal, had been lucky. The wretches who had not perished were singing arias of agony for the Mindak's questioners.

The screams were declining in number. Gathrid wished someone knew where the Sword of Suchara lay. The knowledge could be traded for swift, merciful death.

Gathrid was trying to reach the gap Nieroda's sorcery had blasted through the wall. He was close enough to see stone that had run and lumped like tallow on the flank of a candle. He fought his impulse to jump and run.

There was no fight in him anymore. His only desire was to live.

His insistence on fighting now seemed like a childhood dream that had held no cognition of the horror of reality.

He could see the vineyards through the hole. Maybe he could risk the dash. . . .

Ventimiglian armor clanked nearby. He froze. Dark greaves appeared beyond fallen, fire-blackened timbers. He tried to crush himself deeper into ashes and broken stone.

The Toal moved stiffly, jerkily. The Twelve had done so even in battle. Yet each had been a killing machine no mortal had been able to match. And Nieroda had been worse.

They said even the Mindak feared Nevenka Nieroda.

This one was hunting survivors. They never gave up.

The thing that wore the corpse of a man stopped a dozen paces away. It turned. Gathrid held his breath. The dead eyes probed his hiding place. A black gauntlet rose to point. . . .

Gathrid sprang up. He hurled a fist-sized chunk of masonry, broke for the gap in the wall. The chunk hit the outstretched hand, wrenched the aiming finger's point aside. The remnants of a stable shed coughed, collapsed.

Gathrid had just time enough to reach the hole.

His mixed luck held. He skidded on slippery puddled stone and fell. The Toal's second spell-bolt chuckled in the wall. New-made gravel stung Gathrid's face.

He ran blindly till burning lung and leaden legs slowed his pace and quickened his thinking. He slowed to a dogged trot, turned toward the nearby finger of the Savard Hills. He and his brothers had played and hunted those wild slopes and valleys often enough. He should be able to disappear there.

He glanced back once.

A dark thing on a dark horse cantered from the ruins.

Gathrid increased his pace. It was a mile to the nearest cover.

He slipped into dense scrub a hundred yards ahead of his pursuer. On hands and knees he scooted through brambles like a rabbit. His heart pounded as hard as it had the moment he had met the Toal's gaze.

Was the Dead Captain playing with him? It could have caught him. . . . Maybe the Toal wanted the amusement of a boy-hunt. Or thought he might lead them to the Sword.

Their search for the fabled Sword was baffling. But the Mindak and his wizard generals had shaken other fell and forgotten things out of the earth in their mad drive to revive the ancient sorceries. Among them were Nieroda and the Twelve Demon Kings from ages so eld even they had forgotten them. There were rings of power and amulets of protection the like of which had not been since the Golden Age of Anderle. They had recovered bows that could speed soul-devouring shafts the length of a kingdom. And swords against which little could stand. But none of those were Daubendiek, the Great Sword.

The pressure eased once Gathrid entered the tortuous and steep ravines of the Savards. The dark rider came on, but the advantage had shifted to the man afoot. Gathrid gained ground.

Late that afternoon, almost too exhausted to care anymore, he found a low cave mouth. It exuded no animal fetor. Too tired to worry about becoming cornered, he slithered inside and fell asleep.

He dreamed terrible dreams, of warfare and vengeance, of hatred and treachery in olden times, before the Fall, when Anderle's reach had encompassed two thirds of the continent and the Immortal Twins had ruled over a Golden Age. He dreamed of the winged tempter, Grellner, who had trafficked in whispers of unshared power.

He dreamed of mad, mysterious Theis Rogala, he of

the quicksilver loyalties and golden, slippery tongue; he who had been esquire, servant and companion of the Swordbearer. He and Aarant had been more hated than the Tempter himself.

The Rogala of legend had claimed that Daubendiek chose its own master and cause. The question of treason was irrelevant. He was faithful to the blade.

Gathrid had never been so miserable. Even during the polio epidemic he had felt less distress. His muscles were coals of pain. His stomach was a nest of vipers. His bad leg throbbed. His mind . . . He feared he was no longer sane. Shock still absorbed him, but tendrils of hatred had begun trickling through the mist of unbelief. Every thought of Nevenka Nieroda initiated a promising, "Someday. . . ."

Such emotion frightened him. It could become compelling, could make of him a man as bleak and driven as the fabled Aarant.

He was too stiff to walk. He crawled toward sunlight. It blinded him briefly when it splashed into his eyes. Outside, morning birds sang solar praises, infuriating him with their indifference to what had happened at Kacalief. A squirrel chattered. For the first time he let his thoughts touch on his mother and sister.

The younger women had been spared. The Mindak had dragged them off to Katich.

Gathrid wanted to rend, to tear, to make the Ventimiglians bleed for Anyeck, for his parents, for his brothers and for Gudermuth.

His vision adapted to the light.

One of the Twelve, still as a statue of an ebony general, sat his dark horse not fifty feet beyond the brush masking the cave. A sparrow settled onto its shoulder, chirruped in surprise, fluttered to a nearby tree. It alternately scolded and cocked its head questioningly.

The Dead Captain's head slowly turned Gathrid's way.

Terror hit him like a blow from a giant's fist. They could not be escaped! He scrambled back, scraped his scalp on the cave roof. He fled into darkness, crashing from one cavern feature to another till his reason returned. By then he was thoroughly lost. The more immediate threat of the cavern banished his fear of the Toal.

He wandered for hours, occasionally pausing to indulge in a fit of tears. So many angers, fears, losses, frustrations. It was not fair.

The last time, after wiping tears with the backs of grimy hands, he noticed a pale, ghostly light ahead. With hope and fear writhing together like wrestling snakes, he crept toward it.

His fingers, brushing the cave walls for guidance, caressed scars left by ancient tools. They encountered beams supporting the invisible ceiling. He frowned. There were no mines in the Savards.

He stepped into a bedroom-sized chamber, manhewn from poor limestone. It contained two pieces of antique furniture. They were illuminated by a sourceless witchlight. One was a small, heavy chair. The other was an open coffin.

In the chair slept a gnarly, dusty dwarf. He was half buried by a beard in which crawling things nested.

Gathrid wanted to believe that he had found one of the mythical creatures who, with trolls and elves and giants, supposedly haunted the forests and hills and night.

But in the coffin, on dusty cerulean velvet, lay a long black sword. Its edges were nicked and crusted.

Gathrid stood, one hand scaling his mouth, vainly trying to contain a cough. It all fit the legends.

His free hand strayed to the weapon's hilt.

Sparks. Power flooded his arm. Pain and fear evaporated. His weak leg strengthened. The dead side of his face quickened and joined the other in an expression of wonder. The blade vibrated in his grasp. Dust danced off its dark gloss.

And the dwarf opened his eyes.

The gaze of a Toal was warmer.

''Daubendiek has chosen.'' Theis Rogala spoke softly,

chillingly, with a curiously jerky accent, like the sound of bones being crushed far down a long cold hallway. "There will be blood for Suchara."

Gathrid tried to drop the Sword. His fingers would not open.

The question of which had been master and which tool pervaded the legend of Tureck Aarant. As the Sword, against his will, rose in salute, Gathrid suffered the despairing suspicion that it had been Aarant who had been the controlled.

Bones creaking audibly, Rogala dropped to one knee. In the same death-edged voice he croaked, "Suchara's will be done. Her servant swears fealty to her Swordbearer till Daubendiek severs the bond. Suchara's will be done."

Nothing in Gathrid's sixteen years had prepared him for this. Beyond daydreams he had never really wanted to be a warrior. Nor did he want to be a slave. Most of all, he did not want to replay the tragedy of Tureck Aarant. Though Aarant had been a warrior of a stature equal to any boy's daydreams, his existence had been lonely and choked with despair. He had known no friends, no lovers, nor even a country he could call his own. He had traveled a road of blood and tears. Death had been his only friend, Daubendiek his only lover, Theis Rogala his sole companion.

Yet Gathrid felt the seductive caress of power, heard its soft siren call. Bearing Daubendiek, he need not fear the Twelve. Nor Nieroda. Nor his own handicap. Even the Mindak would fear him. What fell vengeances he could wreak. . . .

He was a fish writhing on a hook. Even at that moment he knew he would not shed Daubendiek till the Sword itself willed it. He had been taken.

Rogala creaked as he rose. "Damned bones. Must've been years." He turned stiffly, began kicking dusty accoutrements from beneath his chair. "How goes the war, boy?"

"Kacalief fell," Gathrid mumbled. "The Mindak has

gone on to Katich. Unless Malmberget, Bilgoraj, and the rest of the Allies move soon, Gudermuth is lost."

"Eh? Gudermuth?" The dwarf frowned, his face becoming all crags and gullies. "Never heard of it."

Gathrid was puzzled. Never *heard* of Gudermuth? But . . . oh. Rogala had slept for centuries. There had been no Gudermuth when the dwarf had gone into hiding. "Kacalief was the castle of my father, the Safire of Kacalief, a knight protector of the Savard, which is a March on the Grevening frontier. Gudermuth is our kingdom. Katich is our capital. The Mindak of Ventimiglia is our enemy. Malmberget and Bilgoraj are the major states in the Torun Alliance. They pledged war and wizardry if Ventimiglia invaded from Grevening, which Ahlert and the Toal conquered last year."

The dwarf dropped into his chair. He combed his beard with his fingers and muttered, "It must have been longer than I expected. An age. I never heard of any of those places." His mien became so sour Gathrid backed a step away. "But there is a war on? We need a war." His eyes burned wickedly. "You'll have to explain as we go." He rose, gathered his gear, strode off as if he knew his destination.

"There's a Toal out there!" Gathrid croaked.

"Eh? So?" Rogala kept walking.

Gathrid tried to explain. Memories of defeat released anger and hatred. The Sword stirred. His emotions paled immediately.

"Then Daubendiek will drink," Rogala snarled.

"But. . . ."

"But me no buts, boy. Suchara has chosen. The Swordbearer can but fulfill his destiny."

Gathrid resisted for a moment—then remembered he was lost. Sighing, he followed the dwarf. Rebellion would have to wait.

Daubendiek measured five feet from pommel to point, yet felt weightless. Gathrid gave it a trial swish as he stood back from the cave mouth, letting his eyes adjust.

He recalled sham duels with his brothers. Clumsy as they had been, they had beaten him regularly.

Squatting in the entrance, studying the Toal, Rogala resembled a huge toad. Gathrid shuddered. The dwarf had not shown the cruel coldness of the legendary Rogala, yet something suggested that the myth was but a shadow of the truth. Gathrid sensed an alienness in his companion, as if the dwarf were in reality an engine of destruction camouflaged in human form.

The Sword was restless and eager. It moved in his hand.

"A strange creature," said Rogala, returning. "Old beyond reckoning. Bound about with a hundred sorceries and armed with a hundred more." He seemed unsure. "Still, Daubendiek needs a taste of death. Go kill it."

Gathrid remembered the Toal raging like blood-drenched black killing machines amongst the defenders of Kacalief. He shook his head.

"The Swordbearer refuses a challenge? Nonsense. Go on. Slay it. Let Daubendiek drink. The blade is thirsty. It's weak with the sleep of ages."

There may have been sorcery in the dwarf's speech. Or a compelling hunger in the Sword. Or an uncontrollable will to revenge in Gathrid himself. He stumbled toward daylight. "No blood," he croaked. "Theis, the Toal. . . . Dead men."

He burst through the brush concealing the cave mouth. The Toal's head turned.

The Sword eased the physical processes of fear without softening intellectual trepidation. He could not help remembering that these monsters had slaughtered champions far greater than he.

His martial training was limited almost entirely to what he had seen his brothers learn, and to imagination. How could he fight this thing?

Daubendiek sprang to guard. Surprised, clumsy, Gathrid stalked the Toal.

THE SWORDBEARER

It seemed puzzled by his challenge. To have the quarry turn. . . . That was beyond its experience.

Its gaze shifted to the Sword. It nodded as if all were explained. It turned to face Kacalief. Ice-eyes stared thither for a long moment, then returned their fell weight to Gathrid.

A spellbound blade as long and dark as Daubendiek whispered from its scabbard. The Toal's mount came to life.

Gathrid's mind remained paralyzed by fear, but his body acted. He leapt to his right, to take the Toal on its shieldless left arm. Daubendiek clove air with a joyous howl.

The Dead Captain leaned away, kicked with a spike-toed boot. Gathrid's ribs received a painful caress.

The youth's next stroke reached for the turning horse's hamstrings. The beast staggered. The Toal plunged off.

Gathrid charged. His opponent's movements were as jerky as ever, but so swift and sure that it was on guard, waiting, when he arrived.

Daubendiek rose like a headsman's blade, descended too swiftly for the eye. The Toal's blade blocked it with ease.

The swords met with a thunder far surpassing steel kissing steel. Sorceries clashed. Cold agony climbed Gathrid's arm. For an instant that became a subjective eternity, the weapons clung like magnets. A dark wind howled about Gathrid. Leaves and branches fell from trees behind the Toal as though invisible giants wrestled there. Daubendiek whined like a whipped dog.

The Toal's sword screamed like a roasting infant.

When the blades separated, Gathrid knew he could win. His weapon bore the more dreadful sorceries. Nothing could defeat him! He released a shout of exultation.

In one corner of his mind something whispered that he was being seduced by the Sword. He didn't care. Not then, not with a savage revenge for his parents attainable.

With his whole being he wanted to slash and tear and deliver pain.

Amazement filled the Dead Captain's eyes. It took a step backward, glanced toward Kacalief, for an instant seemed to listen. Then, as if bowing to a distant command, it resumed combat.

Its blade danced like a wind-whipped flame, darted like a viper's tongue, searching for that fractional gap in Gathrid's defense that would allow it to prick him with its evil. Daubendiek anticipated every maneuver. The swords wailed and screamed. The Toal's avoided meeting Daubendiek squarely.

Gathrid began to feel uncertain. The invincibility of the Sword might not guarantee victory, only that the Toal's blade would not reach him. Rogala had hinted that it had slept too long.

In lulls when the weapons were not singing their grim chorus, the silence was fraught with unpleasant promise.

Then Gathrid heard distant hooves.

Nieroda was coming to claim Daubendiek.

He glanced at Rogala, silently pleading for guidance. The dwarf was in a trance, enchanted by the struggle. He did not respond.

The Sword sensed his desperation, hurled itself against the Toal's blade, wove lightning nets of death, drove the enemy back in sparks and pain. The force of the blows jarred Gathrid into a moment of rationality. How could Daubendiek control him so easily? In his way, he had become as possessed as the Toal.

For the moment he had no choice. He could not run. He had to fight, and win, or die. Or worse, let Daubendiek fall into Nevenka Nieroda's bloody hands.

They might have been giants, flailing one another with lightnings, smoky towers lashing one another with invisible whips both deadly and long. Their wild slashing and chopping ruined brush and trees. Streamers of smoke coiled up from the leafy forest floor and misted thinly as swordstrokes ripped them apart. A sapling murdered by

Daubendiek glowed as redly as a living ruby. Long furrows striped the earth in mad, zigzag patterns.

The Toal retreated, circling slowly. Gathrid realized it was trying to turn his back to Nieroda's approach. He could overcome the maneuver only by forcing Daubendiek through the thing's guard and destroying it.

Always there was the doubt. The Twelve had remained undefeated since the Mindak had raised them from the Hells where they had lain since time immemorial, when ancient sorceries had struck them down.

And Nieroda. What of Nieroda? What *was* Nieroda? Controlling spirit of the Toal now, but something Ahlert had drawn from the dreaming sorceries of yet another age, similar to the Toal in aspect and invincibility, but a thing possessed only by its own inner evil. The shade and bones of someone who had been a Power equaling that which the Mindak hoped to become. A worldshaking evil so antique time had devoured all memory of its native age—except within the archives of the mysterious Library rumor said that Ahlert had discovered and turned to his own wicked purposes.

By what dread power did the Mindak bind Nieroda's fell spirit? Only the Library could reveal that dark secret.

A second Toal appeared.

Gathrid had thought Daubendiek a swift and wild thing already pressed to its limit, but again it intensified its assault.

Now he received intimations of the weapon's own uncertainties. It was expending its ephemeral energy prodigally. It was confident no longer.

But the Toal's defenses were weakening. It withdrew more rapidly, trying to keep its blade from being beaten back into it. Again and again Daubendiek probed deep enough to sear the Dead Captain's armor. Occasionally little chunks flicked away.

Two more Toal arrived. Like statues they sat watching.

Why did they not interfere? Would they let their fellow be destroyed?

Daubendiek pushed past the Toal's blade, sliced armor, for an instant lightly caressed the dead flesh within.

At one time, long ago, that would have been the battle. But the Sword was too weak to do more than sip.

A shock unlike any Gathrid had ever experienced coursed through his arm and body. Daubendiek surged triumphantly. He wanted to reject the feeling, to put it away from him, as a monk might the orgasmic experience it resembled. Yet he also lusted for it, as would the monk. He sensed its narcotic quality.

From the Toal came the first sound he had heard one make, a low, distant moan. Its fellows, now four strong, jerked as if stung, but did not interfere. Their heads turned toward Kacalief.

Gathrid knew he had to take control. He could not let Daubendiek rule him completely. He would become an observer riding an automaton existing solely as a device by which the blade could kill. But how to do it? And when? Fighting the Sword would be suicidal with the Nieroda-fate drawing near.

He inserted himself into the fight by feigning a stumble. The Toal immediately sprang to the attack.

Gathrid retreated toward Rogala, fighting Daubendiek more than the Toal, making himself appear clumsy with weariness. The Dead Captain tried to bring the battle to him.

More Toal arrived.

Gathrid gave Daubendiek its head. The Sword screamed, instantly drove past its opponent and pinked the Toal through its armor. So sudden did it strike that the Toal was, for an instant, stunned into immobility.

In that instant Daubendiek delivered the killing blow.

Gathrid screamed. And screamed. And screamed. For the Dead Captain.

For, after a moment of renewed pleasure, he had become one with the thing whose unnatural life Daubendiek was devouring. The entire experiences of one Obers Lek—loves, hatreds, losses, joys, fears, hopes and the silent despair of being possessed—flickered across his consciousness. He relived the totality of Lek's life. The child and man became part of him while his vampire blade nursed the teat of a soul.

That was terrible enough. But following exposure to the man came immersion in the thing that possessed his body. It was a thing so evil and alien that Daubendiek itself was repelled. The blade sprang back. It glowed. Steam and noisome smoke trailed from the wound it had rent.

Gathrid watched the Toal collapse. It began burning as it fell. A tower of black smoke rose above the clearing, its top taking on hints of the shape of a terrible face. From the remaining Toal came what sounded like a chorus of sighs.

Gathrid wasted no time. In spite of, or perhaps because of, the horror worming through his brain, his reason seized control. The other Toal would not wait long. Nieroda was near. In his weary, bemused state he could not hope to survive. That he had done so till now was a miracle.

He had to run again.

Daubendiek agreed, though it groaned its reluctance to leave a fight. Gathrid whirled to flee.

Rogala seemed trapped in some interior universe of fear and pain. He, too, had gotten a taste of the thing that had possessed the Dead Captain. Gathrid considered abandoning dwarf and sword—if the latter would permit it—before he realized just how much he needed both. Rogala knew the caverns. They were his only hope. And Daubendiek he needed for protection.

Shoving Rogala ahead of him, he ran for darkness.

As he plunged into the cave, he glanced back. His gaze crossed that of Nevenka Nieroda. That cold, cold feeling hit him again, and he knew the horrors had only just begun.

Chapter Four
Caverns

"These caverns run for miles," Rogala said. A sourceless glow lighted their way. The dwarf was evasive when Gathrid asked about it. Rogala was evasive about everything. He either knew no answers or just hated questions. He ignored or sidestepped every query. Gathrid had a thousand. The dwarf continued, "I know most of them."

He did seem to know where he was going.

"Whenever an inappropriate Candidate stumbled onto us, we had to move," Rogala said. "Furniture and all. That damned coffin weighs a ton. But that's all over now, Suchara be praised. The time has come. The blood will flow again. What's the matter?"

"Did you hear something?" Rogala had remarkably acute senses when he bothered to pay attention.

"No." The dwarf listened intently. "I don't hear anything."

"Maybe I didn't either, then. I thought something was behind us." Gathrid now wore Daubendiek scabbarded down his back. It no longer fed him false courage. He was just a confused, frightened boy pretending self-assurance. He prayed Rogala would not sense his growing dependence.

The dwarf, bad company as he was, kept the youth from dwelling on his family's fate. Yet Gathrid could not force Anyeck out of mind completely. Poor spoiled child. . . .

Oh, but his leg ached. He wanted so badly to rest.

Rogala's grim eyes probed the darkness behind him. "I don't think they're down here. They could be following upstairs. Don't worry. We'll shake them."

Later, Gathrid asked, "Why did you pick me?"

"Daubendiek chose." It was the same answer to the same question asked the dozenth time. There were many more that Rogala simply refused to hear. How long ago had he been chosen? Plauen seemed to have suspected something. Had the blade drawn him to it? Had it drawn the Mindak to Kacalief?

Rogala would not talk.

"Why me?" Gathrid demanded.

"The will of Suchara."

That was all he could get.

About who or what Suchara might be the dwarf remained determinedly vague. Gathrid did learn that Suchara was female, probably creatrix of the Sword and possibly a goddess. She had something to do with seas, or overseas, and was bloodthirsty.

Though Suchara was mentioned in the legends of Tureck Aarant, she was even more vague there. Gathrid was bewildered by all the mystery.

The dwarf did not make the ideal traveling companion. He would not talk for conversation's sake. He spoke only to give instructions or to ask about the world to which he had awakened. His few waste words were complaints about his own lot. "The curse," as he sometimes muttered.

With every minute and hour that passed Gathrid felt

more empathy for Tureck Aarant. Aarant had had to endure the dwarf for more than a year.

Time lost meaning. Gathrid kept track by sleeps.

Those were not pleasant. Though he collapsed in exhaustion when the dwarf permitted a break, he never slept the sleep of the innocent. His dreams were nightmares in which some formless, shadowy evil stole after him, always seeking a chance to devour his soul. He could not identify the stalker.

Sometimes he thought the dreams symbolic of his association with the Sword, or with the puppet master Theis Rogala, or with the mysterious Suchara. As often, he suspected his subconscious was reacting to being hunted by Nevenka Nieroda.

Whatever, it cost him invaluable rest. He became nervous and irritable. He engaged in growling matches with Rogala. The dwarf began watching him closely, obviously puzzled.

Shortly after the eighth sleep, Rogala announced, "We go topside in an hour."

"Finally. I hope it's daytime." His spirits rose. His strength and will returned. "I've had enough of these caves to do me the rest of my life."

"Don't get your hopes up, boy. We might have to come back down." Rogala always looked on the dark side.

"Daubendiek. . . ."

"Has its limitations. It's not ready for another of those . . . those . . . whatever possessed that man. We have to stay out of their way till it is."

Gathrid thought of Anyeck, of Kacalief, and grew angry. Yet the pain and loss had begun to pale. Others of his feelings seemed oddly weak too. The effect puzzled him.

"Theis," he asked, "does the Sword? . . . Will it kill my emotions?"

"Eh? The contrary, I'm told. Makes them more intense."

"Then why don't I feel? . . ."

"Ah. How much can a man bear? How much of the agony of another life can he assimilate? You'll feel it later, boy. When there's time. The mind is remarkable that way. Knows when it can indulge and when it can't. It can't now. It's got to worry about staying alive. That what's been bothering you?"

"No." He did not elaborate. His nightmares seemed foolish by day.

Day was hurrying into bloody sunset when they resurfaced. A thick layer of smoke deepened the red. Around the horizon, like the pillars of the sky, smoke rose from countless fires.

"They're burning Gudermuth to the ground!" Gathrid cried.

"Quiet!"

Then Gathrid, too, heard the faint sound of approaching hooves. A Ventimiglian patrol passed nearby and continued on toward a small encampment near the smouldering ruins of a village. A picket of crucifixes surrounded camp and town. The easterners had shown no mercy.

After a long look, Rogala asked, "It's always like this?"

"I guess. The stories out of Grevening were grisly."

The dwarf had seen grim doings during the Brothers' War, yet the savagery of the Ventimiglians seemed to shake him. "But why? Why slaughter a beaten people? Especially harmless peasants?"

"The Mindak swore he would destroy or enslave everyone. The only buy-off was to surrender the Sword. We didn't believe it existed."

Rogala's face twisted into the cruelest expression Gathrid had ever seen. It smoothed out in an instant. "He'll get it. Between the ribs. But that'll wait. Where are we?"

"I don't know."

"It's your country, isn't it?"

"I never traveled much."

"What's forty miles southwest of the place where we met?"

"The grain-growing counties. Small towns, small castles. We didn't do anything big, though. Katich is the only real city in Gudermuth."

"Don't apologize. There's a lot to be said for the rural life. The city. What direction is it?"

"West. Thirty or forty miles more, I guess. I don't know for sure. I'm sorry."

"Another apology. The Swordbearer doesn't apologize. Men apologize to him. Remember that. Be arrogant. It's expected. So. Make it forty miles just to be sure. I've had enough walking. We'll steal horses. Can you ride?"

Gathrid scowled. The dwarf seemed to think him a total incompetent. "Yes. But Katich would be under siege. It may have fallen."

"Not to worry. Best place to hide from an enemy is in his shadow. Gives you the chance to watch over his shoulder. And stab him in the back if the mood hits you. Don't give me that look. You want to stay alive, Sword or no, you'd better learn this lesson. You get your enemies any way you can. Fight fair, play the brave chevalier, and you're going to get your guts spilled."

Darkness settled in fast. Soon the Ventimiglian encampment was distinguishable only by its campfires, gleaming like bright little stars. . . . Gathrid glanced eastward. Yes. "Theis, look at that." He pointed.

"What?"

"The comet."

The dwarf cursed and muttered and groaned. "That again. It's going to be another rough one."

"Was there a comet before the Brothers' War?"

To his surprise, Rogala answered him. "Yeah. The same one. The same damned one. It's going to be rugged, boy. 'Bout time to visit our friends over there."

"I don't think I'm up to horse-stealing right now, Theis. I haven't got the strength. All my body wants to do is sleep.'' As he said it, his underbrain whimpered, cringing away from the inevitable nightmares.

''You've only been up . . . Oh, all right. We have to wait till they're settled for the night anyway.''

Gathrid collapsed. The last thing he saw was Rogala sitting on his heels, a toadlike silhouette against the glow of distant fires. A flareup in the smouldering village set illusive fireflies playing through his tangled beard. He seemed more interested in the comet than in the camp.

Did the dwarf never tire? Gathrid had not seen him sleep since the wakening of the Great Sword. He drifted off wondering if Rogala suffered *any* of the weaknesses of mere mortals.

The nightmare returned, this time while Gathrid was in that stage of semiawareness preceding wakening. It was a time when he was accustomed to manipulating his dreams. Since earliest childhood he had a facility for backtracking, revising and redirecting.

The nightmare would not respond. The dark pursuer remained, closing in, reaching out. . . . A haunting, seductive, yet somehow pathetic and hungry longing kept touching Gathrid's mind.

There was a familiar flavor to it. . . . He recognized it. It was the thing that had possessed the Dead Captain. It still lived. And it was determined to have him as its new host.

''Theis!'' He jerked upright, grabbing for the dwarf.

Rogala had disappeared. Gathrid jumped up. He began blundering through the brush.

Rogala ghosted out of the darkness. ''Be quiet!'' he hissed. ''And get down.''

''It's after me!'' Gathrid babbled. ''It's getting closer. It almost got me this time.'' He was getting loud, but could not stop himself.

Rogala ended his hysteria with a slap. Startled, Gathrid plopped down and rubbed his cheek. There had been a remarkable strength behind the blow.

''Now explain. Quietly.''

Gathrid did so, softly but urgently.

"You should've told me before."

"You could've stopped it?"

"No. But I would've had time to think before it got dangerous. I'll worry about it after we finish tonight's work."

"Eh?"

"Our horses. I've been scouting. There're twenty-three men down there. None with Power. All second-line soldiers led by a lazy sergeant. There were three sentries. I've cared for them already."

"Then we'll have no trouble stealing horses and . . ."

"The horses come afterward."

"But. . . ."

"Daubendiek is weak. It's starving after meeting that thing. It has to be fed."

"Theis, no. I couldn't."

"What?"

"Kill men while they're sleeping."

"Best time. They don't fight back. You remember who they are? They could be the men who tortured your mother. Aren't you hungry? They have more than horses. Boy your age usually eats a ton of fodder a day."

Gathrid needed no reminder. His navel was grinding against his backbone. But to kill men over something to eat. . . . He was not that hungry. Not yet.

The horror of the Ventimiglian invasion had not purged youth's pacifism and idealism. He still saw the world through the lens of should-be. That distorting lens was chipped now. It had a big crack across its middle. It would shatter before long.

"Ideals are a handicap," Rogala insisted. "If you're not flexible about them."

"But. . . ."

"You're going to get your head lopped off, boy. You fight fire with fire in this world. You don't see these Ventimiglians counting scruples, do you?"

"If we sink to their level, we're no better than they are."

"What gives you the idea you are? Human is human, boy. There are two kinds of people. Wolves and sheep. Is the sheep better than the wolf because he bravely lets himself be gobbled? Hardly. These Ventimiglians are pragmatists. I don't yet see their logic, admitted. I don't know their goals. They do have the determination to achieve them." He launched a rambling discourse about great pragmatists he had known.

Gathrid shut him out. He could not stomach the dwarf's primitive philosophizing.

As he talked, Rogala edged nearer the enemy camp. He spoke in an ever softer voice.

Gathrid felt the presence of his haunt. He crowded Rogala.

The cynical old dwarf knew how to motivate him. He talked about Anyeck. Gathrid immediately conjured visions of his sister suffering. The dwarf kept poking that sore spot. Though short-spoken, he could wax colorful when he wanted.

The boy's anger kindled. Rogala fanned it. Hatred conceived in the ruins of Kacalief fed it.

Even so, Gathrid tried to go directly to the horse picket.

Fate intervened.

A sleepy Ventimiglian, leaving his tent on some nocturnal mission, stumbled into the youth. The sleepiness left him. His eyes grew improbably wide. His mouth opened. . . .

Gathrid seized the Sword's hilt and flung the blade around.

For a vertiginous instant he relived the entire mean, small life of Grems Migneco, who had known little joy till Ahlert's conquests had allowed his brutal nature full play. It ended on a high, piquant note of terror.

Daubendiek hummed softly, pleased, but was not satisfied. Having tasted blood at last, it lusted for more. Much more. Rivers. Oceans.

And Gathrid could not deny it. Mastering the blade eluded him. Tired, weak in spirit, eager to escape the thing that pursued him, he welcomed its control and exultation.

The soldier's gurgling death brought three more victims from the tent.

Ventimiglians slept lightly, Gathrid reflected. Maybe there had been other night attacks. Gudermuth would not have submitted passively.

Their quick response did them no good. Swift as an adder's strike, death darker than the darkness, Daubendiek penetrated their guards and flesh, slashing and slicing as if against no resistance at all. The Ventimiglians accomplished only one thing: they wakened their company. Sleepy men rushed toward Gathrid and death.

He was involved no longer. He had become an adjunct of the Sword, a sickened observer watching the ultimate power manipulate his hands.

The first rush gave him no trouble. The Ventimiglians were expecting other raiders. Then they realized he was alone, decided he was a madman making a suicide attack.

Alone? Gathrid thought. What happened to Theis? He was right behind me a minute ago.

Daubendiek screamed joyously. The Ventimiglians grew pale, but persisted. In brief flickers Gathrid and his weapon drank wretched, unhappy lives, yet lives in which, inevitably, there was something joyful, some treasured memory that made each soul unique among so many others of similarly mean origins. The Sword now needed but to wound lightly to slay. Bodies piled round Gathrid.

From his perch behind the eyes of a body that had become a murder machine, Gathrid tasted the sour flavor of their pasts and pitied them. They came of a class where hopelessness and pain reigned supreme. They had made the Mindak's dream their own. It promised escape from the endlessly repetitive, dreary march of their days.

Understanding one's enemy, Gathrid had been told, was the first step to conquering him. Or bringing him to the peace table.

They were all around him now. Guarding his own back was hopeless. And it would not be long till someone thought of using a bow.

A scream ripped from among the Ventimiglian mounts. A dozen horses stampeded. As many cursing soldiers pursued them. Gathrid remained facing three wary foes. They would not venture within Daubendick's reach.

Where was Rogala?

The animals that had not spooked began rearing and screaming. Rogala burst from the herd astride one, reins in his mouth. He clutched a weapon in one hand, led a second mount with the other. He ploughed into Gathrid's opponents.

The youth attacked while they dodged the dwarf. Only one man escaped.

Rogala told him to mount up.

"No saddle."

"I'm sorry, Your Lordship. I had Hell's own time just getting the bridles on."

That was as near a reference to his own height that Gathrid had heard from the man.

"Come on, boy. They won't wait all night."

Gathrid jumped, got his belly over the horse's back. Several Ventimiglians came charging out of the darkness. Some had recovered mounts. Rogala whooped and took off. Gathrid clung for his life, almost losing the Sword.

The Ventimiglians cursed and howled. A javelin plunged past Gathrid's nose. It electrified him. He dragged himself astride the animal.

Wars and adventures, seen from the inside, were no fun at all.

Chapter Five
Round Katich

The region round Gudermuth's capital had been torched and scourged. Even the birds, animals and insects were dead or flown. Rubble and ashes were the lone monuments to ages of handiwork by Nature and Man.

Katich's old gray walls and towers, smoke-stained, rose in unbroken defiance amidst the encircling Ventimiglian host. Royal banners trailed proudly in the smoky wind. And that explained the desolation. The Mindak was a bitter enemy.

Rogala was impressed. "No half-measures for your Mindak. There isn't a cockroach alive out there."

"The Brotherhood must have sent help. Otherwise the city would have fallen. I guess they're buying time for the Alliance." He was puzzled, though. With Nieroda and the Toal to back him, Ahlert should have smashed any Brotherhood deputation long since. And where *were* the allies? Something should have been seen of them by now.

Siegework was in progress. The Ventimiglians were pushing trenches toward the walls. No doubt they were mining, too. The operation showed more patience than was customary with the easterners.

"Don't look like much magic from here," Rogala said.

"Maybe they're all out hunting for us." Shuddering, Gathrid looked around. He saw nothing but wasteland and a few Ventimiglians on the east road, shepherding their army's supply trains.

"This Ahlert isn't much of a general," Rogala observed. "When your army is going to be rooted, you don't waste the countryside around it."

"He probably didn't plan to stay long. He's not used to resistance."

"This was done for spite, boy. Pure spite."

Rogala had been garrulous since they had stolen the horses, though he only talked about geography and politics. He still ignored Gathrid's questions.

Perforce, Gathrid had done a lot of thinking about himself, his future, Daubendiek, Rogala and this war. The Sword could be invaluable to the Alliance.

He did not want to be the man wielding it.

Rogala was adamant in refusing to answer questions about Tureck Aarant and the Brothers' War. He did, grudgingly, admit that Aarant had been one of several previous Swordbearers. "Suchara chooses," he said. "We mortals can but obey. There are greater plans, higher destinies. Some of us have to sacrifice our homes, happiness, lives and even our souls to them." He looked first sad, then rebellious. Then he shrugged. "When the Powers lay their hands on us, we can but obey and hope."

"You've seen it," Gathrid said of Katich. "Now what?"

"There's a war on. We're on the side of the people inside there. We'll try to help them."

"Two men?" Gathrid had changed that much. He had begun to think he had the makings of a man.

"Two men and Daubendiek. I said Ahlert was a poor general. We'll make him pay for his mistakes."

"Those convoys are guarded."

"By second-line troops. We'll start tonight. You kill. I'll torch."

Gathrid protested. Guerrilla raiding did not seem fit employment for the Great Sword. In the stories Tureck Aarant had borne the blade in the great charges, or had sought out enemy champions and had slain them in single combat. Labruyere, Vuichard, Hanschild, Ingebohs, even Grellner himself had met the Swordbearer and had perished. Now Rogala wanted his new Swordbearer to murder nameless kerns. Partisan warfare was a pursuit for gutless peasants.

His thoughts must have shown. "One thing you learn about war," Rogala told him. "You use the weapon at hand and you kill the enemy where you find him. And you do what you have to to win."

"That sounds like three things."

"Whatever. We can't get into the city, so we do what we can from here. To me that reads make the other side hungry."

Gathrid wanted no more fighting, but had run out of arguments. Flat refusal did not occur to him. He had been led all his life, by his parents and brothers, teachers and sister. He was accustomed to giving in when persuasion failed. Moreover, he was a Gudermuther of noble class. He was responsible for the defense of his kingdom and people.

They made their first raid by moonlight, hitting a square of four fat wagons defended only by sleepy drivers and a half-dozen unready soldiers. The slaughter was swift and complete and, at Rogala's insistence, included the Ventimiglian animals. Afterward, Gathrid was sick. The emotional debts had begun to overtake him.

With the sickness came disorientation. His mind had not yet learned to quickly accept the life experiences of Daubendiek's victims, nor to integrate them smoothly with his own. When the Sword released its hold, he felt fragmented, unsure of his identity.

Tendrils of greed, feelers from the thing that pursued him, nibbled at the edges of his soul. His whole being fought for its existence. In pushing the demon out, his personality reasserted itself.

Maybe he was too weak to cope with magicks of these orders.

They raided again. Both the killing and assimilation became easier. That frightened Gathrid. Over and over, he told himself, "I won't become another Tureck Aarant!" He did not want to be remembered solely as a man who had trafficked in bloodshed.

He and Rogala took what supplies they needed, went to ground during the day. Gathrid found daytime sleeping less punishing. The demon seldom stalked him then.

The third night Rogala insisted on making two strikes. "Why are we bothering?" Gathrid asked. He peered at the ominous comet. It did not seem to be growing larger. "The men and supplies we've destroyed weren't a drop in the river they're moving up to the city."

"Because their logistics are strained," Rogala replied. "The thread we pull may be the one that unravels the whole siege. And because you need educating. This is your novitiate, your apprenticeship. You don't become Swordbearer simply by taking up the blade. You and Daubendiek are like bride and groom. You have to get to know one another. You have to meld into a single inconquerable engine of destruction. That takes time and practice."

"Why?"

The dwarf looked bemused.

Gathrid kept his disgust to himself. Rogala was deaf to any protest.

The fourth night the enemy mounted patrols along the road to Katich. The wagons they attacked were stoutly defended. They spent the remainder of the night skirmishing with and fleeing from patrols which had begun closing in during their raid.

Gathrid could not count his worries. But one old one was important no longer. His body felt healthier than he could remember it ever being. His leg bothered him not at all.

Their fifth night of raiding was one more of confusion than one of action. "Their patrols are everywhere," Gathrid complained.

"You expected them to put up with us forever?" Rogala snapped. "Of course they're starting to come back at us."

The youth studied the encampment they were scouting. It was the third they had approached. "We can't take this one either." The guards were numerous and alert.

"We'll try another one." Rogala sounded grim. He was determined to attack. His enemies were not cooperating.

The tale was the same everywhere. Ahlert's people were waiting.

"All right," Rogala grouched, "if you won't play out here, we'll just rag your main camp. You won't be looking for us there."

"Are you crazy? You don't go whacking a hornet's nest with a stick."

An hour later, as they stole nearer Katich and the vast Ventimiglian encampment facing the capital, Rogala yielded to Gathrid's incessant importunities. "All right!" he snarled. And muttered, "Gutless children." He led the way in a long arc around the city, growing sourer by the mile.

Sunrise found them departing desolation for more hospitable countryside north of the Gudermuther capital. An hour later they were hidden in a wood.

"Get some sleep," Rogala said as Gathrid consumed the last of a cold breakfast. "Pretty soon we won't get much chance."

Gathrid needed no more encouragement.

Shouts and the clash of arms wakened him shortly after noon. At first he thought them part of his dreams. When not being stalked by the slain Toal, he relived fragments of the pasts of Daubendiek's victims.

The noise continued after he opened his eyes. He looked for Rogala. The dwarf and his horse had vanished.

Was Theis in trouble?

The racket came from beyond a low rise west of the thicket where they had concealed their encampment. Keeping low, Gathrid scurried to the crest.

Ventimiglian and Gudermuther infantry were locked in a death struggle on the far side. The outcome was beyond doubt. There were fifteen Ventimiglians, only eight Gudermuthers. Men from both companies lay dead or wounded. It looked like the culmination of a hunt for fugitives from some battle already fought. A Ventimiglian junior officer, mounted, watched boredly from a safe distance.

Gathrid withdrew, ran to camp, cinched his recently stolen saddle, mounted, returned—and at the crest, after having revealed himself, had second thoughts. He halted. All eyes turned his way.

The officer drew his sword, spurred his mount in the youth's direction.

Gathrid drew Daubendiek.

He had no idea what the combatants saw. Whatever, they fled, the officer outdistancing them all. Gathrid slew one Ventimiglian, regretted it immediately. There had been no need. He had accomplished his purpose by scattering the fighters.

He fretted all afternoon. Where was Rogala? Why didn't he show up? What would happen now?

The dwarf sensed trouble the instant he arrived. "What happened?"

Gathrid explained.

"Should've stayed out of it, boy. Now they don't just

suspect, they know. Plenty of witnesses. You think we were on the run before, you haven't seen anything.''

"They were my people.''

"You'll learn. You're the Swordbearer. You don't have any people now. You have Daubendiek, Theis Rogala, Suchara and Death.''

Just what Tureck Aarant had had. And Suchara promised nothing in return. "But. . . .''

"You'll learn. Come on. We've got to get moving. They're probably closing in already.''

They were. The first time the pair approached the edge of the wood, near where they had entered, they found a Ventimiglian battalion preparing to sweep through. The ensign of a sorcerer-general accompanied the unit standard.

"Bad,'' Rogala muttered. "He spots us, our only hope is to outrun them. And that'll be impossible if he's in touch with the others. Better put your scruples away, boy, and get ready for a fight. A real fight this time.''

"What's wrong with scruples, Theis? They . . .''

"Because you'd be the only one at the party with them. They're going to get you hurt if you don't turn loose.'' The dwarf wheeled, led the way to another verge. The enemy had not yet appeared there, but dust clouds were approaching.

Rogala had flown to the spot like a pigeon to its coop, Gathrid reflected as they cantered across open terrain. They escaped the closing circle only a quarter mile ahead of galloping horsemen. In his way, in his field, Rogala was certainly competent. Useful, if one had need of a bloodthirsty dwarf.

"What're we going to do?'' the youth asked.

"Make a run for the border. Get over into this kingdom you call Bilgoraj. Maybe we can shame your allies into doing something.'' The dwarf kicked his mount into a gallop.

The chase was on. It continued throughout the night, growing painful and exhausting. Rogala was in his element, running like a fox before hounds, enjoying himself hugely as he matched wits with the Ventimiglian commanders. He strove to keep a southwest heading, toward where the border made its closest approach, but torch-bearing riders kept turning them west and north, toward a border twenty miles more distant. Rogala conceded the ground.

Once they skirmished with a party of four, and took fresh mounts, but lost ground to the growing pursuit. Above the night, a waning moon ghosted westward like a mocking grin in cloth of diamond-studded black felt. The ominous comet led it by thirty degrees. The latter was twice the size it had been when first Gathrid had seen it.

As false dawn sketched the horizon behind them, where fires glowed and pillars of smoke wandered up to mask the lower stars, Rogala shouted, "We're not moving fast enough. They're guiding us. Watch for trouble."

Trouble found them as, moments later, they crested a hill. Across a shallow, misty valley a lone dark rider waited.

A Toal.

Where one could be found others were likely to appear, including the master devil himself.

"Ride over him," Rogala ordered.

Easy to say, Gathrid thought.

The Toal awaited them in full knight's regalia, every piece some sorcery-haunted relic unearthed from the Mindak's mines of the past. The Toal's lance caught the light. It was crystal alive with internal fire. Its shield was a swirling surface from which one or another of Hell's tenants occasionally leered forth. Its armor was the familiar black, and proof against mortal blades.

But its mount most inspired Gathrid's awe. Dragon was the name that came to mind, yet it only vaguely resembled the huge, sinuous, winged monster of artists' conception. It stood horse high. It was heavily scaled, and a third longer than a horse. Its legs bowed remarkably. The Toal sat far forward, almost astride the beast's neck. Wings protruded behind the rider, lying close against the beast's flanks. Gathrid wondered if they were functional. Nothing that large ought to fly.

"Guide right," Rogala shouted as they roared toward the Toal. "Make him swing his lance across his body."

Gathrid tried, almost collided with the cursing dwarf. He wondered how he was supposed to get inside the lance's reach, and what the devil, without shield or armor, he was doing attacking.

The Toal swung with him. Soon he and Gathrid were riding parallel, swirling the low patches of mist in the deepest part of the vale. The youth had failed. It was he who had to swing his weapon across his body.

The Dead Captain's mount was preternaturally quick. It darted in and out, trying to catch him off guard.

At each lance thrust Daubendiek lightninged over. Each meeting produced a thunderclap, noisome smoke and a numbing shock in Gathrid's arm. Yet Daubendiek felt no distress.

The Toal was playing with him, he realized. It was keeping him occupied while awaiting unwitting help from his mount. Over the rough ground, still concealed by the mist, his animal would stumble sooner or later.

Gathrid put all his strength into an attempt to shatter the fiery lance. He succeeded only in making the thunder louder.

But Rogala, too, was in the fray. The dwarf drifted round to the Toal's left quarter. Gathrid redoubled his assault on the Dead Captain's lance. Rogala planted his short blade in the dragon's haunch.

The beast was swift. It stopped dead, leapt into the air. Its wings flashed and slapped, making a gonglike crash. It slew Rogala's horse with a single snap of traplike jaws. It barely missed Rogala as he threw himself over his mount's rump.

The Toal lost its seat too, yet recovered quickly. Gathrid wheeled for the kill. He found the thing setting its lance like an infantry pike.

"Forget him!" Rogala bellowed. "We've got to get out of here!" He pointed. Crossing a distant ridgeline, airborne on a beast resembling that just injured, trailing a fluttering black cloak, came help for the Toal.

"Nieroda!" Gathrid urged his mount toward the dwarf, scooped him up, kicked the animal into a gallop. The thing that Rogala had wounded bit a chunk from its own flank as they passed, became more enraged. The Toal had to slay it in self-defense.

"Hope that wasn't a family heirloom you left back there," Gathrid shouted over his shoulder.

"Knives I can replace, boy. My skin I can't. Shut up and ride."

The youth glanced back, saw the Toal's arm thrust their way. It was about to use the weapon Gathrid had seen at Kacalief. He tightened his grip on Daubendiek. A chuckle redolent of the thing that haunted his dreams seemed to echo from everywhere around him.

A blast of light took his sight away.

Daubendiek quivered, groaned, absorbed the sorcery.

Gathrid looked back again, vision quickly regained. Nieroda was closer. His flyer seemed slow and clumsy.

They crested the far wall of the valley and saw that this would not be a long race. The Bilgoraji border was nearer than they had suspected. Astride a road which wandered in from their left stood a city of tents, a forest of standards. "We've struck the Torun Road," Gathrid guessed. "That's the Alliance army." Gasping, he identified the banners of most of the Allied kingdoms, and those of several Brotherhood Orders.

Rogala grunted with each piece of information absorbed.

"Why haven't they done something?" Gathrid wondered.

"Get us there and we'll find out!" Rogala snapped.

Nieroda had seen the army, too. He put on more speed

by steepening the angle of his glide. He closed fast. Gathrid struggled to ready himself and the Sword.

There was a stir ahead. Knights and men in the robes of the Brotherhood rushed toward the frontier. They remained just beyond the customs shed delineating the border. That puzzled and angered Gathrid. A scrupulous respect for Gudermuth's already shattered sovereignty suggested political intrigue. "There'll be an accounting," he muttered.

"We're not going to make it," Rogala told him. "He has room for one pass. I'll tell you when."

They were little more than a hundred yards from the border when Rogala growled, "Get ready to swerve. Now!"

Gathrid yanked his reins. His horse screamed. Rogala flung himself off, lit and rolled like a professional tumbler. A bolt from a crossbow lying across Nieroda's lap blistered the air where Gathrid's mount had been, struck earth at Rogala's heels, left a fist-sized, smoking black hole. The dwarf responded with mountain-moving curses.

Daubendiek lightninged up and opened a yard of the flyer's belly.

The creature's soul was as alien as the thing that had possessed the slain Toal. Gathrid sensed only coldness, bloodthirst and a feeling of the thing having spent ages asleep. It was another of the Mindak's past delvings.

The thing screamed. Its wings beat like gongs. The very air seemed to try fleeing. Nieroda roared angrily. Mount and rider hit earth in a thrashing tumble.

The Dark Champion got off another bolt while falling. This one Gathrid could not evade. Daubendiek could not turn it. Gathrid jumped. His horse took the impact, moaned, collapsed. A charred flesh smell filled the air.

The earth came up too fast. Gathrid *knew* he would be knocked senseless. Yet he managed to land lightly, on his toes and free hand.

Nieroda stood twenty paces away, blocking his path to

the border. He swelled into a black giant behind which loomed an even larger, nebulous entity.

For an instant Gathrid was frightened. Then Daubendiek's power flooded him as never before. He suffered a moment of disorientation.

The earth dwindled beneath him. Everything human faded into insignificance. He existed alone with his Enemy, and had a self-confidence that was godlike. Never had he felt so alive, so competent, so inconquerable. With a laugh that echoed mockingly off the hills, he brought Daubendiek up to salute his dread opponent.

This was how Tureck Aarant must have felt before his great combats. Daubendiek must have come into the fullness of its Power.

To one side a small, hairy something groveled on the earth and whined, "Suchara be praised. Suchara be praised. Your servant no longer doubts."

"Come, Hellspawn. Come, Nieroda. Receive the kiss of Suchara," Gathrid thundered. He put his lips to the quivering blade of the Great Sword. It had grown hot.

Over the border the Alliance ranks began to show gaps as fainthearts fled. Even those in the colored robes of the Orders looked ready to panic. Gathrid saw, and did not care.

But he could not see himself.

From across the frontier they saw Nieroda huge in an envelope of Cimmerian mist, and past him a blinding man-shape of fire surrounded by aquamarine haze. The haze had about it suggestions of a woman's face. Some even saw blood-red eyes burning over the Swordbearer's shoulders.

Daubendiek, too, had its apparent growth and backing aura. For a moment the Swordbearer had a fist filled with blades, as if Daubendiek itself were but the iceberg tip of an enchantment spanning multiple dimensions.

For Gathrid the world continued to diminish, to narrow, to become unreal, till his universe contained but one concrete object. The Enemy. The thing that called itself Nevenka Nieroda.

A vagary crossed his mind. Had Nieroda ever been human?

The darkness and its content remained motionless, waiting, ignoring Gathrid's challenge. It seemed indecisive, as if no longer certain that its own challenge had been wise.

With a Daubendiek that seemed a half-dozen yards long Gathrid clove the Nieroda-darkness. A bolt like that which had slain his horse ripped into the haze surrounding him. He laughed. It tickled.

More than ever, Daubendiek demonstrated a life and will of its own. It moved in deadly patterns no mortal eye could follow, punishing to the limit the weapon which strove to turn it. That was a blade brother to the one once borne by Obers Lek. It had no hope of victory. It screamed out its life as Daubendiek chopped shrapnel from its edge. The Sword sang in a high, exultant voice.

The end came swiftly. Nieroda's blade died with a despairing wail, becoming mortal metal which Daubendiek cut as easily as spidersilk. With a berserker's one-handed backhand swing, Gathrid removed Nieroda's head.

The dark mist faded. A headless little man collapsed. A susurrus of awe ran through the Alliance army.

And Gathrid knew that he had been cheated. He had won a hollow victory. He had slain another man already dead. The thing that had been Nevenka Nieroda had abandoned the body moments before the mortal blow. It remained alive to work its mischief elsewhere. They would meet again, and next time Nieroda would bear crueler weapons.

Gathrid looked around. Whence he had come a half-dozen Toal on dragon mounts had turned their backs and were departing. He would not be able to catch them even were he so inclined.

The small, hairy thing pranced and babbled at his feet, pointing westward. Gathrid stalked toward his motherland's frontier with her protector, Bilgoraj. "Kimach Faulstich, you great King, why have you forsaken your neighbor?" He hoped his words thundered off the hills behind the Alliance army. He was in a vicious rage. King Kimach had failed to keep faith. There would be a reckoning.

They sensed his wrath, over there, though they did not hear it. Hundreds fled. Thousands remained, rooted in their fear.

But as he drew closer the aura and Power leaked away from him. He dwindled. He took his first step into a foreign land as Gathrid of Kacalief, a bewildered sixteen-year-old Gudermuther completely unhappy with the fate that had singled him out.

Calculation replaced fear in the eyes of one Brotherhood observer. He was a fat man all in red. He summoned his henchmen.

Certain allied Kings did the same.

Chapter Six
The Allies

Rogala stared at the map Gathrid had drawn, committing it to memory. The youth said, "It's pretty rough. It's been two years since I studied geography. Right now we're about two hundred yards inside the Bilgoraji border, here."

"It's good enough. The shape of the land hasn't changed, just the borders and names. Not much left of Anderle, is there?"

"You didn't leave a lot to build on. The Hattori and Oldani barbarians came out of the north and overran what was left. They set up a lot of little kingdoms of their own. Those have been banging away at each other for centuries, trying to take each other over. There're only a few of the original royal families left. Then the Emperor plays one King off against another, trying to weaken them, hoping to resurrect the Imperium's old glory. All the Kings say, yeah, it's great to have the Empire around—as a referee in their squabbles—but they don't want it making a real comeback. When you add the

Brotherhood to that already thick soup, you have a real devil's stew.''

They had been given a tent near the edge of the Alliance camp. Elsewhere, captains and Kings were trying to adjust to the presence of the Swordbearer and, perhaps, arrogating to themselves decisions concerning his fate.

Gathrid had wanted to storm through camp raising hell because the Alliance hadn't rescued Gudermuth. Rogala had restrained him, had made him sleep, and now was trying to unravel an international political structure so confusing, so byzantine, that even lifelong participants became bewildered by its complexities. Gathrid's map demonstrated the schizophrenia of present-day boundaries and loyalties.

''Whenever there's a wedding, cities and castles and counties are given as dowry, so all over you have these speckles of one King's territory surrounded by another's. Somebody is always at war with somebody else. Sometimes it looks like they're fighting themselves. Almost chaos, but not anarchy. And the Reds and Blues keep stirring the pot for their own reasons, which most of the time nobody can figure out. The Red Magister, Gerdes Mulenex, wants to be Fray Magister, or chief of all the Orders. A Blue has that job now. Klutho Misplaer. I don't think he'd just give it up.''

''How many of these countries belong to the Alliance?''

''Most of them, directly or indirectly. Like, say, Kimach Faulstich is part, because this is Bilgoraj and he was one of the founding Kings. Even if they're not here in camp, everybody who's related to him, or protected by him, will get pulled in whether they want to or not.'' Gathrid leaned over, tapped the map. ''The really complicated area is west of Bilgoraj and Malmberget. In Gudermuth we missed the worst of it. We minded our own business. Everybody looks west, mostly, toward

Sartain. Anderle isn't what it was, but its capital is still the cultural wellspring of the west.''

Rogala shook his head, muttered what may have been, ''A classic case of feudalism gone to seed.'' Louder, ''Somebody's coming. Let me do the talking.''

Gathrid listened. Several seconds passed before he caught the metallic rhythm of soldiers in cadence. The tramp-tramp stopped not far from the tent. One man moved closer.

Rogala folded the map. ''Just follow my lead,'' he said. ''Try not to give away how green you are.''

''My Lords?'' a voice called. ''The Council of Torun has convened. Will you attend?''

''Be arrogant,'' Rogala whispered. He threw the tent flap back. Gathrid slipped outside, stared at the knight who had come for them. The man was shaky and pale and avoided his eye. His men-at-arms were just as cowed.

''So let's go!'' Rogala snarled.

''After me, my Lords.''

''Don't let them bully you, boy,'' Rogala told Gathrid as they approached the heart of the camp. ''They'll look at the length of your whiskers and try. Just remember, they're more scared of you than you are of them.''

The knight glanced back, frowned. Rogala was dragging his heels, forcing the impatient soldiers to pause again and again. ''The pressure starts getting you, rest your hand on the Sword. Just rest it. Don't draw it unless you need to kill somebody.''

Gathrid wondered at Rogala's game. Why was he stalling? He was not overawed. He had kept company with men far greater than any they would meet today.

''Tell you a secret,'' the dwarf said, divining his thoughts. ''Always be late. It irritates them. Fogs their thinking. You can get the best of them, long as you keep a clear head yourself. And it works whether you're dickering over sausages or provinces.''

Gathrid nodded, though he was not really listening.

He was awed by the men they were about to face. The most important man he'd ever met was his father's liege, the Dolvin.

"Whew!" Rogala spat suddenly, halting. "Will you look at that?" They had come in view of the compound of the Kings. Doubtless Rogala had seen greater opulence in ancient Anderle, but hardly amidst a march to war. "These people aren't serious," he said. "They're just making a show. Running a bluff. Better get a grip on the Sword now, boy. They're going to put us through it."

Gathrid did grasp Daubendiek's hilt after adjusting it so it hung crosswise behind his waist instead of down behind his shoulder. Just a light touch on that grim hilt gave him instant confidence.

He wondered if it really were the Sword, or just something in his head.

Comings and goings round the big tent ceased. "Good. Good," Rogala said. "They're impressed. Give them another touch. I'll teach you yet."

The dwarf surged forward, past the startled knight. He bulled through hangers-on. Gathrid scampered after him.

Rogala shot into a huge tent. Immediately inside lay a curtained receiving room where guards and worktables formed a barrier between world and council. The guards moved to intercept Rogala. They froze at a frown from Gathrid. They hadn't the nerve to stop him.

How good that felt!

The knight yapped at his heels like a worried pup. Gathrid glowered over his shoulder, won some silence. This was his first taste of power. He savored it even though he knew he was being seduced by the Sword.

He and Rogala shoved into the heart of the tent.

Men were shouting at one another there. Fists shook. Threats filled the air. Kings cursed one another for being hardheaded or stupid.

A chamberlain intercepted them and babbled in their faces. His face was bleak with terror. Rogala shoved him inside. Someone in authority bellowed, "Guards, seize those two." Gathrid located the speaker and locked gazes. The man went pale and began to stammer. The guards ignored his instructions.

Gathrid caressed Daubendiek's hilt.

"Got them," Rogala chuckled softly. Into the sudden silence he bellowed, "The Swordbearer. The Chosen Instrument of Suchara. All rise."

Several men did so, sank back angrily.

Gathrid scanned the gathering, keeping his fingers near the hilt of the Sword. Never had he felt so young and clumsy and out of place. Only in wild daydreams had he ever pictured a moment like this. In the dense human press of that tent he saw seven crowned heads. He saw four Brotherhood Magisters, the heads of every Order but the Blue. Dukes and barons attended the great ones. . . . Again and again his fingers went to Daubendiek's hilt.

One spare, grisled old man caught Gathrid's eye. His uniform marked him as a high officer of the Anderlean Empire's army. He seemed amused by the interruption. Only he met Gathrid's gaze without flinching. Here, the youth thought, is a man of substance, of character. Who is he? What is he doing here, treated as an equal by the others? For them contempt of the Empire was as fashionable as it was false. Had the Ventimiglian threat made them admit that Anderle was still the spiritual and cultural axis of the west?

Without knowing quite why, Gathrid nodded to the Imperial officer. And it was to the Imperial he addressed himself when his feelings burst forth.

"We have lately come from the environs of Katich, in Gudermuth, capital of a kingdom shielded by Articles of Alliance pledged at the Council of Torun last autumn, and recently reaffirmed in the Treaty of Beovingloh. Perhaps our eyes deceived us. We are young and inexperienced. Perhaps we did not see what we thought we saw. Perhaps in our youthful bemusement we only imagined that a foreign army stands leagued round Katich's walls, and is wasting the countryside, while beyond Bilgoraj's border Gudermuth's sworn allies bivouac and disport themselves with sweet wine and silk-clad courtesans. We are, we admit, inexperienced in these matters and possibly easily deceived. Kimach Faulstich, you great King, where are you? Where is the sworn protector of my homeland?"

No one admitted to being Kimach Faulstich, though that King and his Bilgoraji entourage were amply in evidence.

Gathrid was surprised at the depth and strength of his voice and emotions. He had felt very tentative, launching into the Old Petralian. Plauen had taught the language with dedication, but with despair because his students mangled it so.

Old Petralian was the language of the Anderlean Empire of olden times, of the Imperium of the age of the Immortal Twins. Today it was a highly formalized and formularized tongue reserved for occasions when the vulgate was considered either gauche or insufficiently precise. For Gathrid to have elected its usage before his betters had chosen to do so could, in diplomatic terms, be construed as mildly insulting.

"In Gudermuth the wine has soured. The silks have been torn asunder. The beautiful women weep at the feet of the conqueror. And their men wonder what became of the brothers who pledged them succor at Torun. What became of the swords and lances so boldly rattled then? The wise men, the old warriors, who fought for other Kings in other wars in other lands, and who know the ways of alliances, tell them it takes time. It takes patience. They tell them that they need but hold a while longer.

"But even they have begun to wonder." Gathrid turned slowly, sweeping his gaze round the gathering. His anger disturbed them, but they were thinking he was only a man, even armed with the Sword. Their attitudes were clearly cast on their faces.

Springing from his subconscious, like a leaping dolphin, came the realization that he was not speaking his own words. These were borrowed. He had translated and adapted them, but the originals had been voiced long ago by Obers Lek, before a similar council in another age.

Though he did not yet believe it, did not yet *feel* it, in a sense he was becoming superhuman. He possessed a vast experiential reservoir. He simply had to learn to tap the memories of the men he had slain.

Kimach Faulstich, the Bilgoraji King, upon whom Gathrid was prepared to lay the blame for Gudermuth's demise, chaired the convention both because its army had assembled in his dominion and because he was one of the Alliance's founders. He rose, awaited a lull in the outraged chatter, then answered Gathrid. He, too, spoke Old Petralian. "Who are you, that you dare come among us uninvited, questioning the acts of Kings?"

Kimach had regained his composure quickly. His counterburst calmed the others. They turned hard eyes on Gathrid. One fat Magister eyed Daubendiek with a lust almost obscene.

"The Esquire spoke for me," Gathrid purred. His gaze dared the Magister.

Thus it had been for Tureck Aarant. His closest allies had lusted after the Great Sword. He had endured and survived countless attempts to steal it. He had dared turn his back on no man but Rogala, and even that had proven fatal in the end.

Rogala answered Kimach with an arrogant snort. The Bilgoraji was wasting time. He strolled to a low table facing the lustful-eyed Magister of the Red Order. He kicked a woman aside, dropped to his hams, seized and began gnawing a piece of roast fowl.

The Magister turned as red as his clothing.

With preternatural accuracy the dwarf had chosen a victim sure to be offended. This Magister was the infamous Gerdes Mulenex, the most violently storied member of the Brotherhood.

Mulenex's reputation had run by whisper and innuendo throughout the west. His arrogance and viciousness were legend. His enemies within his own Order, who had tried to thwart his rise, had come to cruel and lingering ends. In his way he was as nasty and ambitious as the Ventimiglian Mindak, though he was a weaker, less imaginative man. He could not endure the sacrifices necessary for one who would seize powers matching those attained by Ahlert. He was limited in his own mastery of the sorceries. He inveigled more competent, less ambitious men into performing his thaumaturgies for him. He was not above stealing their credit.

There was just one upward step Mulenex could take within the Brotherhood, the Fray Magistery or crown of mastery, over all five Orders. No one, and the present Fray Magister, Klutho Misplaer, least, doubted that he meant to try taking that step.

Emperor Elgar, of the Anderlean Imperium, was a friend and political ally of Klutho Misplaer. Both resided in Sartain, capital of the Empire since prehistoric times. The seat and symbol of Brotherhood Power was a grand old palace called the Raftery. The Imperial Palace and the Raftery both had long been braced for a Mulenex intrigue.

Mulenex had confounded everyone by appearing to remain content with his present status, devoting himself to profligate living and hurling scorn at the objects of his ambitions.

Theis Rogala seized a knife. He stabbed a particularly succulent morsel off Mulenex's own plate. Mulenex reached for his own knife.

Rogala stabbed the tabletop between the Red Magister's fingers. "Don't overreach yourself."

Not a whisper could be heard.

Gathrid grinned. The dwarf had done his bullying smoothly.

The officer in Imperial uniform laughed. He nodded amiably when Gathrid glanced his way. There was no love lost between Mulenex and Emperor Elgar XIV. Rumor said Mulenex had eyes for the Imperial Palace.

The dream of Empire had not perished in Sartain. There the true believers went on, ever certain that someday the Golden Age would return. In fact, the dream was not far from the hearts of many of the western ruling class. There were endless intrigues aimed at usurping the Imperial throne, in hopes of founding a rising dynasty.

Gathrid drew a deep breath and thundered, "Where are the allies who spoke so loud and bold?" Politics, he thought in youthful naivete, could be set aside before the threat of a common enemy.

The Emperor's man replied, "Two cohorts of the Guards Oldani are in Katich now, Lord." He smiled at the puzzled, surprised, angry looks he received from his companions in council.

The Guards Oldani, so-called because in olden times they had consisted of barbarian mercenaries, were the Anderlean Emperor's praetorian troops, the cream of the Imperial army. Their ferocity was legend. Their professionalism was respected everywhere. Enfeebled though the Empire might be, neighboring kingdoms seldom warred with it.

The Blue Magister's representative added, "With the Guards are four cabali of the Blue, Lord. Little enough, I grant you. But their captain is Honsa Eldracher himself."

Mulenex roared in outrage. He leapt to his feet. His great jowls wobbled as he thundered, "My Lords! What woe and deceit have we here?" His arms flapped like the wings of a flightless bird. Rogala backed toward Gathrid. He wore an expression of bemused awe. Mulenex was a showman, sure. The man launched a long-winded, vigorous, extemporaneous denunciation of the Emperor and Blues for having intervened unilaterally.

Gathrid whispered to Rogala, "The Fray Magister is

72

from the Blue Order. Honsa Eldracher is his daughter's husband and his stand-in as Blue Magister. This explains why the Blue Magister isn't here."

Rogala nodded. "Would you say the Emperor and Misplaer are trying to embarrass the fat man?"

Gathrid shrugged. "I don't know. Probably. When a Red says black, a Blue usually says white."

Rogala grinned at Mulenex. "He does go on, doesn't he? Taking it personal, too."

"Honsa Eldracher is the Brotherhood's crown prince. He takes over if anything happens to Misplaer. Mulenex doesn't like it, but there isn't anything he can do. Eldracher is supposed to be the greatest thaumaturge ever produced by the Brotherhood. He don't want to lock horns."

Rogala nodded thoughtfully. He didn't waste much attention on the pyrotechnic Red Magister. He scanned the faces of the audience instead. Gathrid wondered what he read there.

"*Politics* have fettered this army," the youth muttered. He made the word "politics" a curse. "They're going to sit here till Ahlert stomps them like bugs. And they'll die squabbling and intriguing."

Rogala asked, "You under the impression Katich would be in friendly hands if it weren't for politics?"

"No. What gets me is, nobody *cares* what happens in Gudermuth. It's just an excuse to grind their own axes."

"That's what it's all about, son."

"And Ahlert is going to take advantage."

"He'd be a fool if he didn't." The dwarf sneered. "He'll sit over there, scrupulous about respecting frontiers, and laugh his tail off while these clowns use Gudermuth as a counter in a power struggle that may tear their Alliance to shreds. And when the moment ripens, he'll jump all over them. I'm beginning to find human greed, duplicity, weakness and dearth of imagination boringly predictable."

"You shouldn't play games with human lives."

Rogala gave him a strange look. "You're serious, aren't you? You really are as naive as you put on. You're really offended."

"Of course I am!" Gathrid glared at the dwarf. "Enough!" he shouted, breaking in on Mulenex. "A compact was made. If Gerdes Mulenex and his toadies want to renounce it so they can forward their personal ambitions, let them say so. If the rest of you want to use an ally as a piece on a political chessboard, say so. Stop the hypocrisy. Show your true colors. Repudiate the Treaty of Beovingloh. And be accursed by the dying while Ventimiglian brigades trample your fools' dreams."

Rogala threw him a series of savage looks. He was being *too* forthright. He was not supposed to make enemies, he was supposed to goad these men into accepting a will not their own. Of course, Gathrid did not know that. Suchara did not confide in her Swordbearer.

The dwarf did not care a fig for Gudermuth, except insofar as its fate could be used to twist someone's arm in accordance with Suchara's desires.

Gathrid's speech drew scattered applause. Kargus Scanga, King of Malmberget, responded. "Your shaft strikes near the mark, Swordbearer, though I find your phrasing too bold and your companion boorish."

"Boorish?" Rogala squealed, stamping his feet. He grinned as attention focused on him again. "I'm not a great man, I admit. Nor do I stand as tall as some. Yet I ask you, is boorishness strictly a province of class? Are the high and the mighty above *common* courtesy? Is gentility a cruel fiction foisted on the masses by monsters such as this?" He indicated Mulenex with a thumb jab.

"That's entirely possible," Scanga replied. His grin was as broad as the dwarf's. "When I see him in these councils I certainly think so. To the matter at hand. I think we'd all agree we made a mistake at Torun. Not in hammering out an Alliance, but in forging it in such unwieldy form. Swordbearer, it's unfortunate, but we

THE SWORDBEARER

agreed unanimity was a prerequisite for armed action. Naturally, that leaves the decision-making process at the mercy of opportunists." His scowl transfixed Mulenex. There could be no doubt that his accusation was specific.

"Opportunists?" Mulenex howled. "You dare denounce opportunists when just last month your cousin seized the Red livings in Dharsyn and had three Red Brothers put to death? Shame!"

Scanga replied, "That isn't relevant here."

Arnd Tetrault shouted, "Sit down, fat man. You come into my domain and you'll get the same. I hang thieves no matter who they are."

Shifting his ground, Mulenex snapped, "You're obscuring the issue here. . . ." The mood of the council jelled. He made no headway. Who was and who was not obscuring issues was obvious. Even more obvious was Mulenex's increasing unpopularity. The others shouted him down.

Tetrault's voice broke through the uproar. "Let's impale the pig. He's tied us up for the past three days."

Gathrid doubted that Mulenex alone was responsible. Some mechanism in the group unconscious had tripped and, suddenly, the Red Magister had been elected to bear all their sins.

Mulenex turned bright red. He roared. He fumed. He howled and threatened. And every twist of showmanship only dug the hole deeper.

Gathrid suffered a dismaying insight. The debate had a foregone conclusion. The parties were toying with one another, playing for a position of vantage. His intervention, his anger and indignation, were not germane.

Mulenex was stubborn. He invested an hour in verbal attack and grudging retreat before he yielded to the inevitable. By then Gathrid knew he wanted war as much as did his adversaries. He was simply looking for a payoff in return for abandoning his negative stance.

He got in the last word. He thrust an indicting finger Gathrid's way. "I warn you," he cried, voice dramatically atremble. "If we take up this instrument, it will turn in our hands. As well grasp an adder."

Rogala nodded as if conceding the argument.

The Emperor's representative rose. The uproar declined. "My Lords. Magisters. Envoys of principalities great and small. The thing is decided. We march. As it was agreed in treaty, I'll command in the field. Now I want to propose a temporary mechanism whereby we can smooth the functioning of the Alliance, in the face of an implacable, malignant force totally indifferent to our customary squabbles and differences. Till we agree that the eastern peril has abated, let us all acknowledge the supremacy of the Imperium and unite behind the Emperor's standard as though we were Anderleans of old. Let's show this Ventimiglian pestilence a single face crimson with righteous wrath."

Snickers and incredulous whispers fluttered about the assembly. It was a transparent ploy. The Emperor would never yield a single ounce of power acquired.

Gathrid suspected the man's suggestion was offered at the command of his liege, that he had no real hope for the proposal.

"Anderle is dead," Rogala countered, startling everyone. "Your empire is a political fiction, a specter that won't lay still in its grave—though you people seem to find it a useful ghost. Ventimiglia is no fantasy and no spook. Anyone here fool enough to believe Ahlert is going to be satisfied with Gudermuth? Step up here. I'll kill you so the rest of us can get on with our job."

"Here's a reality for you, buffoon," growled the King of Calcaterra, one Arnd Tetrault, a cousin of Kargus Scanga, the King of Malmberget. "The morning despatch from our agent in Gudermuth says that besides himself, his Toal, Nieroda, and his sorcerer-generals, Ahlert now has him a witch-woman who can manipulate the moon-magic. A renegade Gudermuther, at that, and a strong one, though supposedly she isn't yet trained. That puts two elemental powers inside Ahlert's purview.

What do we have to face that? The feckless support of Suchara? These shiftless Orders? I'd sooner trust Ahlert than the likes of Mulenex or Ellebracht. The Mindak comes out and tells you what he wants.''

Ellebracht was, apparently, the Blue representative. Gathrid recalled having heard the name. A relative of the Emperor, closely allied with Klutho Misplaer and Honsa Eldracher.

Mulenex rose to protest. His peers shouted him down. Their language was brutal and offensive.

A Gudermuther woman turned renegade? Gathrid thought, appalled. After what Ahlert had done? Impossible. ''Who is she?'' he demanded. He pictured some gap-toothed crone. Some peasant malcontent eager to requite Gudermuth's nobility for fancied slights.

''The Ventimiglians refer to her as the Witch of Kacalief.''

Witch of Kacalief? He reeled. That said so much. . . . Anyeck. Had to be. . . . Who else could it be? The Mindak had taken several prisoners there, but only his sister would fit the charges. He caressed the Sword, eager for its comfort. His sister. . . . It would be Anyeck's style. She had the black streak. She could turn her back on her past.

Her problem was wanting. Wanting too much. And being unable to see any reason not to do whatever she wanted getting. Rules were mere vexations, perhaps applicable to lesser souls, but to be ignored by her. A desertion to the enemy would be a logical escalation of past selfishnesses. He wondered that he had not expected this from the beginning.

Yet how could she, so quickly, forget what had been done to her family?

He did not doubt that she could. She had little concept of yesterday, and not much more of tomorrow. She existed entirely in the now, incapable of discerning a connection between current events and future consequences.

The youth concealed his shock. He did not want these

people to know who he was, whence he sprang. It was grim work. He succeeded only because the Sword's touch calmed him, because Rogala captured attention by demanding that the Brotherhood smash this witch instantly. The dwarf was quick to make the connection, based on what Gathrid had told him of his home life.

He spoke with a great passion. Gathrid assumed he was covering for him. Had he been less self-involved at the moment, he might have wondered at Rogala's fervor.

"The great Eldracher is on the scene," Mulenex countered. "Let him handle her."

This once the assembly went with the Red Magister. Rogala shrugged at the decision.

The die was cast. Gathrid had what he wanted. The Alliance would enter Gudermuth. And what had his effort profited him? He had nudged a host in the direction of his only living relative. He wore a sad smile. Plauen would have been amused by the irony. Poor dead Plauen, whose candle had been extinguished by the Mindak's whirlwind.

Rogala said, "Time to talk terms, Gentlemen. Suchara has her needs. She won't let Daubendiek serve for free."

There was no debate. The council backed Kimach Faulstich unanimously. He responded, "We're not stumbling into that trap, Rogala. You won't do us the way you did Anderle."

"So be it," the dwarf said. He stalked out of the assembly. After a moment of indecision, Gathrid followed.

What was the dwarf doing, walking out now? There were things to be said, questions to be asked, decisions to be made. . . .

"It's not our problem," Rogala said. "We needed a war. War there'll be. That's sufficient."

The youth had a thousand questions banging around inside his head, but Rogala clammed up when he tried to ask them.

"Be patient. They'll get back to us. They'll want to make sure Daubendiek doesn't go over to the other side."

Gathrid shook his head. Theis did not understand. He and the dwarf seemed to exist in two different realities, so contradictory were their ways of thinking.

An hour earlier Gathrid would have scoffed at the suggestion he might serve the enemy. Now he was not sure. He shared Anyeck's fallible blood. He might become as feckless as Aarant had been.

"We'll stay here till the army moves out," Rogala told him. "We need the rest. And the free meals. Don't wander off. Don't trust anybody, no matter what they say. Don't ever think you're safe. Gerdes Mulenex wasn't the only viper in that snakepit."

Once they reached their tent, Rogala produced pen and ink. "Let's review. We've walked into a complicated setup. Let's see who's who here." He scribbled quickly, producing a list with four columns. "The four major factions I detected," he explained. "One revolves around Kimach Faulstich, our gracious host." His voice dripped sarcasm. He did not think much of the hospitality extended them.

"Yeah," Gathrid agreed. "This is his council, really. Half the assembly were his relatives. Bathon of Bochantin. Forsten of Tornatore. Doslak of Fiefenbruch. Danzer of Arana. All cadets of the House of Faulstich. Forsten and Danzer have Scanga wives, though, and they say Danzer is ruled by his."

"Scanga heads my second faction. Him and the guy who shot off his mouth about the witch."

"Tetrault. Arnd Tetrault. He has a reputation as a hothead and troublemaker. Kargus has only been King for a couple of years. He's been trying to break the old cycle of constant skirmishing over rich cities and counties. Tetrault has been more harm than help."

Rogala silenced him. "I don't need to know all that. Two more. The Empire and the Brotherhood. The Blue faction of the Brotherhood sides with the Emperor. Part sides with Mulenex. Part looked like it didn't want anything to do with anybody."

"The spokesman for the Blues was Bogdan Elle-bracht. He's related to Emperor Elgar, and he's tight with Misplaer and Eldracher. I can't tell you much about the Yellow, Green or White Orders, except that they claim to be what the Brotherhood was really all about when it was founded."

"Son, you're proving a favorite point of mine."

"What's that?"

"That everybody knows more about everything than they think they know. I have a pretty good picture of the lineups now. Motives. . . . They're still a little shadowy. The trouble with trying to map them is, most people don't really know what they want themselves."

"What do you mean?"

"Think about it. Even when you think you know why you're doing something, is that always the real reason? Is that the reason you admit? No. Not very often. Here. What about the old man? The Imperial soldier. I have a feeling the Empire is going to become very important before we're done."

"I didn't hear anybody say who he is. He's not the Emperor, though. Elgar is supposed to be so fat he can't get out of the palace."

"Make a guess."

Gathrid drew a blank. He could not recall Plauen having talked much about the modern Empire, except to label it a weakling, lost in fantasies of its past, battling for life in a hostile age, constantly stalked by hostile intrigues.

"The ones to watch are him and Mulenex," the dwarf mused. "Mulenex is ambitious, but only in a small-minded, predictable way. Dangerous only if you don't keep one eye on your back. The other, though . . . I couldn't read him at all."

Rogala's head jerked up. "What's that?" His ears almost wriggled. He whispered, "Get the Sword."

"What is it?"

Rogala tapped his ear.

Then Gathrid heard the stealthy feet, too. The tent was surrounded. Men were closing in.

Someone cut a rope. The tent began to topple. Gathrid swept Daubendiek round in wild strokes that ripped fabric away, negating the trap. He attacked out of the ruin. Two lives fed the Great Sword. Other attackers fled.

"Short and sweet," Rogala said. "That's the way I like it. You're learning, boy. Got any idea who sent them?"

"In broad daylight." The sun stood directly overhead. "No. They didn't know. What should I do? Where are you?" Rogala had disappeared. The youth saw flickers of hairiness between tents as the dwarf dogged the fleeing assassins.

Ignoring bystanders, Gathrid dragged the bodies together, then attacked the apparently vain task of restoring the tent. He kept a wary eye out for would-be plunderers. He wanted to examine those corpses before anyone else touched them.

I'm starting to think like Theis, he thought. Always suspicious.

The jangle of panoplies approached. He turned toward the sound. And smiled puzzledly. The Emperor's man had come visiting.

He would have expected Mulenex first.

The crowd evaporated. Gathrid turned to the bodies. He doubted they would tell him anything, but a search had to be made.

His doubts were well-founded. Each man carried gold minted in Bilgoraj, but that told him only that they had been paid exceedingly well, not who their paymaster was. Only a fool would have paid them in self-damning coin.

"Trouble, son?" the Imperial officer asked.

Gathrid glanced up, looked around. Imperial soldiers surrounded him, facing outward. Protecting him? Or? . . . "Only for these two." He was becoming accustomed to his role. "Rogues from Torun, disguised as soldiers."

"What happened?"

Gathrid sketched the story.

"So. It's begun. They're after the blade already. Rather sudden, eh?"

"They were here on retainer," Gathrid said, retrieving snatches of their memories. "They expected to be used in an assassination attempt, but not this one. As to what they expected to accomplish with me . . . I don't know." They had not known that themselves. Their leader may have, but he was one of those who had gotten away. "Could it be they were sent to get Rogala out of the way so somebody could talk to me alone?" He locked gazes with the old soldier, could not tell if he had hit the mark. The man had a face of stone.

He did not believe his suggestion. His had been a random bolt loosed to see what might flush from the brush.

"I know whom you represent," Gathrid said. "But your identity has escaped me so far."

"Yedon Hildreth. Count Cuneo. Commander of the Guards Oldani and Chief of the Imperial General Staff."

"Ah. I should have guessed, shouldn't I? The former mercenary. Battle of Avenevoli, and so forth. You're a Count now? You've done well for yourself. Yes, I should have guessed." Yedon Hildreth was the most widely known Imperial soldier, and a man with a hard reputation. Gathrid was astonished by his own temerity. The Sword was making him bold. "Yes. Who else would the Emperor have sent?"

"The Imperium rewards those who serve it with trust." Hildreth showed the same humor as during Mulenex's discomfiture. Gathrid had an unpleasant suspicion the man was divining his thoughts.

Hildreth's reputation made him appear capable of the maneuver Gathrid had suggested. But he would not fling assassins into the breeze, the way Gerdes Mulenex might. He would be careful and cunning. He would do nothing that could be laid at the Emperor's door. He was said to be Elgar's, heart and soul, and a devout advocate of Imperial resurrection. He was believed by many to be Elgar's chosen successor.

The Imperial crown did not pass down patrilineally. Since time immemorial Emperors had chosen their successors from among their most able subjects, usually with the consensus of the people of Sartain. When the latter did not accept the choice, the Imperial capital would rock with civil strife till some strongman elected himself and squelched the rioting.

"Now we know who I am," Hildreth said. He chuckled as if at a weak joke. "So tell me, who are you? What are you?"

"Sir?"

"Look at the situation from another viewpoint, son. You came out of a land under Ventimiglian dominion. You bear a blade that should have stayed buried. We don't have the slightest guarantee that you're not an agent of Ahlert. That little show at the border could have been staged."

"But. . . ." On second reflection, Gathrid saw Hildreth's point. They did have nothing but his word. His and Rogala's, and for ages Rogala's had been worth nothing

Hildreth continued, "I accept you at face value, proof or no. But does that make any difference? Not really. Your show in council only betrayed your essential ignorance of what's really going on west of Gudermuth. Obviously, you see politics only at its most primitive level. You dared chastize Kings and mock princes of the Brotherhood without knowing what you were talking about. That worries me."

"Sir?"

"It makes me wonder how wise you are, son. About whether or not you're in the dwarf's thrall. Are you another Grellner? Another Tureck Aarant?"

"I'm what you see, Count. Becoming Swordbearer wasn't my idea. Rogala didn't like it much either. In fact, he was more disappointed by the Sword's choice than I was. Yes, I'm naive. I wasn't trained for this. I didn't plan to take up the Great Sword.''

"Neither did Tureck Aarant.''

"I repudiate the paths of Grellner and Aarant, Count. Yes, I know the old tales. *My* path will remain honorable.'' A small weakness, a touch of his fear, leaked through as he added, "If Suchara wills it.''

"That's the catch, isn't it?''

"It looks like it from here.''

"You're a likable sort, it seems. I'll give you that. A word, then. To you. To Rogala. To Suchara herself if she can be bothered. The Imperium won't let itself be ruined again.''

Gathrid smiled. He forebore observing that Anderle had no power to threaten. He said only, "Let's not become enemies over possibilities, Count. We all have too many realities to face right now. Don't worry about Daubendiek.''

"But I have to, son. The thing has a cruel history.''

Gathrid hoped he concealed his feelings as he remarked, "So it does. I hope it's less so this time.''

"And the Empire?''

"A dream that slumbers. I don't believe it'll waken in my lifetime. I don't really care either way. Gudermuth is my main concern.'' The youth congratulated himself for having fashioned a sound noncommittal answer.

"Good enough. For now.'' Hildreth stared piercingly, then led his retainers back toward the center of camp.

Rogala appeared a moment after the Count departed. "Well done, lad. You're learning fast.''

"I thought . . .''

"I turned back.''

"Why didn't you? . . .''

"Wanted to watch you handle yourself. You did fine. Get some sleep. We'll have to be on our toes tonight. They'll try again. Once isn't enough to convince that sort. Here. Let me take care of this mess. That's what an esquire is for.''

The sun had not drifted far westward when Gathrid was wakened by an argument. One voice was Rogala's. The other was unfamiliar, and spoke too softly to be understood. When the dwarf slipped inside their resurrected tent, the youth asked, "What was all that?"

"Messenger from Gerdes Mulenex. Old fatty summoned us to the presence. *Ordered* us to attend him. Whatever you say about him, he's not short on nerve."

"What did you say?"

"Told him he knows where to find us if he wants to talk."

"Sounded like you said more than that."

Rogala laughed. "A little. The man's attitude irritated me. The others were at least polite."

"Others?"

"Sure. Heard from almost everybody in camp. Some of them had some interesting propositions. But they all had nothing but their own gain in mind. You'd think they never heard of Ventimiglia."

"Depressing, isn't it?"

"There are times when I think the gods ought to scrub the whole human race and start over. Go lie down. Night will get here all too soon."

Chapter Seven

Gudermuth

A gentle hand wakened Gathrid. Another covered his mouth. "It's time," Rogala whispered.

It was dark. He had been more tired than he had thought. His haunt had not bothered him.

How did Rogala manage?

They crept from the battered tent, concealed themselves in a firewood dump nearby. The camp was still. The fires had burned low. Crickets and nightbirds called against the darkness. Scurrying clouds masked the moon.

Gathrid reflected on himself while he waited. He had changed. He had grown, had gained self-confidence. He had begun looking for ways to seize the helm of his own destiny.

For instance, he had decided to do something about Anyeck. And he still owed Nieroda. There would be an accounting with Ahlert's Dark Champion.

Anyeck puzzled him. He thought he knew his sister. He believed himself free of illusions about her character. He had been her confidant. How could she have possessed the Power and have kept it hidden?

Maybe he was wrong. Maybe he had jumped to a conclusion only because he *thought* he knew her. She could not have kept the Power hidden. She was too greedy and compulsive not to have used it. Wasn't she?

Who else could the witch be, then?

His thoughts drifted back to childhood years, to silly, blind years of games and little pleasures, when the most difficult moral dilemmas had been the decision whether or not to tell the truth when a question about Anyeck's conduct arose. . . . There had been a noncom in the garrison who had informed their father of one of her misdeeds. Gathrid had forgotten the exact circumstances. He did recall that the soldier had, immediately afterward, been stricken dumb. No one had been able to explain. Then there had been the time . . .

"Here they come," Rogala whispered.

Gathrid chivied himself out of the wilderness of memory, peered round the woodpile. Men with drawn swords were stealing toward their tent. He took the Sword's grip. . . .

Rogala's touch stayed him. "Let them be disappointed. Let's see who they run to."

"Good thinking."

Finding no prey, the assassins withdrew. They did not panic, nor did they forget to cover their backtrail.

The army had begun stirring. It was to move out at dawn. Tracking the assassins proved difficult. A series of interlocuters made tracing the heart of responsibility almost impossible.

"Levels," Rogala muttered. "He's no fool."

Between them they managed to maintain contact. The trail ended at the pavilion belonging to Gerdes Mulenex.

"Tit for tat," Rogala promised solemnly. "But we have to wait our turn. We've got to move with the army."

"Thought we were letting them fight their own battles."

"We are. But I want to be there to watch."

The camp crawled like an anthill as the noncoms turned their men out early.

Gathrid's homeland had changed. The smoke had cleared. The birds sang across the countryside, celebrating the gods knew what. The few Ventimiglians he and Rogala saw were hurrying toward Katich. The Mindak was gathering his forces outside the capital's walls. "He knows the Alliance is moving," Rogala averred.

He and Gathrid did not move with the army itself, but parallel to it, within a few hours' ride. They avoided Ventimiglians, Alliance patrols, and all but one group of refugees. Those they quizzed. They learned that Ahlert had bragged he would reduce Katich and destroy the Alliance army the same day.

"That much arrogance might become its own reward," Rogala observed as they rode off to well-wishes from folk with whom Gathrid had shared his meager supplies. "A man makes brags, he'd better deliver. A couple failures and some ambitious general will take a shot at snatching his job."

"He could have the power and know it."

"Of course he could. He obviously thinks he does. But a wise man does his deed, then he brags. There's less chance of looking a fool that way. What's kept him out of Katich so long? A quick victory there might have awed the Alliance into backing down again."

Gathrid returned to an argument they had been pursuing since he had revealed his suspicions about Anyeck. "Theis, I meant it about stopping my sister. It's something I have to do. I don't care if it is free help for the Alliance."

He kept bouncing back and forth between that and his question about what profit he could expect for his misery as Swordbearer. Rogala answered curtly when he would talk at all. At that moment he entered his sour and silent phase again.

"All right. All right. A man does what he has to. Do

88

what you want. You won't listen to me, and I'm getting sick of listening to you.''

Gathrid grinned. The dwarf's scolding reminded him of his mother's. . . . The memory left a bitter taste. They had been close, he and she.

Vengeance was necessary.

Alliance patrols became more numerous. They saw more bands of Ventimiglians. Occasionally they came across the wrack of skirmishes, then a field where a small, fierce battle had been lost by Malmbergetan infantry.

"One of the Toal was here," Gathrid said. A trail of corpses marked its path through the action. "No ordinary blade would have cut that deep."

His Toal-shadow, lurking at the edge of consciousness, became excited by the supposed proximity of its fellow.

Rogala shrugged. "There hasn't been much sorcery so far. I find that interesting."

"So far. Maybe it hasn't been needed. Weren't we here before?''

"Yes. There's a plain the other side of that ridgeline. I'd guess they'll meet there. A set battle. Lots of blood. Victory to the stubbornest. No strategy, no finesse. The only soldier I saw in that lot was Count Cuneo, and they gave him command in name only. They'll interfere all the way down the line. Politicians!'' He snorted, shook his head, growled. "If war is too important to trust to generals, then policy is too important to trust to politicians.

"Well, that's neither here nor there. Right now I want a look from yon hill. Katich is only ten miles on."

"Where's the desolation?''

"You'll see plenty from the hill."

Rogala, Gathrid reflected, had a remarkable memory. "Has the land changed much? I mean, since the Imperium?''

The dwarf frowned, shrugged. "Some. It's wilder now. Unkempt, you might say. During the High Imperium, while the Immortal Twins reigned, the Inner Provinces were like parks. In those days they weren't preoccupied with wars, politics or juggling the Treasury. Life wasn't iffy till Grellner showed up. After that all you had to do was look around to see what was coming. The land started getting wooly, the way a man gets sloppy when he's preoccupied.''

Rogala's loquacity puzzled Gathrid. How could he keep the dwarf talking? He might let some answers fall.

It also made him suspicious. Rogala seldom took a deep breath without having an ulterior motive.

They climbed the hill Theis had chosen, picking their way up slopes scattered with bodies and scolding ravens.

''Here we have an allegory of most warfare on the mortal plane,'' the dwarf growled. ''The Ventimiglians had a force posted here. The Bilgoraji decided they wanted the hill. So they took it. And after all these lives were spent, they changed their minds.''

''What?'' Rogala was sliding out of character today. He was criticizing a bloodletting? This sounded like the pot calling the kettle black. What was going on?

Each time the man opened up, he became more a mystery. Gathrid sometimes felt there were three or four personalities behind the dwarf's haunted eyes. Or one so complex no mortal could hope to comprehend it.

The youth gasped, awed, when he saw the armies spread out beyond the hill.

To the west, gaudy as peafowl, lay the Alliance forces, spreading till their flanks climbed the sides of the hill-walled plain. The Ventimiglians, to the east, looked like a dun-flecked black glacier making an inexorable journey westward.

''So many!''

''I've seen larger.'' Rogala seemed far away. He stared intently. ''The Alliance looks stronger, numbers-wise. But Ahlert has the advantage of a unified command.''

Troops of cavalry roamed the plain between the hosts.

''Why aren't they fighting?'' Gathrid asked.

"They are. Skirmishing. Testing each other's nerve. They'll rest and bluff and look each other over today. The fighting will start in the morning."

They watched the horsemen race around, taunting one another, trying to isolate one another at a disadvantage. Nothing much happened.

"Not the best site, this," Rogala observed. "Just ground where chance brought them together. Nobody has the sense to back off to a better place." He glowered at both camps. "The sorcery might make a difference. From the feel of them, I'd say Ahlert has the edge there."

The dwarf muttered along in total detachment. He was no more involved than if this battle to be were one that had taken place centuries ago, between nations which no longer existed. He seemed unable to connect with the blood and tears about to be spilled.

"We've got to do something," Gathrid insisted.

"They turned us down, remember? Anyway, you want to see about your sister. Right? Okay. That means we've got to travel. All night, maybe, to get around Ahlert to Katich."

"You don't waste time on life's frills, do you?"

"Frills?"

"Eating. Sleeping. Little luxuries like that."

Rogala grinned. "We're getting a sharp tongue on us, aren't we?" Then his humor evaporated. He muttered something about getting his debt paid as soon as possible. He added, "In troubled times no head rests easy, neither just nor unjust."

Dawn found them deep in the desolation round Katich, atop a rise facing the city. Since they had seen the city last a major effort had been made to breach its walls. Stains and wounds of fire and sorcery marred its ramparts and the surrounding earth. "The defense held," Rogala said. "But it looks like it was a close thing."

Countless biers, elevated on poles in the Ventimiglian fashion, stood ranked outside the combat zone. Beneath each, numbered according to the importance of the dead, were the bodies of natives who had been slain to provide the warriors with slaves when they reached the other shore.

Gathrid averted his eyes. The necropolis had taken the fight out of him.

"Gruesome custom," Rogala conceded. "But this is an old world. It's seen even stranger. Remind me not to ride downwind."

Gathrid ignored him. He was worrying about Anyeck. Her perfidy, if the witch were indeed she, had to be countered.

Where was the witch? He saw nothing unusual amongst the Ventimiglians surrounding the city. "You think she went with Ahlert?" he asked.

"No. There." Rogala pointed.

Gathrid saw it now, a gibbet-size platform that faced Katich's main gate, beyond the range of conventional weaponry. He had missed it because it was camouflaged by countless siege engines.

Rogala pontificated about the wisdom, or lack thereof, of placing one's dead where the enemy could count them. Then, abruptly, he demanded, "What're you planning?"

The query caught Gathrid off balance. Theis seldom asked. He told. "You'll back me?"

"I have no choice. It's my job. My fate. My curse. But try to finish in time for us to catch how the big battle turns out."

He was so calm about it. So bloody indifferent. . . . Uncertainty racked Gathrid. How *would* he handle it? Deciding to stop Anyeck was easy. Doing so was something else. He had had no luck at home. Nothing swayed her once she made up her mind. "What can we expect?"

"Only way to find out is the hard way. I suggest you get started before we're noticed." He pointed.

There was activity round the gibbet now. Trumpets blared. A sedan chair came from among the Ventimiglian tents. That was the kind of thing Anyeck loved, he thought. Pomp and honors. If she was the witch, she would make sure there was plenty.

"I'd better go down."

His heart hammered. His hands shook. Perspiration beaded his forehead. Afraid Rogala would see him and mock him, he spurred his mount.

His mind darted off in a hundred directions. All he could extract from the chaos was an urge to flee. He seized the hilt of the Sword for comfort.

The horns became stilled. A curtain of silence swept across the world. A thousand faces turned his way. The sedan paused in its passage. A face peeped out. He could not be sure at this remove. It was pale enough. And Anyeck was vain. She always protected herself from the sun.

Sound returned to the earth. Horns and drums howled and growled in Katich. Their voices were defiant. A gate opened. A knight in glowing blue armor surged forth. He rode a prancing charger. It was the biggest animal Gathrid had ever seen. The warrior's lancehead seemed to have been wrought of living fire.

The Ventimiglians ignored him.

"That would be Honsa Eldracher, eh?" Rogala shouted as he pounded up beside Gathrid. His yell seemed to come from far away.

"Probably." Gathrid found his own voice unnaturally loud.

"Watch the moon!" Rogala bellowed. "She's the lady of the moon."

Several Ventimiglians started their way.

Gathrid glanced toward the western horizon. The silver of the moon hung a half hour short of setting. The comet looked like a silver blade stabbed through the fabric of the sky.

Rogala laughed. "Looks like they don't want us hanging around."

Gathrid wondered why the dwarf was amused, then realized that, of his own volition, he was carrying Daubendiek unsheathed. Sharp disgust fluttered across his mind. No wonder Rogala was cheerful. There would be blood for Suchara.

The blade had seduced him into wielding it without thought.

He rebelled. For just a second. Then he thought, this once Suchara's interests are my own.

There was little he could do anyway. Daubendiek would not be sheathed unblooded.

The feeling of growth came over him. He gazed with scorn on these puny mortals who would dare try delaying him. When he dismounted and stalked toward them, a susurrus of awe swept the Ventimiglian encampment.

They were afraid.

He whirled Daubendiek overhead and laughed as he strode toward the witch.

Silence gripped the land. Fifty thousand chests ceased heaving in mid-breath. The sliver of setting moon waxed brighter, till it rivaled the sun. Sudden ropes of silver danced around the witch. Her arms rose. Her fingers moved in intricate patterns. Her liquid voice seemed to come from everywhere as she sang forth her Power. The ropes wove themselves into brilliant nets. Soon she was a singing spider at the heart of a scintillating web.

Around her, in a faint mist, a huge feminine face could sometimes be seen.

From one of Gathrid's stolen memories came the thought that the spider image was apt. No man without great Power could hope to escape soul-devouring destruction once in the web's grasp. In that way it was like Daubendiek.

A strand snaked his way, questing like a blind serpent. It lashed out. Daubendiek severed it. The loose end darkened, scorched the earth, faded into mist.

Then there were a dozen attacking strands. Daubendiek became a blur. Gathrid continued toward the platform, trailing reblackened earth.

The web thickened till he could no longer discern the

woman. Daubendiek moved so swiftly that it destroyed strands faster than the witch could spin them.

Occasionally one strand would penetrate his guard and for a moment touch him with a draining coldness. The Sword's power shielded and fed him, but each touch left him a little weaker. In snippets he felt what it was like to receive Daubendiek's cool kiss. His leg began to ache, his eyelid to droop.

He saw with clarity greater than ever before, as if the cold caresses were freeing his mind while Daubendiek took complete bodily control. He discovered ways he could regain control if he desired, but dared not attempt lest he divert the Sword's attention. Their purposes were one just then. Anyeck had to be rescued from her folly.

He was sure his sister stood at the heart of the web. There was a flavor to it redolent of her personality.

The web drew inward as the witch realized she faced no easy foe. She formed a dense silver chrysalis around herself, adjusted the web till the only strands remaining were those attacking Gathrid. Their number increased.

He wondered if she knew whom she faced.

He also wondered if this were the sorcery intended for Katich. He could picture the web crawling over the city, sending strands into barracks and homes. The Blue Brothers and Honsa Eldracher might protect themselves, but ordinary, Powerless citizens would be slaughtered. She would grow stronger. The Ventimiglians would move in, unresisted, to finish with steel those engrossed in surviving the sorcery.

Almost imperceptibly, Daubendiek weakened. Deep as it had drunk since awakening, it did not have the strength to withstand this forever. Gathrid felt its first faint stir of uneasiness.

But the witch's power was waning too. The strands grew fewer and slower. Her remaining strength she used to maintain her chrysalis. Gathrid was now just twenty feet away.

Beyond the silvery glare, the moon began sliding behind blackened hills.

She knew, went entirely defensive.

Singing victoriously, Daubendiek drank the lives of fear-frozen Ventimiglians, renewing itself. Then it flew into desperate play against a last surprise assault by the witch.

A beam of silver speared from the chrysalis. The woman's protection evaporated as its power fed the beam.

Daubendiek absorbed it, its voice changing from song to moan. Ventimiglians by the thousands fell to earth, clawing their ears.

The moon sank lower and lower.

Weariness devoured Gathrid's sword arm. The feeling of giganticism faded. His leg burned. Daubendiek had begun drawing on him.

He saw Rogala rushing toward him. Probably to salvage the Sword if its Bearer fell. To pass it on, he thought.

The upper limb of the moon perished behind the hills. The witch's power frayed. Her spear of light faded.

Gathrid forced himself forward, limping. His leg hurt more than when he had been stricken with polio. His sword arm sagged, dragging the silver beam with it. Daubendiek's bloody tip began tracing a line in the barren earth.

He faced her from the foot of the platform. Anyeck, definitely. She recognized him, too. She showed more fear than surprise.

They exchanged stares. Defeat had stamped out shadowed hollows in her once beautiful face. Her golden hair had become a moonlike silver. She looked older than their mother had on the day of her death. And the surrender of Kacalief had aged their mother terribly.

Gathrid felt no sense of triumph. He was tired and disappointed and profoundly sad. He had clung tight to a wan hope that this moment would not bring him face to face with his sister.

Communication came in almost imperceptible gestures. Gathrid frowned questioningly. Anyeck responded with a slight shrug. She did not know why, only that she had been drawn. Chosen. Just like her more successful brother. She frowned a *What now?*

He nodded, meaning she should come down.

Strength, flowing from the final reserves deep within himself and the Sword, gradually eased his weariness. His leg ceased aching. He regained control of his eye.

From his saddle, Rogala observed, "We'd better get moving. The natives are getting frisky." He pointed with a dagger.

The Vontimigliano were coming out of their daze. And Honsa Eldracher was making a sortie from Katich. He looked likely to rout the easterners.

Minor sorceries began clashing nearer the city.

"I suppose. Where's my horse? And round one up for my sister. We'll take her with us. She may serve the Alliance better than she served the Mindak."

Rogala shrugged. Gathrid thought he saw an evil little smile cross the dwarf's lips.

Anyeck set foot to earth. Nervously, she awaited his will.

Daubendiek struck.

It was sudden, unexpected, and surprised Gathrid completely. The blade simply flashed out and plunged deep into his sister's body.

Their shared screams seemed to echo on forever. The taking of her went on and on and on. As she became a part of him, her pain and anger took effect. Her hatred joined his and became a thing almost superhuman, almost as powerful as the Sword itself. He sensed a faint apprehension in the blade.

She died her little death with a single soft cry. Gathrid cried out at the same instant, hating himself for the pleasure he felt through the misery.

The moment passed. The Sword's control slipped.

Gathrid whirled. He charged Rogala.

The dwarf was quick as a cat. He rolled off his mount an instant before Gathrid's stroke clove air over his saddle. His eyes were huge and his teeth were bare. Only continued preternatural quickness saved him from his horse's hooves.

Gathrid slew the animal and started round after Rogala.

A Ventimiglian got in his way. Gathrid dropped the man. Another replaced him, then another and another. The besiegers were running from Honsa Eldracher. Out of his head with anger, Gathrid raged among them, punishing them for his loss.

He kept trying to reach Rogala, but the dwarf was too quick for him. He soon disappeared.

Chapter Eight
Ventimiglia

Honsa Eldracher won a resounding victory outside Katich. Hardly an easterner escaped. The story would course through and excite the kingdoms of the Alliance, though thoughtful folk would shudder when they heard about the reappearance of the Great Sword. Its return portended grim times.

The outcome of the battle fought nearer the Bilgoraji border overshadowed and obscured the victory at Katich. There the presence of Nevenka Nieroda and the Toal tipped the balance. While the sorceries of the Orders, and of Ahlcrt and his generals, negated one another, the men with swords and spears decided the outcome. For the most part it was a bloody, unimaginative slaughter.

The Alliance Kings refused to subordinate themselves to their one competent commander. Count Cuneo, Yedon Hildreth, might have won the day.

Nieroda and the Toal concentrated on the junctures between national forces. By nightfall the Kings had lost their arrogance. They knew they were doomed if they continued into the morrow. They surrendered themselves into Yedon Hildreth's safekeeping.

Hildreth repeated the ploy he had used at Avenevoli. He built the campfires high, then forced the exhausted troops to decamp. He force-marched back into Bilgoraj and dug in astride the Torun Road where the brushy north slopes of the Beklavac Hills crowded against the fetid immensities of the Koprovica Marshes. Ancient, bleak strongholds, perched on basaltic crags, frowned down on the high road. The Beklavacs themselves were steep-sided and densely overgrown. Forces smaller than Hildreth's had held those narrows against armies more vast than the Mindak's.

Ahlert's pursuit was indecisive. He had to keep one eye on Honsa Eldracher. Failure to fulfill his boasts had shaken his confidence. Consequently, he failed again.

A bold, swift follow-through would have carried him through to Torun and might have shattered the Alliance. Instead, he camped below the Beklavacs, tried to draw Hildreth out and sent home for fresh levies.

The Alliance Kings called for more soldiers too.

Gathrid was, by then, far away. He remained angry and desolate. He loathed himself for not having controlled the Sword. He wandered aimlessly, avoiding both sides.

He stole a horse and drifted eastward by back roads and out of the ways. For a time he bore Anyeck with him, intending to return her to the family mausoleum. The irreversible progress of nature forced him to abandon the idea. He consigned her to the earth near Herbig. He drifted onward.

He did not know where he was bound, or why. He did not much care. Movement was what mattered. It separated him from the scene of his despair, of his sin against his own blood.

He could not outrun the pain. He could only numb it with physical exhaustion.

He crossed the Grevening border without noticing.

One region of Ventimiglian occupation looked like another, though the farther east he traveled the more the land had recovered.

His thoughts became fixed on Tureck Aarant. He began to understand the man. Aarant, too, had slain his kin. He had murdered his own mother near the beginning of his tale.

Gathrid wished the Sword's history were better known. What he did know had been set down by Imperial scholars with other matters on their minds. The blade's past lay behind a veil of artful shadow.

Was the kin-death a rite of passage engineered to separate the Swordbearer from his earthly ties? Had Rogala known the moment would come? The youth drank deeply of the sour wine of suspicion, judging Suchara, the dwarf, and himself in the harshest terms.

His brooding gradually came to a head. His unfocused anger coalesced. He set himself a goal. He would try to rid the world of abominations like Daubendiek. And Nicroda. And the Toal.

The notion was vague and grandiose. Only belatedly did he realize that it could cause him great pain. Had he not taken a step along that road by slaying Anyeck?

The voices within him mumbled and muttered and propounded a curious question: Had Tureck Aarant come to the same decision? He seemed to have ranged himself on the side of the weaker Power whenever he had done battle.

Every question and every decision lured Gathrid back to the same puzzle. Was he following the path of Aarant? Was it all foreordained, choreographed by the mysterious Suchara?

Where should he begin this self-appointed mission? Great Powers had gathered in the west. Left to their contention, they might destroy one another. He needed but wait, then go after the victor.

There seemed little doubt that Ahlert would triumph

eventually. His mining of the past had put too much might into his hands.

Therefore, Gathrid reasoned, the Mindak should be weakened before their inevitable confrontation.

That dark shadow which once had been the controlling spirit of a Toal remained with him. He could feel it there, over his left shoulder, watchful and patient. It no longer strove to supplant his soul. It hovered on the border of awareness, full of fright and hopelessness. It could not find another host without guidance from the Mindak.

These days Gathrid was more disturbed by its patience than by its presence. It was immortal. It could wait forever. In its unbleak moments it seemed to be telling him that its chance would come. It would give him time. Someday he would relax a little too much.

And yet it feared. . . .

It had taken this new, less aggressive stance after his confrontation with Anyeck. It had been impressed by the Power he had wielded then.

Days became weeks. He wandered into lands where Ventimiglian peasants had begun colonizing. They were a hardy, determined breed. They were more ambitious than the peasants of Gathrid's own Gudermuth.

He began to suspect that his separation from Rogala was not as complete as he had hoped. A horseman seemed to be shadowing him from afar. He set an ambush. No one rode into it.

That in itself was suggestive. Rogala always knew what was going on. Gathrid gave up with a shrug. He had to assume the dwarf would follow the Sword. The two were inextricably linked.

Gathrid began to think, to plan. The thought of a Rogala pursuit jarred him into it. His gaze swung eastward, drawn like a compass's arm.

From Grevening he passed into Rodegast, then Silhavy, then Gorsuch. Each was another small principality like Gudermuth. He saw no one but the occasional Ventimiglian colonist. In Gorsuch colonization was well advanced. New cities were growing where old had fallen.

The Nirgenau Mountains rose across his path. Beyond their high, bleak passes and chill peaks lay Ventimiglia itself.

The Nirgenaus were tricky. Levies bound westward crowded the one good road across. They were cheerful young men eager for plunder and glory. Some were as young as he. They reminded him of his brothers, or even of himself in that ridiculous time when he had *wanted* to go to war.

The pain reached in and squeezed his heart. Childhood had come to an end. He was a singleton now. He had nothing and no one. . . . He had slain the last of his kin himself.

The long, lonely weeks did not go solely to remorse. He practiced integrating and learning to tap the memories given him by the Sword. From them he learned of secondary trails seldom trod by the Mindak's soldiers. Following those, he reached Camero Marasco, the high, barren peak that marked the easternmost boundary of ancient Anderle, and the western frontier of modern Ventimiglia. From its wind-tortured, snowbound heights he studied the storied fortress called Covingont.

Covingont of the three pink towers, mistress of the Karato Pass, where Tureck Aarant had slain Cashion the Blind in the first blush of the Brothers' War. Covingont, where the gnaw of elder sorceries had left the Karato's granite walls permanently scarred, where even time had been unable to banish the dread memorials of the fury that had brought Cashion's doom.

One of Ahlert's predecessors had rebuilt the castle. It looked as formidable as the Covingont of yore. Gathrid touched the Sword. It remembered. The fighting had been grim. It had fed well.

Having slain Cashion, Aarant had vanished into the east. He had been gone a year. Grellner had kept the cauldron of war boiling. His whispers had sabotaged every effort to reconcile the Immortal Twins.

Then Tureck Aarant had come across the Karato again, a changed man. His sojourn in the east remained forever unilluminated. Never again was he Tureck Aarant the young warrior. He had become Tureck Aarant the Swordbearer, and friend to none. He had become a force, not a man.

He had hunted the sorcerers of both sides with an implacable ferocity, barely pretending to be anyone's ally. His legend had come into being during the following year. It was a story that looked a decade deep when seen from centuries down time. No man should have done so much in so little time.

Then Tureck had died. He was not yet twenty. Rogala still stood accused of his murder.

Gathrid stared at the pink granite towers. He shuddered. The chill of the Karato had little to do with his shaking.

Once again he was following a trail blazed by Tureck Aarant. Was he meant to share that previous Swordbearer's fate?

He thought he heard a ghostly chuckle over his left shoulder. He whirled, hand flying to Daubendiek's hilt. He saw nothing.

"The Toal," he murmured. He had forgotten the Dead Captain. It could have stolen into him. . . . He shuddered again.

And again the Toal expressed mirth.

Gathrid spat in disgust, slapped his hands together to get his blood moving. Had Aarant ever felt the way he did now? Like the walls of reality were pressing in? Like he was being herded down a long road between two facades that, instead of coming together because of perspective, were really constricting the way? His options were dwindling. He had few moments in which to occupy himself with anything but Rogala, the Toal, Ahlert, Nieroda, and just plain staying alive.

His lack of choices angered and frustrated him. He thought he understood why Tureck had become so violent and vicious. A mocking history may have rewritten spiteful savagery as heroic battling.

He had done nothing yet himself, Gathrid thought. Unless murdering Anyeck counted as a mighty deed. Surely the forces toying with him had a greater purpose than that.

Again he heard the ghostly chuckle of his haunting Toal.

Traveling Ventimiglia without drawing attention proved difficult. Gathrid discovered it to be a crowded land of countless feudal estates, all lying cheek by jowl. There was very little untamed land. Hiding places were scarce. The nobility, men of Power from among whom Ahlert's officers were drawn, lived in squat, dark fortresses within sight of one another. Each fortress was surrounded by peasant hovels like a hen surrounded by chicks. Neat networks of rammed earth road formed the boundaries between neighboring manors.

Ventimiglia, Gathrid concluded, was a land shaped by generations of military success and by devotion to order. Everything seemed as perfect as an illuminated manuscript. Even the woodlots—in one neat square for each manor—were parklike. Every plant, animal, man and structure had its place.

That stood at odds with stories he had heard in Gudermuth. He had been taught that Ahlert was an emissary of chaos and destruction.

In a sense he might be, though the chaos existed only along Ventimiglia's frontiers.

Gathrid had his difficulties, but found ways to slip through the countryside. He abandoned his horse early, sure it would give him away. He traveled by night. Days he usually spent sleeping in trees in woodlots, or beneath the bridges on the roads.

By the time he had put a hundred miles behind him he had concluded that good and evil were matters of perspective. Ventimiglia was a peaceful, happy, prosperous land, not the hell he had been schooled to expect.

The voices of the dead reminded him that there were perspectives and perspectives. What he saw had been purchased at great cost. He was not seeing all of Ventimiglia. Few of the men he had slain had sprung from these bucolic environs.

The conflict between preconception and reality only confused him. He coped by rejecting all conclusions.

Months passed. He slipped past cities named Lobiondo and Bozeda. He was approaching Senturia, the Ventimiglian capital. All three cities were supposed to be nests of the darkest sorcery. He had seen nothing to support or refute the charge.

Senturia was a mighty city. It was said to be populated by more than a million souls. That was more people than had lived in Gathrid's native kingdom. He could not comprehend so many people having gathered in one place.

Two hundred miles beyond, to the northeast, lay the city Dedera. It crowded the feet of the Chromoga Mountains. Somewhere back in their ore-rich canyons, rumor claimed, lay the mouth of the tunnel Ahlert had discovered. At its nether end lay the subterranean ruins the Mindak mined for his Power.

Gathrid thought of the place as a library of past evils. A place where all sorceries had been recorded.

Gradually, without conscious consideration, the Library had become his destination. There were things he wanted to learn. About Nieroda, about the Toal, about Suchara and about the Sword. He was sure the information could be found there. Ahlert had uncovered most of it already, hadn't he?

His extended run of luck ran out east of Senturia.

He had, after all those miles and weeks, finally found himself a forest. It was a tamed and tended wood, but still the best cover he had seen since leaving the Karato. Its keepers had allowed large sections to remain semi-feral. Though it was inviting, it made him nervous. It had the air of a hunting preserve. Still, it gave him a chance to travel by day. He had not been able to since leaving the Nirgenau Mountains.

It began shortly before noon one day, when he thought he heard the distant-faint bray of horns. He paused, listened intently. Finally, unsure, he resumed walking.

He heard the sound again an hour later. It was much closer. This time he had no doubts. He was in the path of a hunt.

His trepidation was shared. Trees rustled as squirrels went into hiding. Rabbits dashed here and there, their white tails bouncing. A boar, then a stag, crossed his path. Each broke into panicky flight after spying him.

"Better hide," Gathrid muttered. He glanced round, ran after the stag. He needed a remote thicket or cave.

Proper thickets were scarce. He hadn't the speed or wind to stay with the stag long enough to discover its hiding place. He did find a cave, but beat a hasty, ignominious retreat upon finding himself nose to nose with a she-bear and her cubs.

The horns sounded again. The hunters were getting close. Was he the quarry? That did not seem possible. They were coming from ahead, not from his backtrail. And even Ahlert hadn't the arrogance to announce his coming to the Swordbearer.

Pure dumb luck was about to betray him.

He had to move fast. After a moment of dismay and indecision he flung himself at a post oak. He shimmied up and transferred to a larger beech, which he climbed till he could crawl out a branch and get into another oak. This was a many times grandfather of the first, and one of the largest trees he had ever seen. Sixty feet up he settled into a fork and watched a brook gurgle along a dozen yards from the tree's base.

The horn again. He listened for hounds, heard no baying. A good sign, he thought. They would not stumble onto his trail.

The horn again. Then the quarry passed beneath him, exhausted, staggering toward the brook. "A girl," he said softly. He leaned for a better look.

She was ragged, scratched and bruised, and hardly older than he. Though he considered himself a poor judge, she appeared reasonably attractive.

She paused to scoop water from the creek. She was in command of her wits. She turned downstream after drinking.

And slipped on a slimy stone. She fell with a little wail of despair and pain. She stayed down. Though she tried valiantly, weary muscles and a sprained ankle refused to be tortured further.

Gathrid started down even before the hunters arrived. He froze while they passed beneath him, exchanging quips about their prey. Having absorbed Ventimiglian from Daubendiek's victims, he understood. The girl was an escaped sacrifice meant for a slow, painful death in rites that would give them command of a familiar spirit.

There were five of them. Behind each rode an esquire. They were cruel young men who inspired Gathrid's loathing. They dismounted, surrounded the girl. They taunted her, laughed at her, kicked her down again when she tried to rise.

Gathrid crossed to the beech. One of the esquires turned, cocked his head then resumed watching his master's sport.

Sometimes, Gathrid thought, you have to compromise a moral resolution to meet the demand of a greater obligation. He had been determined never to draw Daubendiek except in self-defense.

Rogala would have called him a fool for interfering.

He dropped the last dozen feet, landed quietly on the soft grass. The sharp-eared esquire turned again. Gathrid drew the Sword.

The esquire tried to shout, could only gobble.

Gathrid felt the familiar growing sensation, the eagerness of the blade, the momentary vertigo as Daubendiek drank a soul. The Ventimiglians froze when they sensed the surge of Power.

Gathrid raged among them, slaughtering all the esquires and two of the nobles before they could defend themselves. The others, after crossing the brook, began some hasty sorcery. Two moved toward Gathrid's flanks while the third retreated. A red mist roiled in the pocket thus formed. Within that mist an anthropoid, bow-legged, squat, long-armed, hairy and toothy thing took shape. It looked at the girl and grinned.

Despite its origins it did not seem all that remarkable till Gathrid splashed across the creek and attacked it.

Daubendiek behaved like an ordinary blade swung into a hardwood post. It cut, but with no more effect than that ordinary blade would have affected that mortal oak.

Though Gathrid was startled, Daubendiek was not. It beat about the demon in an almost invisible storm. Chips of monster flew. The Sword clanged like a beaten gong.

The demon seemed astonished that it was vulnerable at all. Rocking with each blow, grin waning, it kept trying to reach Gathrid. The three who had summoned it kept yelling in amazement.

Gathrid remembered the field where his father and brothers had practiced with their horses and weapons. The demon began to take on the target-post's well-hacked look.

Daubendiek would strike for the creature's neck, then go for a leg when it raised an arm protectively. The Sword fell into a rhythm of high and low, staying a move ahead, till one demon leg parted at the knee.

Daubendiek howled gleefully.

While the demon sat staring at its severed calf, Gathrid slew the nearest Ventimiglian and charged after the other two.

He caught one, but the last captured a horse before Gathrid overtook him. He escaped as a scream drew the youth's attention back to the brook.

The demon was after the girl, stalking her on all fours,

looking like some weird wolf spider awaiting the right instant to pounce. The girl kept scooting away. She seemed unable to take her feet.

Swinging Daubendiek with both hands, Gathrid severed the demon's head from its neck. It rolled down into the chill water. Its mouth broke the surface and began cursing in fractured Ventimiglian.

The decapitated body crawled round the slope, hands feeling for the missing head. When it encountered a stone of appropriate size, it tried settling that atop its shoulders.

Gathrid turned to the girl. She cowered away from him. She seemed more terrified of him than she was of the demon.

Though the Sword protested, Gathrid forced it into its scabbard. He offered the girl a hand. She accepted as if afraid refusal would bring reprisal. Gathrid did not know what to say, so said nothing. Ventimiglian words would not roll right on his tongue anyway. He helped her climb the bank, leaned her against a sapling while he rounded up horses and examined his enemies' gear. He found their memories more interesting than their equipment. They knew the way to the Library. It was there that the Mindak had gifted them with their demon.

Said demon kept cursing in the streambed.

He was wasting time. He helped the girl onto a horse. Then, on impulse, he scrambled down and salvaged the talking head. He bound it to his saddle by its wiry hair. It chattered right along, telling him what it thought.

The girl spoke for the first time when Gathrid started to leave. "What about me? What am I supposed to do?"

He looked into her dark, frightened eyes. He shrugged. "Whatever you want. You're free now."

She understood despite his recalcitrant tongue. "No. I'll never be free. I've been dedicated." She indicated the head. "The thing's masters will compel them. They can't break their bargain with it. Nor it with them. The one who escaped. He'll bring friends. Powerful men. The high sorcerers. The fathers of the ones you slew.''

Gathrid shrugged again. What could he say or do? He had not thought beyond her rescue. "Come on." His plans had no room for companions, yet he could not abandon a responsibility once assumed.

She hesitated. She was afraid of him. She did not want to remain near a man so deadly. Yet he had saved her from the devils she knew.

Shortly after he shrugged a third time and started off, exchanging unpleasantries with the head, she called for him to wait.

Chapter Nine
Round Dedera

The girl's name was Loida Huthsing. "Any relation to Franaker Huthsing?" Gathrid asked.

"My father." She seemed startled because he knew the name.

The demon was Gacioch. The girl was seventeen, the demon ageless. Loida had been part of the plunder the Mindak had sent home from Grevening. Gacioch was the lackey of a demon-lord in the service of high Ventimiglian nobles.

The youths Gathrid had slain belonged to the Mindak's own household. They had been sons of cousins and nephews. Loida told him to expect a cruel death. Gacioch gleefully confirmed her contention.

The demon let up on the cussing and fussing. His game, now, was to describe at length, and in loving detail, the sophistication of the tortures to be found in the Mindak's dungeons. Ahlert's family was sacred, at least by their own decree.

"Don't you ever shut up?" Gathrid demanded. "Right now Theis Rogala is looking good."

The demon grinned and babbled on.

Gathrid shrugged off the threats. "Ahlert can't want me any worse than before. Loida? Your father is *really* Franaker Huthsing? The infamous Sheriff of Rigdon?"

"Infamous? Look, friend . . ."

"He was infamous on our side of the border." He had been afraid his identity would frighten the girl. She grew relaxed instead.

"Heck, we're neighbors. Almost kin. What went on between our fathers doesn't seem very important now, does it?"

"Not when you look at it from a forest in the heart of Ventimiglia, no."

The exchange of identities occurred during their second day together, while they paused at the forest's edge and Gathrid quietly debated going afoot once more. Before, Loida had tagged along in silence while Gacioch had done the chattering. For his part, Gathrid had been too preoccupied to worry about the girl or demon.

By now an alarm would have spread throughout Ventimiglia's ruling class. The hunt would be up. Could he reach the Library before the pursuit overtook him?

The city Dedera was the obstacle. Daubendiek should see him through the countryside. Out here, sheer distance would keep the enemy from gathering in number. But the city, with its quarter million people, could throw an army across his path.

He saw no way, now, to conceal his presence and destination. He decided to retain the horses and try for speed.

A dozen riders passed through a field a quarter mile away, boredly watching the wood. To Gathrid's surprise, Gacioch kept his mouth shut while they were within hearing.

"Why didn't you yell?" Gathrid demanded.

"I like you, boy. I've gotten attached to you."

"Liar."

"Goodie! You noticed. That'll be a plus mark on my

record when I come up for promotion.'' He snickered evilly. ''Actually, I'm just lazy. When they do catch you, they'll catch me, too. Means I'll have to go back to work. You should only know how rare vacations are in my corner of Hell.''

Gathrid gave the head an uncertain look. It was hard to tell when the demon meant what he said, or was just joking. Then he laughed.

It was the first time he had done so since the Mindak's invasion of Gudermuth. ''Then your wickednesses include sloth?''

''My strong point.'' Gacioch spoke sourly. He had lost interest in conversation.

Gathrid turned to Loida. ''It's going to get rough. I'm going to try to outrun them.''

Her fear and awe were evaporating. ''I can keep up with any Gudermuther.''

''Is that the kind of crack I'm going to have to live with from now on? Maybe I should've left you where I found you. Let's go.''

They had ridden less than a mile when they encountered another patrol. Though armed and aware that they had found their quarry, the Ventimiglians refused combat. They drifted off into a field while Gathrid passed.

''Why did they do that?'' Loida asked.

''I don't know. I don't like it.'' He watched the patrol return to the road a respectful distance behind them. ''They're showing too much good sense.'' They were, his more experienced memories assured him, acting according to some prearrangement. There would be big trouble nearer Dedera. ''I may have made a mistake.''

Gacioch broke into laughter. ''That you did, boy. When you were dumb enough to interfere with the girl hunt.''

Gathrid glanced at the sun. It was a long way from setting. He had miscalculated. He should have stayed hidden till nightfall. If they guessed his destination . . . They would waste no time chasing him. They would wait at the Library.

He recalled the flight from Gudermuth to Bilgoraj. Theis had done all the thinking. . . . He was on his own now. The Ventimiglians were in no hurry this time. They were confident. Because he no longer had the dwarf to help outwit them?

He hated admitting it. He missed Rogala.

He would do without! He wasn't stupid. And he had scores of advisers perched on the shoulders of his mind. He had the dead to guide him. He was a necromancer who divined within himself.

His Toal chuckled.

The party trailing him grew stronger. Dust clouds rose on roads paralleling his own. Several times he saw men in dark armor waiting off the highway, forewarned and ready to join his escort. How long before they felt strong enough to close in?

Their plans did not seem to include immediate engagement. The party behind closed up as darkness gathered, but made no threatening move. Gathrid estimated their number at two hundred.

A tidbit of stolen memory bobbed up in his mind. The Hudyma River lay only a few miles ahead. It was one of Ventimiglia's greatest rivers. This road would span it on a narrow, fortified bridge. The fortification would make a good anvil against which to hammer him.

But there was a tributary to be crossed first, a mile this side of the Hudyma.

It was thoroughly dark when they reached the first stream. Gathrid had galloped ahead of the Ventimiglians. Now he swung off his mount, helped Loida descend, grabbed Daubendiek and Gacioch. He slapped the horses back into action. He knew they would not run far. They were exhausted. But even a quarter mile would be a help.

They concealed themselves beneath the bridge. The horsemen who poured overhead seemed to form an endless stream. Gacioch again held his tongue.

Gathrid knew he had very little time. Clutching Loida's hand, he ran downstream. "Come on. Hurry."

"I'm tired," she complained, then saved her breath for flight.

They were lucky. Gathrid stumbled onto a boat not far downstream. It was well-hidden and guarded by a quiet but savage dog. "The owner of this thing can't be no solid citizen," Gacioch observed. "A fisherman would keep his boat pulled up by his hut."

The dog growled till it got wind of Gathrid. Then it slunk silently away. Gathrid pushed Loida into the boat and shoved off as the Ventimiglians returned to the bridge.

The current kept Gathrid ahead of the pursuit. He reached the sluggish Hudyma within an hour. Clumsily, he started rowing for the far bank.

"I knew it was too good to last," Loida grumbled as he beached the craft. "I was hoping we'd drift for a while. This river is headed home."

"I'm not going home."

"I was afraid you'd say that."

"If I might make a suggestion," Gacioch interjected as Gathrid started up the bank. "They won't get onto your trail as fast if you shove the boat back out into the current."

Gathrid looked to the east. A procession of torches was snaking across the fortified bridge. He did not have the adventurer's mentality, he concluded. It seemed cruel to waste a man's boat. Stealing it had been bad enough.

"Do it!" Loida snapped.

"All right, already!"

"This isn't my first escape," the girl said.

"Don't put too much faith in her experience," Gacioch rumbled. "She's never gotten away."

Gathrid spent a moment watching the boat slide off into the darkness. What was the demon's game? Gacioch was doing his best to avoid his masters. Why?

He had to move. The torches were approaching. Perhaps his underminds could resolve his questions while he concentrated on escape.

He did not expect the Ventimiglians to remain out of touch long. Locating Gacioch and the Sword should present no problem for a sorcerer. Both would strain the fabric of this plane.

Gathrid tramped along head down, silent. He missed Rogala. He told himself that was because he would find the dwarf's perception of distant events useful.

The voices down inside him chuckled. They always did when he lied to himself.

Gacioch kept up an abrasive commentary. It made Rogala's reticence appear ever more attractive. Gathrid suffered through all the latest gossip from the courts of Ventimiglia and Hell. Then the demon offered to do his scouting. All he had to do, Gacioch claimed, was decorporealize him. Any fool could manage the necessary spell.

Alarm bells clamored in the depths of the youth's mind. "No. I don't need any help. Thank you."

A ghostly, merry tinkle of Toal merriment assured him that the offer had been a trap.

Rogala remained in his thoughts. What had become of Theis? He no longer had that feeling of being followed from a distance.

If he wanted to reach the Library, he had to start thinking like the dwarf. Eschew mercy. Make the goal everything. Don't let anything else matter. Be willing to sacrifice anyone and anything. . . . His stomach knotted. His thoughts disgusted him.

Near midnight they came upon a manor. Gathrid found himself feeling an inexplicable homesickness. Ah. Some of his souls belonged to men who had begun their lives here. Their emotions were bubbling. He drew their memories to his forebrain.

Using their knowledge, he traveled westward till he reached a manor famous for the horses it bred. He stole two. He rode away wondering how soon their loss would be noted, and if it would be connected with him.

After a time he turned northward again. He planned to make a grand swing, west and north, around Dedera. That should be less predictable than his former, more direct route.

Fate, luck or the masking hand of Suchara herself, served him well. Even by day no one challenged his party, though they passed manor after manor and hundreds of people glanced at them incuriously.

He pushed hard all day. Loida became too tired to complain. Late in the afternoon he started following roads tending eastward again. By dusk he and Loida were directly north of Dedera. The peaks of the Chromogas looked like bloody teeth in a horizon-spanning jaw as the setting sun illuminated their snowy peaks. Gathrid kept pushing.

Then a Toal appeared on their backtrail.

Whence it came Gathrid had no idea. He glanced back and there it was, gleaming black astride its black stallion, keeping a respectful distance. It had not been there minutes earlier. He thought it was the one he had dueled near the Bilgoraji border. It had the same feel, and the lance it bore blazed against the gathering darkness.

Attack seemed far from its mind.

"Oh, it won't," Gacioch grumbled. "It's just here to keep an eye on the Sword."

"I'll still end up fighting it." Gathrid shuddered. He did not want another of those dread entities drifting along behind the corners of his vision. Would they squabble over him like jackals over a carcass? "Loida can't go much farther."

He expected a Rogala-like suggestion that the girl be ditched. Gacioch disappointed him. "Then stop and let her rest. He isn't going to bother you. In fact, he'll make sure nobody else does."

"What?"

Gacioch's great failing, as he himself confessed, was that he talked too much. "He has orders to make sure the Sword doesn't get snatched by the wrong people. He can't do anything but follow orders."

"How do you know?"

Gacioch sniggered. "You'll just have to take my word."

Gathrid took the chance. It was not as much a matter of trusting Gacioch as of doing what had to be done. He abandoned the road for a woodlot. In minutes Loida was snuggling against him for warmth. The tireless Toal took a sentry post a hundred yards away. Gathrid tried hard to remain awake, but sleep quickly took him. He had a dreamless night. His haunt may have been communing with its fellow.

He was surprised to waken unharmed and still his own creature, with the Sword still in his possession. Or vice versa.

The Toal stood statue-still, stone-patient. Its eyes remained fixed on the road. Gacioch's hints about someone other than the Mindak wanting to lay hands on the Sword began to make sense. Gathrid got a feel of the shape of it from his haunt.

All was not right in Ventimiglia. Nevenka Nieroda and the Dead Captains were out of control. They were acting behind the Mindak's back, and not in his interest. It looked like they wanted to keep Daubendiek away from Ahlert.

Why?

His Toal haunt projected that infuriating mirth.

"Gacioch." He was unsure whether or not demons slept. Gacioch put on a good show of waking grouchiness.

"What?"

"What's going on out west?"

"Folks are sleeping. It's night out there. They'd be sleeping here, if certain people didn't . . ."

"In the war, I mean."

Gacioch had no shoulders to shrug, but gave a definite impression of having done so. "Not much. Ahlert is bogged down. Involved in a war of attrition."

Gathrid recalled Rogala's assessment of the Mindak's generalship. "A master warlock but an indifferent captain?" he suggested.

"In a nutshell."

It became more clear. "And the troops are getting restless?"

Gacioch would say no more. Gathrid suspected he had hit the mark. So. The politics of disunity had reached the enemy camp. Ventimiglia was not a monolith anymore.

Nieroda had to be the focus. Dissension is a contagious disease, he thought. He would have to redouble his vigilance. Two factions would be after the Sword. Neither would care what became of Gathrid of Kacalief.

Maybe he could use *them*. . . .

The important goal remained the Library. In fact, reaching it now seemed absolutely essential. Was that an intuition? Might it be a subliminal instruction from Suchara?

He wakened Loida. "Time to go, girl."

She glanced round, spied the Toal. "It's still here."

"It's still here. I'm afraid it'll be with us for a while."

Breakfast was quick and cold. The horses were lacking in a properly enthusiastic attitude. Gacioch talked at length when Gathrid questioned him, but had nothing concrete to say. It was not an auspicious beginning for the day.

"Let's go, Loida. We've got a long way to go." The map in his mind was daunting, though his shared souls assured him the journey was easier than it looked.

Gathrid set a hard pace once more. Not only did he want to reach the Library before the Ventimiglians thought to seal it off, he wanted to get there before Nieroda appeared. He suspected restraint on the part of the Toal reflected its expectation of the controlling spirit's imminent arrival.

They entered the foothills of the Chromogas shortly before noon. They started collecting new followers there. These soon formed a veritable parade. Gathrid drove the horses harder.

A flying thing appeared. It circled high overhead. It did not resemble the dragon thing Nieroda had ridden in

Gudermuth. Who bestrode it Gathrid could not tell. It did carry a rider, he believed.

The Toal remained a fixed two hundred yards behind him, changing its pace when he did. The Ventimiglians stayed that far behind it. Gathrid wondered where their loyalties lay.

By now, he thought, there could be no doubt of his destination. This was the wildest country he had seen since leaving the Nirgenaus, though even here there were manors. They perched atop the terraced hills. He searched his encyclopedia of memories. The Library was the only thing on the map of his mind. They could not think he was bound anywhere else. . . .

They were letting him go where he wanted, then. To their purpose. They wanted him at the Library. Was he doing Nieroda's work? Was he killing these animals and punishing himself and Loida for nothing?

Logic battled emotions long keyed to danger. Once again he wished Rogala could advise him. "Take a chance," he said aloud. He had played hunches before. He slowed to a walk.

The procession did the same. No one made a threatening move, though the Toal did station itself closer.

People were watching from the hillside farms. The peasants were not working today. They were lined up as if to observe the passage of a parade. When he appeared, some retreated. Some fled toward places of hiding.

He experienced that feeling of power which heretofore had come only with the drawing of the Sword.

Then he came to the Library, sooner than he expected. And found the answers to several riddles. Why his progress had not been interrupted. Why the serfs were on holiday.

The Mindak Ahlert was there waiting for him.

Chapter Ten
Ansorge

Gathrid's hand leapt to Daubendiek. He spurred ahead. Gacioch laughed. The feeling of growth came over the youth. Daubendiek whined in its scabbard, begging to be freed.

The men with the Mindak, captains and sorcerers all, backed away. Gathrid's horse reared, hammered the air with its hooves. It screamed, came to earth prancing.

The Mindak was not intimidated.

This was the first time Gathrid had seen the man unarmored. At Kacalief he had been but another suit of dark plate, indistinguishable from the Toal. Today he had eschewed all warlike gear save a ceremonial dagger. He was afoot, wearing clothing more suited to court than the field.

Have I guessed right? Gathrid wondered. Is this really Ahlert? Or might he be some viceroy?

Gathrid spied a circlet half ridden in the man's heavy, dark hair. It was a simple gold serpent with a ruby egg in its mouth.

The minds within the youth reacted, saying the coronet was another product of the Library. It was the infamous Ordrope Diadem, which had been Grellner's secret weapon. It gave its wearer the ability to look into minds, to ferret out character flaws and hidden dreams which could be twisted and manipulated. Anyone who looked into the jewel became entranced.

Only the Mindak would wear the Diadem. It was one cornerstone of his power.

Ahlert slowly spread his hands, showing himself unarmed. He peered intently, trying to draw Gathrid's gaze.

The temptation was too much. Gathrid glanced at the ruby.

Ahlert moaned and reeled back, throwing a forearm across his eyes. Gathrid swayed. He almost fell from his saddle. For an instant he felt a great vacuum sucking at his mind.

They exchanged stares. Ahlert's men withdrew to a safer distance. The Toal moved nearer Gathrid. A shadow fluttered along the ground. Gathrid glanced up at the flyer.

Then he examined Ahlert more closely.

He had expected an elderly caricature of Gerdes Mulenex. What he saw instead was a thirtyish, lean, dark man with mouth corner quirks suggesting a rich sense of humor. But the man's dark eyes were cold, calculating, the windows of a nighted soul, of a man of boundless ambition.

Gathrid found him reminiscent of Yedon Hildreth, particularly in the aura of stubbornness he exuded.

Ahlert spread his hands again. "Come down, Swordbearer. Let's talk."

Daubendiek quivered hungrily. Loida begged, "Kill him while you have the chance. He'll trick you."

"No doubt. Or I might fool him." He believed he was safe. The Mindak had something on his mind. Conquering his memories of Kacalief, Gathrid said, "Speak."

"Here?"

The youth glanced around, understood. "Into the Library, then. You and me. Alone together." He met

Ahlert's eye, squeezed Daubendiek's hilt. "Maybe only one of us will return."

Gacioch laughed again.

"The Library?"

"The underground city. The place where you dredge up these horrors." He indicated the Toal.

"Ah. Ansorge. Come along, then." The Mindak seemed to be a man of few words.

Loida was not pleased. "Don't leave me here! They'll sacrifice me."

Gacioch leered and jeered.

The Sword, though undrawn, made itself felt. Gathrid could summon no emotion concerning the girl's welfare.

"No one will harm you." The way the Mindak spoke, while surveying his officers, made that sound like a statement of natural law.

Gacioch wanted to go, too, but argued with no special vehemence. "Don't buy any cats in a sack, boy," he said by way of parting.

"You're certainly a puzzle," Gathrid told him.

"Glad to hear it. Glad to hear it. I'd stop being fun if I was predictable."

The Toal, too, wanted to go. It asked no permission. It dismounted, took lance in hand and began to follow.

"Begone," Ahlert ordered. "Mohrhard Horgrebe, I command you. Go you forth, whence you came. This I command in the name of Great Chuchain."

The hairs on Gathrid's neck stirred. Chuchain. Where had he heard that name? Something Rogala had muttered. An entity the equal of Suchara. Sometimes her ally, more often her rival.

The Toal came on.

"I was afraid of this," the Mindak said. "The break is complete."

"The name of Chuchain may be impotent, but is the Sword of Suchara?"

"Never mind. Let it come. There's another one here that can't be kept out. It's discorporeal."

Gathrid shrugged, followed the Mindak. The Toal Mohr-hard Horgrebe did likewise. Then it stopped. It seemed to listen. After a few seconds in that attitude, it took three jerky steps to one side and seated itself on a boulder.

Instructions from Nieroda?

Ahlert led Gathrid into a tunnel that showed signs of recent mining. He strode a dozen steps inward, halted, intoned, "The Child of the Father, Great Chuchain, and He Who Bears the Wrath of the Mother, Suchara of the Sorrows; He Who Slew the Son. I say three times, let us pass! Let us pass! Let us pass! In the Name of Great Chuchain."

Something stirred. Something caressed Gathrid's face with spider's silk, with the light, nimble fingers of elves. Unbidden, words formed on his lips. "In the Name of the Mother, Suchara Beneath the Sea."

The fingers of gossamer withdrew. "Come," Ahlert told him.

It was not a long passage, and hardly as miserable as his subterranean trek with Rogala, yet Gathrid was relieved when they departed the tunnel. The sense of presence there, of unseen, hungry things watching, was overpowering.

"Ansorge," the Mindak said. "City of Everlasting Night. City of the Night People. The ones remembered as elves and trolls in your legends. They're all dead now. An unfortunate after-effect of the Brothers' War. Only their guardians remain. Their last project was to collect the wrack of the war. They didn't survive long enough to finish. Daubendiek and the Shield of Driebrant were their most noteworthy oversights."

For a minute Gathrid was just an awestruck sightseer. The cavern and city it contained stretched as far as he could see. Countless thousands of balls of light drifted around, mostly on aimless currents of air. Some bounced and dodged like playful butterflies while others swooped and darted like swallows on the hunt. They came in every color. Occasionally one changed hue.

"What are they?" Gathrid asked.

"We don't know. My best people have studied them. They might be alive, or magical. Or both. They won't hold still for a close examination. If you cage them, they die, and leave behind nothing you can dissect. Maybe we'll find out once we learn to decipher the underpeople's writing."

"You can't read their records?"

"Only their pictographs. The exploration has been haphazard. We're like barbarians looting a temple. Like the Oldani and Hattori during the Sack of Sartain. We're probably missing the most interesting things simply because we don't recognize them." He stopped walking. "Earth. Air. Fire. Water. And this. A fifth vision, perhaps? Greater than the others? But it was neutral. Always neutral. And now it's dead."

What was the man talking about? "You brought me here for a reason."

The Mindak resumed walking. "You asked. I came. We're here together. Chuchain and Suchara have moved us. We pawns can but go to our squares."

"A quote cribbed, no doubt, from Theis Rogala." Gathrid surprised himself with his boldness. He did not *feel* bold. He wondered if all self-assured men were just nervous, frightened boys hiding behind well-schooled facades.

"There is Purpose in our coming together," Ahlert told him. "The hourglasses have turned. The tides have shifted. I'm not the man I thought. I'm no general. I'm not much of a leader. I excel only at thaumaturgy. I'll tell you something, Swordbearer . . . though you'll learn it for yourself, the way we all do. All ambition is self-delusion. It comes. You overreach. Then you find yourself in a death-struggle, just trying to hold onto what you had at the beginning."

Ahlert reminded Gathrid of his boyhood teacher. "Nieroda has challenged you," he said.

"Nieroda, the Toal, and men whom I believed were

loyal captains. Because I showed so poorly in the west. No. I didn't fail there. I could've won. But I was too timid. And I didn't get the help I should have from Nieroda. It puzzled me then. I understand now.

"I was frightened of Yedon Hildreth. I thought I could handle him easier by stalling because he couldn't avoid politics. I didn't realize that I couldn't avoid them either. Then, too, there was what you did at Katich. It made me Doubt." He said the last word as though it were the name of some dread deity.

"That, too, is something you'll have to face to understand."

Self-revelation was not what Gathrid had expected. Argument or conflict, perhaps. Or a settlement of the debt of Kacalief. But not having his enemy talk to him like a brother. Nor his own willingness to listen.

"While they were enemies, they were reconciled," he said, quoting something he had heard from Plauen.

"Perhaps. Before foes with whom there can be no conciliation. But not forever."

"Suchara would disapprove," Gathrid murmured.

Ahlert smiled thinly, nodded. "Nieroda was another of my mistakes. I believed I could master her, against all the evidence of history. No one, not even Bachesta herself, can control that daughter of Hell. I realize that now."

"Her? Daughter?"

"You didn't know? I suppose not. There in the ruins of Anderle, you wouldn't. The memories have washed away. The books have been burned. Time is a cleansing rain. Yes, Nevenka Nieroda was female."

"But the Toal . . . And I slew . . ."

"The Toal are sexless. They never were human. They just possess the bodies of humans. But Nieroda was a Queen, in a land called Sommerlath, ten thousand years before the Immortal Twins were born. She was the greatest witch who ever lived. So great she elevated herself to virtual demigod status." They walked a way in silence.

Ahlert was thoughtful. "A lot of people have tried. A lot more will. We all want to grasp the stars. Nieroda came closer than most. But like the rest of us, she overreached and drew back fingers webbed with damnation."

Overreaching had been Anyeck's flaw, Gathrid reflected. That last time she had gotten her hands on pure damnation. "You place your bet and take your chances."

"Exactly. Here we are."

"Here we are where?" They were among crumbling structures now. Gathrid had a feeling these were far older than they looked. There was no gnawing weather down here.

"What I call the House of the Eye." Ahlert stooped to pass through a low doorway. The cave dwellers had been small people.

There was a man inside. Gathrid rested a hand on Daubendiek's hilt.

"Magnolo Belfiglio," Ahlert said. "He lives with the Eye. He's the only one who can manipulate it. He watches the west for me. Any news, Magnolo?"

"Nothing good, Grace. Nothing good. The Sixth Brigade has gone over. Gone over. That leaves the Imperial and the Ninth. The Ninth."

Belfiglio was incredibly old. And shaky. And confined to a wheeled chair. He was the first truly old person Gathrid had seen since entering Ventimiglia.

"The Western army is gone, then. I trust that Tracka and Marcagi have withdrawn."

"They have, Eminence."

To Gathrid, Ahlert explained, "The Imperial Brigade has to support the crown, no matter what. The Ninth is Ahlert family. It was my command once."

The Ventimiglian military was a curiously cobbled structure. Some larger families and trade associations maintained their own privately financed brigades. They were indistinguishable from those maintained by the Empire, but were loyal to their paymasters. The public units seldom took part in private ventures. The private units could be called by the Emperor at need.

There were also mercenary brigades raised by adventurers from among the free peasantry. Such armed associations had made up most of Ahlert's Western army. They had been the first to defect.

The Mindak's western adventure had, in reality, been instigated only by the *man* who wore Ventimiglia's crown, not by the crown itself. Ahlert had been acting not as Emperor but as a plundering warchief.

"And Rogala told me Ventimiglia had the advantage of a monolithic command," Gathrid muttered.

"And here at home?" Ahlert inquired of Belhglio.

"The Corichs have repudiated their war captains. War captains. They know what Nieroda is, although they agree with her arguments. Her arguments."

"Have there been desertions from the brigades? Anyone coming back?"

"Very few, Luminence. Mostly career and family men with home ties stronger than their greed. Their greed."

"Then it'll be Ventimiglian against Ventimiglian. Damn! What think the Corichs?"

"Few will join an expedition, Grace. But none will hinder, nor will any support rebellion. There's been talk of denying the peasantry the right to form associations. Form associations."

"There always is. People change their minds when they need a few hired swords. Did you see any discernible lean anywhere?"

"No, Might. They await the rising wind. Rising wind."

"How does he know all that?" Gathrid asked. "I see no mystic Eye."

"It's all around you," Ahlert replied. "It's the room itself."

Gathrid glanced round. "Unusual. But not that unusual."

"I forget. If you had a mind like Magnolo's, you'd have noticed it right away. But Magnolo is unique."

"Oh?"

"You're thinking that makes him powerful? It does. He is. He's the factor that won me the crown. My enemies would give anything to see him slain. Yet he's only a slave."

Were slaves less subject to temptation than free men? Ah. Of course. Ahlert had the Diadem. He could monitor Belfiglio's thoughts.

"What brought you here?" Ahlert asked.

"I don't know. Maybe I meant to destroy it."

"I see. Moved by Suchara. Want to see more of Ansorge? You'll see how hopeless it would be for one man to try anything."

Gathrid suspected he was being maneuvered away from the Eye. How could he harm it, though? By slaughtering the old man? "Might as well."

Later, he asked, "And why are you here? You should be getting your army under control."

"Those brigades have been written off. A while without pay, supplies or word from home will make them more amenable. But you're part right. I can't wait forever. Sooner or later, Nieroda will turn eastward. Probably after defeating Cuneo, while the troops are heady."

"That's not saying why you're here, only why you're not there."

"The will of Chuchain? I think the Great Ones mean us to be allies."

Gathrid half expected that. Visions of Kacalief returned. The excesses there had been committed by the Toal, but this was the man who had given the order to march.

"I know," Ahlert said. "It's ridiculous. We're enemies. I destroyed everything that meant anything to you. I lured your sister to her death. And you slew my myth of invincibility by slaying her. My throne will never be secure again. I can't raze Ventimiglia to expunge that memory. *And* you stole my chance to control all four Powers before they fully wakened. I had Chuchain, Bachesta and Ulalia. I would've had Suchara but for foul luck. All ambition is vanity.''

''Still . . .''

''Where lies the greater evil?''

It had been laid out like playing cards face up. Gang up on Nieroda. Make alliance with the old enemy, or face the Dark Champion alone.

Gathrid did not like it. It forced another questionable decision. He had faced nothing else since discovering the Great Sword. Nothing in this mad world, now, could be reduced to black and white.

''You convince the mind but not the heart.''

''I know. I have the same conflicts. Let the intellect rule passion for a while.''

Gathrid recognized a rock formation. ''You're headed for the surface?''

Ahlert nodded. ''We'll have to move fast if we do ally. The Toal up there will know instantly. It'll act. We'll have to be there to stop it.''

Gathrid pondered. The Mindak, though harsh, was human. Nieroda was something undead, something come back from the grave to torment the living.

Assuming Ahlert was telling the truth. This talk could be all maneuver. . . . ''How can I believe you?''

''A touchy point. You could wait and see. That's always good. But in this case it would be too late by the time you got proof.''

''It would,'' Gathrid agreed.

''I'm strong. Ventimiglia is strong. But our system makes it impossible for me to command the Empire's whole strength. I depend on the support of the Corichs, the organizers of the peasant brigades. They're frightened. Nieroda is a mistress of elder sorceries. Horrors we can't comprehend these days. If you had time to go down and see the past . . .'' He seemed to disappear inside himself.

"Yes?"

"What? Oh. I can't win alone. She'd seize control of Ventimiglia. With the Empire and her ancient sorceries she would tear at the world like a wounded tiger. She'd destroy everything."

"You've given this some thought."

"A lot of thought." Ahlert stopped walking. "I'm going to place myself in your power. I'm betting you'll resist temptation long enough to learn the truth." Hands shaking, the Mindak removed the Ordrope Diadem. "Squat down here."

Gathrid was frightened. He had an urge to say he believed, and never mind the truth. Then an imp of suspicion whispered at his ear. Suppose that was what Ahlert was fishing for? He dropped to one knee.

The Mindak accepted the challenge.

The Diadem seemed weightless. A man could forget he wore it.

Gathrid rose. Pale, grim, Ahlert stared at the ruby. His dark eyes glazed. His personality hit Gathrid like a sudden storm. The cold power of it drove the youth back against the cavern wall.

He rolled with the force, released mental channels worn smooth by the Sword's predations. He learned more than he wanted to know. He yanked the Diadem off, thrust it at its owner. To live with that continuously, seeing every man's bleak black deeps. . . . It was too much. Ahlert had an incredible will.

"You saw?" the Mindak demanded.

Gathrid nodded. Ahlert had not lied. His Western army had gone mad. It had to be neutralized.

The impossible had become imperative. His conscience allowed him no choice. He and Daubendiek had to serve Ventimiglia in order that he might serve his own people.

The Toal awaited them beyond the cave mouth. It snapped its lance at the Mindak. Daubendiek leapt into Gathrid's hand, slashed across, altered the weapon's path.

But not enough. Its fiery head grazed the Mindak's left arm. Ahlert roared in pain and anger.

A mob fell on the Toal, raging and tearing like wild dogs, wielding weapons both magical and mundane. Mohrhard Horgrebe, possessed, chopped and slashed, its sword a deadly blur. Its armor turned both blades and sorceries.

Gathrid spared but a glance for the Mindak before wading in.

Ahlert neutralized the lance's wizardry with incantations forced through clenched teeth. He saved himself, but not his arm. In seconds it withered to a dry, useless appendage.

But for Gathrid's quickness he would have died. "Damn me!" he muttered. "And I was expecting it, too."

Feeling a hundred feet tall, Gathrid shoved through the Toal's attackers. He let Daubendiek have its head. The Dead Captain held its ground.

Nevertheless, the match was less even than had been their previous encounter. Gathrid and the Great Sword were melding. In moments Daubendiek slew the Toal's blade. It perished with a great metallic scream. Daubendiek drove in over the lifeless steel.

The Toal felt much as had the one taken in the Savards: cold, evil, and under it all a flicker of despair that was all that remained of Mohrhard Horgrebe, once a champion of wide renown.

A shadow rolled over the canyon. A cold wind whipped dust and leaves up in violent little wind-witches. Mocking laughter made the hills shake.

The thing that had circled above raced toward the west, into a blood-red setting sun. With the flying beast, or in it, went the thing that had possessed the corpse of Mohrhard Horgrebe.

The Mindak seized an enchanted bow and spellbound silver arrow. He sped the shaft after the flyer. His ruined arm betrayed him. The arrow fell to earth less than a mile away.

Nieroda had foreseen the alliance. She had planned for the eventuality. Confirmation was on its way to her.

Gathrid's Toal-haunt gurgled merrily.

"Good show, boy. Good show."

"What the devil?"

Theis Rogala pushed through the crowd. He bowed to Gathrid and the Mindak—then sprang back when he saw the light in Gathrid's eyes.

The youth considered running the dwarf down. Then he shrugged. There would be little point. He went looking for Loida instead.

His feelings had been correct. Rogala *had* been tailing him.

Chapter Eleven
Senturia

Three days passed before Ahlert recovered sufficiently to travel. Gathrid spent the time with Loida or wandering through the hidden city. He avoided Rogala religiously. He discovered that the hopes of his eastward journey had been but shadows cast by futility. Excepting Belfiglio's Eye, the rich ore of this motherlode had, it seemed, been transferred to the Mindak's palaces at Senturia. In Ansorge he saw only ruins and more ruins.

The Mindak's people showed him where the Toal had been unearthed, in caverns far beneath Ansorge proper. The twelve crypts were incredibly old. When Gathrid viewed the place where Nieroda had slept he fancied he smelled sour evil still.

He returned from the caverns early the third day, after learning that they would be leaving next morning. As he joined Loida he thought he saw someone slipping through the rocks near their slightly separate encampment. "Who was that?"

"Rogala."

"What was he doing here?"

"Talking to Gacioch."

"There's a pair," Gathrid muttered. "Look, I don't want him hanging around."

"Grouch." Loida made a sour face at him. "How did it go down there today?" She had accompanied him once, had found the ruins too spooky for further visits.

"A whole lot of nothing. What they've found is already gone. What they haven't you can't see. The murals and reliefs and stuff don't make much sense."

"Lord Telani told me we're leaving tomorrow."

"I heard. I'm glad. I'm getting restless." He picked up a stick, drew figures in the dust. "Movement becomes an end in itself."

"You can't run away."

"I know. I tried to leave the Sword down there today. It wouldn't let me. When I got fifteen feet away, I started shaking. It *hurt*. It made me run back and grab it."

"That's spooky."

"That's terrifying. I can't live with it and I can't live without it."

"Don't think about it." She leaned over a small fire and simmering pot. "A soldier gave me a rabbit and some vegetables." She raised the pot lid. Stew smells tantalized Gathrid's nose.

"Smells good."

"Then just think about supper."

"How soon?"

"I don't know. What do I know about cooking? I just did what the man told me."

Exasperated, Gathrid asked, "How long did he say?" He wished she would discourage these soldiers more.

"All right. Another half hour, I guess."

"I'm going for a walk, then."

What he did was run. Strongly and steadily, as he had not been able since his bout with polio. And as he ran, exhilarating in his ability, he reflected that the Sword was not all bad. It hadn't given him a lot, but had given something important.

And he thought about Loida and how her fears and his nagging depression kept them from communicating about anything that mattered, kept them from getting to know one another. She got along better with Gacioch and the young soldiers who kept buzzing round. She and the demon went on like a brother and sister comedy insult act.

He wished he could reassure the girl. He could not. They both knew their fears were not imaginary.

They would be heading for Ventimiglia's capital tomorrow. Loida would be in great peril there. So might he be, though reason said the Mindak had no excuse for treachery yet.

Near the end of his run he glimpsed the dwarf scrambling through the rocks, following him. He grinned. Served Rogala right, having to bust his tail to stay near the Sword. He upped his pace.

All the disorder, squalor, misery and crowding lacking in the country manors was concentrated in Senturia. Gathrid tapped his memories. He knew the slums well. These Quarters produced the soldiers who fleshed out the brigades. No other career offered such opportunities for the poor.

There was plunder to be had, out on the frontiers. A man who survived a tour with his brigade could buy his way out.

Gathrid searched their dreams, their so-small dreams, marveling at those men, and pitying them.

The Mindak's party passed through the slums. People ignored them. Farther in, Gathrid saw buildings and monuments known to his soldier-souls only by repute. There had been a renaissance during the last century. Senturia's heart had been demolished, then rebuilt as the domain of the wealthy. The poor encircled the rich like ramparts of despair.

The city's center boasted a dozen scattered palacios belonging to Ventimiglia's leading families. Between them lay great plazas, imaginative fountains, reflecting lakes and the somber structures of the colleges and universities where wizardry was taught and knowledge preserved. There was a feral park from which deer peeped out as the riders passed. This district denied that poverty could exist in the Mindak's Empire.

"Look at the pigeons," Loida murmured. "There must be millions of them."

One of Gathrid's spare souls snickered. Pigeons were wards of the Twelve Families. It was a crime to harm them. Even so, poor folk of the Quarters made the birds guests of honor at many a meal.

Ahlert's home proved to be a rambling, interconnected mass of baroque structures covering a dozen acres atop a low hill. A few armed men, flashy in family colors, patrolled a walkway encircling a ten-foot wall. They looked bored. On spying their master they became jaunty and arrogant.

"The House of the Five Fountains," Ahlert told Gathrid. "Don't ask about the name. There're six fountains. Four for fresh water. . . . My ancestors must have had grandiose plans."

"More grandiose plans," Rogala muttered. "He calls it a house. I've seen smaller cities."

"How many people live here?" Gathrid asked. Loida had been imprisoned here. He hadn't believed her stories before.

"It varies. We're at a high point now, what with our western venture. Several thousand."

Gathrid exchanged glances with Loida. The girl looked triumphant.

The quiet seen from outside the house proved to be a mask. The House of the Five Fountains was busy as an ant's nest. Loida said, "Those are the clerks and accountants who keep track of profits and cost out west."

Whole courtyards were filled with western plunder. It was decaying for want of buyers. Gathrid looked for something from Gudermuth. He did not find a thing.

Ahlert told him, "I was too successful. I saturated the

138

market. We quit plundering after we occupied Grevening. We're concentrating on long-term projects now. Mainly colonial ventures.''

Gathrid controlled his temper. The reckoning would come. Those who had died to enrich Ahlert would be avenged.

People stared at him. They avoided his eye. They knew him. They were afraid.

The Mindak observed, "Our alliance won't be popular. I don't think they realize what losing control of Nieroda means.''

Rogala grumbled, "Those brigades rebelled out of boyish high spirits, eh?''

"Some people take that attitude. They think they'll come around. They can't encompass the noncommercial aspect.'' Ahlert halted, dismounted, handed his animal to a groom. A platoon of stableboys took the other mounts. "It snuck up on us. We found Ansorge when there were civil wars in Gorsuch and Silhavy. They were weak. We were strong. The wizardries we controlled, augmented from Ansorge, made us think we could enrich the family on the cheap.''

"And you became addicted to conquest.''

"Not entirely. Greed had more to do with it. The Corichs got excited by all the loot. They wanted more. The great families wanted their share. More powerful and effective weapons were coming out of Ansorge. We found Nieroda and the Toal. It looked like nothing could stop us.''

Ahlert led them through long marble hallways filled with bustling clerks. "Then I started changing. A few years ago the title Emperor meant nothing. I took it to heart. I got grand ideas. A world-spanning Empire, at peace. My family mastering its commerce. . . . I hadn't heard of Chuchain or Suchara. I didn't know my delvings in Ansorge were wakening them, or that Chuchain was whispering into my dreams. Sometimes I wish I hadn't found the Hidden City.''

They entered a large hall. The houseboys bearing personal effects spread out, heading in several directions. Ahlert sped his guests hither and yon. Loida and Gathrid followed a half-dozen servants. Between them they hadn't enough possessions to burden one. Gathrid still wore the clothing in which he had fled Kacalief. He looked and smelled it, though he had washed when he could. Loida wore the clothing in which she had fled the Mindak's nephews.

She said, "That man doesn't sound like a mad conqueror."

Gathrid replied, "I haven't met anybody who fit his part. Except maybe Gerdes Mulenex. The others are as reluctant as I am."

"What about your sister?"

"I don't know. She was a special case. Maybe she was like Mulenex. She did fit in with what happened to her."

They climbed several flights of stairs. Ahlert's palacio ceased being showy off the level where visitors were welcomed. Their rooms, facing one another across a bare, narrow third-floor hallway, were windowless, small and spartan. A houseboy told Gathrid, "Don't be alarmed, Lord. The Mindak himself sleeps in a room like this." He leaned close, confided, "It's an affectation of the family. Humble beginnings, you know. They want to remind themselves that it isn't a long way from Five Fountains to the Quarters."

"The more I see of him and Ventimiglia, the more confused I get. Every conclusion I draw gets contradicted."

The servant smiled. "We puzzle ourselves, Lord."

Gathrid kept the man there. He did not mind wasting the afternoon chatting. Gathrid pumped him about the Mindak and his family.

A dozen generations back, Ahlert's ancestors had been mercenaries. Luck, a talent for politics and sorcery, and a run of steel-willed offspring had built Ventimiglia's most powerful house.

"It's happened a hundred times," the servant averred. "That's why Quarters folk enlist. They all think they can make it if they just win a stake."

Hours passed. Someone knocked. The servant looked alarmed. "Don't worry," Gathrid said. "I kept you here, didn't I? Enter."

An elderly woman came in. Her arms were filled with apparel. "Lord, I was told you need fresh clothing. I brought a selection. We'll tailor you something better tomorrow." She surveyed his rags with ill-concealed disdain. She snapped at the houseboy, "Have you shown him the baths?"

"We were about to go. Lord?"

Gathrid got up off the narrow cot and followed the man. "I do need one."

Behind them, the woman shouted, "Maid! There's a bed here needs changing."

"Don't mind her, Lord. She's only had the floor for a month. She's still got the swelled head."

Two days passed before Gathrid saw the Mindak again. He spent his time talking to servants and visiting with Loida. Gacioch disappeared. The girl said Rogala had collected him. She did not mind. Gacioch was beginning to grate.

Ahlert had them attend what he called a small family dinner. A hundred people attended. Brothers and cousins, uncles, and others and others, some of such far remove that in Gudermuth they would not have been considered family at all. The meal lasted for hours, and was an adventure in itself.

Gathrid met the Mindak's wife there. Her name was Mead, she was in her late twenties, and she was the most radiantly beautiful woman Gathrid had ever seen. He was smitten. Her smile melted the hardness growing in him. He hardly heard Ahlert's annoying chatter.

"We'll be here at least two months. I have to mend more fences than I expected. Some members of my syndicate aren't as philosophical about Nieroda as we are. They consider her defection an insult from us.''

Gathrid half-listened while he watched Mead chat with Ahlert's sister. The topic was babies. The sister was extremely gravid. Mead was in the third or fourth month of her first pregnancy. Gathrid would not have guessed had she not mentioned it.

Ahlert continued, ''I'll have to smooth their feathers, then get them to raise another army. So you don't get bored in the meantime, I arranged access to our libraries and historians. Rogala says you're interested in the history of the Great Sword. My people did a lot of research when we thought we could lay hands on it first.''

''Uhm.'' Gathrid nodded. He watched Mead till Loida poked him in the ribs. ''Why'd you do that?''

''It's not polite to stare. And the Mindak is trying to tell you something.''

Embarrassed, he devoted more attention to Ahlert.

''We found a cache of readable books in Ansorge. They span several thousand years. Some are in Old Petralian. Those are the springboard my people are using to translate the rest. You could help, being familiar with Petralian.''

''I suppose.'' Ahlert had become formal and remote. The youth's staring had not won him any affection.

''You seem distracted, Gathrid.''

''It's a strange land. Everything is different. I don't know what to do. I grew up in a remote outpost. This's the first real city I've seen. No one here but Loida shares my background.''

Ahlert smiled. ''I suppose so. That hadn't occurred to me. Well, scholars are scholars. You won't be uncomfortable doing your research.''

The Mindak was right. The men he joined next morning were indifferent to anything but their pursuit of knowledge.

He was a research project himself, Gathrid discovered. He spent half the day answering questions. After lunch they answered his and showed him where to find the histories he wanted to plumb. The pattern persisted for weeks. They drained him of every thought even vaguely relating to the Great Sword.

The first thing Gathrid read was a report delivered to the Mindak two years earlier, "A Summary History of the Great Sword, also known as the Sword of Suchara, also known as Daubendiek." Its style matched that of its title. It contained sketches of previous Swordbearings.

Tureck Aarant had been one of the luckiest Swordbearers. His Choosing had been brief and comparatively painless. It had ended in a quick death at Rogala's hand. That section added little to Gathrid's knowledge.

Aarant's immediate predecessor had been killed in battle. *His* predecessor had committed suicide. Earlier, there had been a Swordbearer who had met his fate at the hand of someone bearing the Shield of Dreibrant, and several who had been as successful as Aarant. There was mention of a Stodreich Uetrecht who, like Anyeck, had overreached. Rogala had ended his stewardship after just two days.

The earliest Swordbearer with a remembered name was one Scharon Chaudoin. His entry was longer than Aarant's. He had been a contemporary and enemy of Nevenka Nieroda when she had been alive. She had used the name Wistma Povich then, and had adopted the name Nieroda later.

Chaudoin had battled Sommerlath and been defeated. Povich had separated him from his esquire and captured him. He had been the longest lived Swordbearer.

His life had spanned a thousand years, the entire lifetime of Sommerlath's Queen. He had spent every moment of her reign imprisoned in a large bottle drifting at the end of a tether over Victory Square in Spillenkothen. He had shared his prison with Daubendiek and a bloodsucking imp. The Sword had remained in his hand. He hadn't had room to use it. He'd simply had to wait till Rogala had found a way to kill him.

After the report, Gathrid read history books. The more he read, the more he saw a pattern. The scholars confirmed his notion.

Evenings involved meals with Ahlert's family. After Gathrid's novelty value faded, those shrank. Rogala and Gacioch became part of the dinner scene. Gathrid avoided the dwarf otherwise, and did not talk to him at table.

Gacioch he saw more frequently. Ahlert's scholars were studying the severed head too. Gacioch made himself difficult. The youth often heard the demon's cursing from his study bench.

He enjoyed being round the scholars. Had the choice been his, he would have joined them. One evening he detained the Mindak after their supper.

"How are the studies coming?" Ahlert asked. "Are they keeping you busy?"

"Hurting and helping, I guess. There's so much pain in it. There're too many parallels between my path and Aarant's. And the others."

"We Chosen follow a script," Ahlert mumbled. "*They* fight the same old fights."

"I don't like it. In fact, I can't stand it. I don't want to follow Aarant's road. I'd rather be a scholar. This's the first time in my life I've ever done something I really enjoyed."

"Why'd you want to see me? I don't have much time. I have a meeting with the Corichs."

Gathrid unslung Daubendiek and proffered the Sword. "Take it. You wanted it. I don't."

Ahlert refused. "It's too late, Gathrid. Suchara is awake. I'm not even tempted. She'd destroy me. It's safer for both of us to play the game out."

"But . . ."

"They call me a lot of names, but fool isn't one of them. Only a fool would wrestle Suchara when She's awake. Sorry. You've been Chosen."

Gathrid cursed under his breath. He cursed again when

he spied Rogala in a doorway, a knowing smirk peeping through his beard.

Ahlert said, "Take your walk with Loida. You'll feel better."

Gathrid departed, stamping his feet angrily.

He and Loida took long walks after dinner every evening. They seldom spoke while strolling. Talk did no good. Just the proximity of another lonely soul was adequate medicine.

"Let's go to the lily pools tonight," Loida suggested. "What happened? You were really happy at supper, when you were joking with Mead." She looked as though she had bitten into a pellet of alum. She made the same face whenever Mead's name came up. Gathrid did not notice. He was not perceptive about women.

Loida Huthsing was blessed with patience.

"I tried to give Ahlert the Sword. He wouldn't take it. He practically laughed at me."

"Oh. Let's go to the lily pools anyway. Somebody said they're blooming again."

"Isn't it late in the year?"

"Sometimes sorcery is good for something besides making war."'

The ponds she favored lay in one of Senturia's wild parks. They were surrounded by exotic trees. Among those there were benches and tables and statuary. The area was popular with young couples. Gathrid never noticed. Perhaps he was too young.

They stayed out late that evening, watching the moon shine off the pools. The silvery orb worked no magic. It only reminded Gathrid of his sister. He talked about her and brooded about his Swordbearing. Loida became exasperated.

"You're so naive!" she snapped. "So self-involved."

"That's not true. I just don't want to hurt people."

"Whatever you say, Mister Imperceptive. I swear, that foul-mouthed demon is better company than you are. Let's go back."

"Loida. . . ."

"Oh, just be quiet."

They played out similar scenes several times. Gathrid never caught on.

He remembered that night only because it was then that he learned that all was not sweetness and light between the Mindak and Mead.

They were in the dining hall when he and Loida returned. Ahlert was in a foul mood. His meeting with the Corichs had gone poorly. He and Mead were arguing about conquests to be undertaken after Nieroda's destruction.

The Mindak argued that genocide was a rational and pragmatic policy. "If we wipe them out, they're no trouble later. We can use our own people to exploit the land." He seemed baffled by Mead's insistence that assimilation was a better course.

"It's inhuman. How can you murder all those people?"

"Murder? That's a hard word, Mead."

"That's what it is."

"Is it murder when we clear a forest to build a new manor? Wait. I guess it is. If you're one of the trees. But we need the land. . . ."

"Piffle. You aren't interested in the land. All you want is profit for the family. You've gotten carried away by your conqueror image. I warned you before. And it caught up with you, didn't it? Your devils all turned on you."

"Mead, please."

"I did warn you. And you wouldn't listen. You started a huge war without the Empire behind you. Now you're scrambling around licking the boots of low-caste Corichs so you can put another army together. That doesn't befit your dignity. Why not take your losses? Just close the Karato Pass. Let the Alliance deal with Nevenka Nieroda."

"I can't. You know that. The investment is too big."

"It's an investment of ego."

"I agreed to protect the people who bought land in Silhavy and Gorsuch."

"So your honor is involved? Your word? What about your word to me? You haven't been a real husband to me since you found Ansorge. You've been running around playing warrior."

Loida took Gathrid's arm and pulled him away from the doorway. "That's enough," she whispered. "Their fights aren't any of your business."

Gathrid tried to pull free. Loida would not let him. "Come on. Off to bed."

He went. And lay awake a long time, hating Ahlert for giving his wife such pain, yet halfway admiring him for concealing the truth of his unwanted commitment to Chuchain.

There came an evening meal when the Mindak was in high spirits. He joked with his relatives and enjoyed himself immensely. He was about to burst with good news. He barely kept it pent till after the desserts. Then he announced, "I sewed up my negotiations with the Corichs today. They've given me all the men I need. We begin moving come the end of the week. The army will assemble at Covingont."

A dour Mead asked, "Isn't it too late in the year? It won't be long before winter closes the Karato."

"Beggars can't be choosers. I had to take what I could get when I could get it."

"And what did you have to give up?"

Ahlert's smile faded. He gave his wife a hard look. She shut up. He told the others, "Finish whatever you have going. We're moving out. Any questions?"

Gathrid had a score, but this was not the time for them. Mead had thrown Ahlert into a black mood. During their evening walk, Loida asked, "Are you leaving me behind?"

Gathrid had not thought about it. "You don't want to stay, do you?" There were those in the Mindak's family who had their eyes on her. She had been consecrated. They meant to complete her dedication. Had she been shielded only by the Mindak, she might have disappeared already. The added threat of the Great Sword kept them at bay.

"Thank you so much."

"What are you upset about now?"

"Never mind. It's not important."

Gathrid kept making the same mistakes. He accepted her word when she wanted to be pumped instead. She became foul company for several days. She reclaimed Gacioch from Rogala, and shared more time with the demon than with Gathrid.

He reacted the way she wanted, and did not realize what he was feeling.

The old voices down inside him kept their opinions hidden. They often teased him, and never told him why. He grew ever more baffled.

And then it all seemed unimportant. He was moving again. He was astride a horse, and that horse was headed west. He and Daubendiek were about to write another chapter in the tale of the Great Sword. He hated himself for being excited.

Chapter Twelve
Covingont

Nevenka Nieroda launched an offensive in Bilgoraj. Sorceries howled and prowled and wasted the Beklavac Hills. Castles tumbled. Strongpoints fell. Yedon Hildreth and the Brotherhood contested every foot of ground. The fighting was merciless and bitter.

Hildreth knew he would lose. His allies were withholding reinforcements, were withdrawing his tactical reserves. Fearing they would lose them, they would not give him the tools he needed to hold.

They had a defeatist outlook. Expecting a breakthrough, they wanted to beef up their defenses at home. Some talked of getting out of the Alliance altogether.

They did not yet know that the Mindak no longer directed their enemies, that this Ventimiglian host was renegade and stood excommunicated from its homeland.

Hildreth held on. He awed his allies with his stubbornness. He held his battered army together solely with the adhesive of will.

Then Gerdes Mulenex withdrew the Red Order.

Death kissed Hildreth's last hope full on the lips.

Nieroda's sorceries began to hurt. The desertions began. They started small, with a man here and there running for home or crossing the lines to enlist with a winner. Then Malmberget and Bilgoraj evacuated their contingents.

It was over. Everyone knew it. Of those left behind, whole companies went over to Nieroda. She welcomed them as prodigals returned to the fold.

Within days Hildreth's command consisted only of his own Imperials and the contributions of the Blues and Whites. As might be expected of small men, his allies indicted him for failing.

Hildreth responded by abandoning his positions. He left behind everything but his animals and men. He marched toward Sartain.

He ignored renewed entreaties from those who had deserted him and were now interested in enlisting his skills in defense of their individual principalities. His answering letters were hard and forthright and sometimes insulting. He made no friends.

Nieroda did not swoop down on Torun. She sent two seasoned brigades to occupy the Beklavac narrows. Her main force she turned eastward. Striking quickly, she drove Honsa Eldracher back into Katich. She stripped him of much of his strength as he withdrew.

Again she disdained the obvious move. Instead of reducing the obstinate city, she marched eastward, into Grevening. Her army now boasted as many western turncoats as Ventimiglian.

Gathrid stood in Covingont's pink granite watchtower and watched Ahlert's new army pass below. An icy wind whipped his cloak and gnawed at his flesh. Winter was clamping down on the high Nirgenaus. For days Ahlert's wizards had been fighting the weather, keeping the pass open.

The youth had been at Covingont three days. Having

nothing else to do, he had spent his time thinking, questioning, wriggling on the hook of his conscience.

Loida joined him in Covingont's chill. "There's so many of them," she whispered. "And when they came to Grevening before, we thought the whole might of Ventimiglia had fallen on us."

"There's more of them. We haven't seen a ghost of their real strength. There're so many people in Ventimiglia."

"What're you going to do when this's over? When peace comes?"

He glanced at her. Could she be that naive? "Try to rest easy in my grave."

She faced him, took his hand. "You're sure you're going to end up like Aarant, aren't you. Why? Do you really have to? Or are you going to make it come true by believing it?"

"The Sword . . . Loida, it's taking me over. I can't get away from it. I can't leave a room without it anymore. Remember the fairy tale about Ash Boy and the Sticking Stone? He would throw it away every night before he went to sleep, and every morning it would be back in his hand when he woke up. That's the way this is. Only maybe I'm the stone. We're going to be stuck the rest of my life. Which won't last long if other Swordbearers are any indicator. I can't get away from Suchara."

Loida squeezed his hand. "The priests never tell us why the gods do what they do. They just say we have to go along."

"I don't think they are gods. That's the strange part. But they can't be human. Sometimes I think they exist only in our imaginations. One old guy in Senturia said they wake up because there's a need in the race. A collective mind that calls them forth."

"My father used to say that about the gods. That they exist only in the hearts of the faithful."

"One thing for sure. Rogala is real. The Sword is real.

Nieroda is real. And they've all been around a long time. Sometimes they used other names. The Mindak's scholars say Grellner was really Nieroda. And she might be the Driebrant who made the Shield.''

"Do you believe in reincarnation?"

"Only the way Nieroda does it. She's a continuous ego. Her identity isn't ever interrupted. Why?"

"I wondered if I played any part in Tureck Aarant's life."

"You believe in it?"

"Yes."

"The only woman in his story was his mother."

"And she would fill the same role as your sister. What you called the kin-death."

"I suppose." He scowled at the soldiers below. Their column seemed endless. He wondered how many would become sacrifices on the altar of this godlike family's game.

He forced a smile. "Guess I've been around Rogala too much. The thing goes on and on, but the scripts aren't fixed. Things are a little different each time. Maybe this time humanity will win."

"Gathrid, were you happy at Kacalief?"

"Most of the time. Why?"

"You take everything so serious. You make everything so important. You want to change everything to the way it *should* be. I thought maybe you had a bad time when you were little."

"You think Rogala is right? That we should just go along? Make it easy on ourselves? Loida, somebody's got to fight it."

"You can say that till the sun freezes, boy. It won't make a whit of difference." The dwarf joined them. Gathrid started to move away. He was doing his best to avoid Rogala still. Loida clung to his hand, holding him there.

"It hurts," Rogala said. "It hurts like hell sometimes. But that's the way things are. Even for us. And we're the shakers and movers. The ones who make things happen. Think how frustrating it must be for the ones we happen *to*."

A nasty chuckle drew Gathrid's attention. Rogala had installed Gacioch in a special carrying case, an ornate box. He carried it in the crook of his arm.

"See you've found a friend, Theis. Enjoy. You were made for each other."

"You don't have to like me, boy, but we're stuck with each other. You could try to get along."

"Try to get along? Why don't you take your own advice?"

"How do you mean? I'm willing to try."

"I've got a name. It's not Boy. I had enough of that from my father. And I'm tired of hearing about how we don't have any choice. A man always has a choice. Suchara can't control us every second. She can't make us live if we don't want to."

"This's serious," the dwarf grumbled. He considered Gathrid intently.

"Why not do a belly-buster off this here tower?" Gacioch asked. "It's been dull for days. Big news. Swordbearer commits suicide. That would liven things up."

"I just might try it."

"Don't be a fool," Rogala snapped.

"Appeal to his better nature," Gacioch suggested. "Remind him that he'll hurt the people he lands on." The demon hooted as if at one of time's great jokes.

"I don't need to," the dwarf replied. "He's right about the choice. Suchara *can't* control him all the time. But he hasn't thought it all the way through. She doesn't need to, thanks to Nieroda." He grinned evilly. "He's got this haunt. It would take him over if he died. And it wouldn't let him die all the way. It would keep him sitting there behind it, watching everything it did with his body."

Gathrid shook in an instant of fury. Rogala was right. It was that impotence which had made the souls of Mohrhard Horgrebe and Obers Lek so difficult to digest. They had spent ages despairing over their usage.

"That's still a choice," he blustered.

"Sure is. And as pretty a one as you'll ever have to face. You up to it, Gathrid? Really up to it? I didn't think so."

The Mindak and his wife came to the tower's top. Gathrid immediately forgot everything but Mead. The woman had a warmth, compassion and understanding lacking in his other acquaintances. Though she was twelve years older, he remained halfway in love.

Common soldier to high commander, Ventimiglians were interested only in survival, plunder and power. Hows and whys and who got hurt were matters of supreme indifference.

Mead cared.

Yet she believed in her husband.

It had taken Gathrid weeks to resolve the apparent contradiction. He finally concluded that the lady agreed with her husband's ultimate goal, an empire free of strife. What she loathed were his methods.

Gathrid bowed to the Lady Mead. She offered him a ghost of a smile. Loida scowled. The youth was more obvious than he thought. He said, "We were just discussing the traps of our lives."

"We're all trapped in our lives," Mead observed. "Either by the Great Old Ones or by ourselves. No use mourning it, Gathrid. Make the best of a bad situation. Try to leave things better for those who will follow us."

"Any success would be devoured by the Great Old Ones," Ahlert told her.

The lady smiled her serene smile.

"What?" Gathrid asked. He had missed something. Had the Mindak finally told Mead that he had been Chosen by Chuchain?

"You're picking an argument, dear," Mead told her husband. "I'm not going to play today." She guided Ahlert to a point twenty feet from Gathrid's group.

The youth reddened. He took a step in the Mindak's direction.

"Just hold it," Rogala growled. "What the hell do you think you're doing?"

Gathrid stopped. He was surprised at himself. "Oh. Yes. All right." He felt a moment of shame. He was becoming arrogant behind his despair. He was getting too confident of his immunity from every peril but Rogala's dagger.

He had not been born with this blade in his hand. Behind it he was nothing but Gathrid of Kacalief, a very unprepossessing youth.

He was getting antsy. He had to get out of Covingont soon. He had to start *doing* something.

Fate granted his wish soon enough. Messenger birds began arriving. Contact had been made with Nieroda. Her rebels were in Silhavy and Gorsuch. Patrol after patrol reported an encounter. The presence of Toal was mentioned in every message.

Nieroda had split her army into divisions commanded by the Toal, hoping to draw the Mindak into multiple engagements. Gathrid saw her strategy. He and Daubendiek could be but one place at a time. She was diluting the power of the Sword.

Selection of a suitable response generated a lot of debate. One of the Mindak's generals suggested, "Let's poke at them till we find out which group she's with, then go after that one."

Ahlert himself said, "I think if we worked out the assignments carefully, our best people could neutralize the Toal with each group while our troops handled hers. The Swordbearer could move from battleground to battleground while we kept them pinned."

Another general said, "I don't like the idea of us splitting up. It's not good tactics. We'd end up scattering our strength too much."

General Tracka, who commanded the Imperial Brigade, added, "Not to mention that that's obviously what she wants. Which makes it a trap of some sort."

Rogala coughed querulously. "Excuse me, gentlemen. It ain't my place to horn in, but you don't give me a whole lot of choice."

The Mindak's commanders looked at him as if he were a roach discovered in a half-eaten bowl of breakfast porridge.

"You'll grant me a certain familiarity with military procedures, won't you? I mean, I have seen a few wars."

"It didn't occur to me to consult you," the Mindak admitted. "Go ahead. Fire away. I'm always open to suggestion."

"Look at the bigger picture before you start your planning."

"Explain."

"Nieroda has committed an unpardonable strategic sin. The general trend of this discussion indicates that you're going to let her get away with it. That you haven't yet noticed."

"I don't follow you."

"She's taken on a war on two fronts. The enemy on each side is stronger. She's risked it thinking she knows you well enough to predict your behavior. She's betting she can whip you before the Alliance gets its house in order. The way you're all talking, she made the right bet."

The generals muttered among themselves. Gathrid caught fragments of sentences involving sentiments ranging from embarrassment at not having seen the obvious to irritation at the dwarf for having interrupted his betters.

"So?" said the Mindak. "What would you do?"

"Make her sweat. Just plain don't fight her. Dig in right here. Hold the Karato. Time is on our side. Every day that passes will tighten the jaws of the vise. Sooner or later she'll have to come to you, and try to finish you, on your ground and your terms. In one place, where Daubendiek can do the most damage.''

Ahlert reflected but a moment before nodding. "Tactically sound, Rogala. But let's note a wee problem. It's not springtime. If I sit my men down in one place, digging trenches and building stockades, how do I feed them? They wouldn't be able to forage. And we don't have the Power to keep the pass open.''

Rogala smiled. "I didn't overlook that angle. I haven't forgotten the old saying that an army marches on its stomach. Nor the considerable likelihood that Nieroda's foragers have already stripped the countryside, the colonials out there being beholden to your family and therefore fair game.''

The Mindak's eyebrows rose. He surveyed his staff. With a trace of sarcasm, he observed, "I don't recall anyone having made that point before.''

One officer blustered, "We anticipated using stocks captured from the enemy.''

"Oh. I see. Gentlemen, I never claimed to be a military genius, but even I can see the hole in that kind of planning.''

"One giant hole," Rogala said, chuckling. "That's desperation planning. Easy! Easy! I've been round the quartermasters. I know what we have, down to the last bushel of oats. We can get through the winter.''

"Would you tell us how?" Ahlert asked. "I know of rations for two months. The Karato will be closed four to five.''

Rogala sucked air between his teeth. "Now we come to the part where I get unpopular." He grinned a big, toothy grin behind his wild beard. "First, there'll be casualties. Nieroda will have no choice. She'll have to attack. That will mean men dying. Dead men don't eat. That'll help some.''

One of the generals muttered something sour about negative attitudes.

Rogala winked and went on. "Mainly, though, the

way to manage is for the officer class to swallow a side order of pride with their meals. This army has almost as many animals as men. Not a lot of them will be useful if my strategy is adopted. So eat the animals, beginning with the non-workers. The warhorses. Then eat their food, that you worked so hard to haul over the mountains. Oats cook up just fine, and a two month supply for one horse will support several men for the same length of time.''

Ahlert's staff seemed to have gone into shock. Rogala's suggestion was so absurd, by their standards, that it took a half minute to fully penetrate and generate an angry stir.

The Mindak raised an admonitory hand. "Wait!" he said. "Rogala, that's asking an awful lot." The warhorse, specially bred and trained to carry an armored man in battle, and extremely expensive if calculated by the man-hours invested in the animal, was *the* symbol of status in feudal society. Rogala's suggestion could not have been met with greater horror, east or west, had it been that they eat their babies.

Rogala clung to his point. "Look at it pragmatically. You won't need the animals. In my scenario you'd fight on foot anyway. Grab replacements from the enemy. . . . Meantime, let the animals forage. They can eat grass and leaves. Soldiers can't. Save the grain for them.''

"What about pursuit?" someone demanded. Rogala had lighted a fire. The Mindak's staffers were wide awake and looking for a dust-up.

"Why worry about it? Where's she going to run? Just sit tight. Make her come to you, but keep her out of Ventimiglia. Let the Alliance mobilize behind her. Let her get desperate, attack and be defeated. Judging her troops by past performance, you won't need to chase them. They'll come begging to join up with you.''

Gathrid followed the exchange in silence, often finding it amusing. Rogala was serious, he knew. Intensely serious, and probably right. The Mindak's officers sensed the logic of his suggestions, and that raised their hackles even more.

Ahlert gave them free critical rein. For a time the meeting turned into an enthusiastic verbal brawl.

Rogala, unfortunately, was blessed with a lack of tact and an ages old habit of not explaining in sufficient detail. Both worked against him now. He answered most objections simply by saying, "You can't whip Nieroda in the field. She's got too much. Believe me." He failed to provide supportive evidence, so his arguments were not accepted. "Not even the Sword will help if you meet her on her terms. Damnit, you have to let her defeat herself. You have to sit here and look like you're going for a draw. You have to let the Alliance become a threat behind her. So she don't dare commit herself completely anywhere. If the alternative was defeat, I'd think getting my feet dirty was trivial. But that's just a coarse little peasant of a survivor's opinion."

Later, after an especially bitter denunciation by one of the conservatives, Rogala observed sadly, "You're always the same. In every age. What do they do to you when you're little? Suck your brains out your earholes and stuff your heads with wool? You always consider your illusions more important than winning. I just don't get it. Hold it there, your undeserved generalship. I'm going to pronounce an oracle on your enterprise, based on a few thousand years of experience. You damned fools are going to get smoked. Nitwits always do."

"Smoked?" the offended general demanded.

"Smashed. Stomped. Decimated. Wiped out."

Ahlert made a gentle, open-palmed gesture in the general's direction. The man subsided immediately.

He still awes them, Gathrid realized. Maybe he hasn't slipped as much as he thinks.

Musingly, Rogala continued, "The Swordbearer and me, of course, we're going to get out of it all right. The lad here, he's emotional. He's going to mourn you all. Your wives and families too. That's the way he is. Me,

I'm just going to laugh. I get a kick out of seeing jerks get what's coming to them.''

Rogala turned to Ahlert. "One other thing, Chief. Assuming somebody has an attack of smarts and listens to me, that gang of camp followers has got to go. Right now. They aren't nothing but eating mouths. The mouths you want to fill belong to your soldiers, not your harlequins and harlots.'' He stamped away. After a few steps, he paused to beckon Gathrid. The youth rose and followed.

Once out of earshot of Ahlert, the dwarf said, "We're not going to have any more luck here than we had with the Alliance Kings. These clowns would let their army get stomped like cockroaches in a cattle stampede before they'd swallow their pride and do what I tell them.''

Rogala misjudged the mettle of the Mindak. The army remained encamped in the mouth of the Karato. Immense earthworks began to rise, more as a means of keeping the troops occupied than for their military value.

Magnolo Belfiglio relayed the news that the west's political problems were settling out. Yedon Hildreth was in Bilgoraj again, clearing the Beklavac narrows.

Nieroda continued to await a response from the Mindak.

Rogala did not win all his points. The horses did not go to the butchers right away. Their destruction was too much for even the Mindak to swallow in a single lump.

Nieroda moved steadily nearer, finally establishing a line of fortified camps five miles west of Ahlert's position. For weeks the only contact between armies came when scouting parties skirmished. Each host awaited the other's first move.

Ahlert lost patience first. He led Gathrid, a grumbling Rogala and a select company of warrior-wizards into no-man's-land, hoping to provoke Nieroda into some ill-advised action.

She refused the bait.

Ahlert tried again. And again. The Dark Lady responded by sending a Toal's brigade to savage the

Ventimiglian right while her opposite flank was being irritated by Ahlert's raiders.

Next morning Ahlert announced, "Word from Belfiglio. She's going to turn our tactic against us. She's coming after our livestock today." Ahlert's party had plundered Nieroda's herds several times.

"You thinking ambush?" Rogala sounded hopeful.

"I am."

The usual raiding party assembled and raced to intercept Nieroda's raiders. The dwarf knew the perfect site for a bushwhacking, but it was far from the lines. They barely got themselves hidden in the brush and washes and gullies in time.

"Damn that Belfiglio!" Ahlert snarled when he saw the enemy approaching. "He didn't say he was going to hit us this hard."

Six Dead Captains led the enemy party. With them rode a mix of Nieroda's best soldiers. Their path would take them to Ahlert's extreme left flank, where the animals were grazing.

Gathrid found himself more nervous than the situation seemingly demanded. There was a wrongness in the air. The fight looked too big. He whispered to Rogala, "I think we'd better call it off."

Rogala was uneasy too. "I'll suggest we hit from behind, after they begin their attack on the main line."

Too late. The Toal entered the ambuscade. Ahlert signaled the attack.

Gathrid muttered, drew Daubendick, joined the charge.

The Toal were not surprised. Six black-gauntleted hands rose, thrust out stiffly. Six Ventimiglian saddles emptied.

Spells previously prepared by both sides lightninged back and forth. The earth churned. The sky darkened. Horses screamed and threw their riders. The companies crashed together, mixed.

Nieroda and the remaining Toal appeared on a nearby rise.

"A trap within a trap," Gathrid shouted at Rogala, pointing. Daubendiek took control, howled about him, murdered sorceries and drank lives.

Nieroda had anticipated the Mindak. Perhaps she had fed Belfiglio disinformation to set her opponent up.

The Toal remained out of Gathrid's reach, but gradually enveloped him. He saw disaster taking shape. The Dark Champion's strategy had one obvious purpose: to strip her former master of his most potent ally.

Gathrid knew he was not invulnerable. Daubendiek had limits. Swordbearers had fallen in battle ere now.

The Toal and Rogala had their limits, too.

A band of the Mindak's warrior-wizards isolated one Dead Captain. Rogala got in among them and with preternatural quickness planted a dagger in the thing's side. The sorceries on his short blade were weaker than those on the thing's armor. His knife burst into flame. But it survived long enough to cripple and distract the creature.

A blurring stroke of the Toal's dark blade, moving faster than the nimble dwarf could dodge, raked Rogala's side. He yipped like a kicked puppy, spurred away.

The Ventimiglians invested six lives in unhorsing the injured Toal. They drove its own witchblade through its heart.

The battle was not going well, Gathrid decided. The casualties were too nearly even. And Nieroda had come a little closer. She might be tempted to get involved herself.

Daubendiek got the reach of a Dead Captain.

This time the disorientation seemed endless. Gathrid's mind threatened to shake loose from its foundations. This Dead Captain, when it had been a man, had worn the name Tureck Aarant.

Staggered, Gathrid thought, Are there other Swordbearers among the Toal? Will that be my fate?

Only eleven of a hundred ninety Ventimiglians survived the skirmish. Nieroda had crafted herself a cunning little victory. Of those eleven, Gathrid was the lone man to escape without a wound.

Of the flesh. The cuts on his soul were deep and painful, and festered immediately.

Ahlert sounded the withdrawal when he saw the Swordbearer go slack in his saddle. He grabbed Gathrid's reins, shouted orders and fled. Most of the men lost died covering his retreat.

Gathrid retreated, too, deep inside himself, where he faced a sad yet grateful Tureck Aarant.

"What's happened to him?" Ahlert demanded of Rogala. "He just seemed to fold up."

The puzzled dwarf replied, "I don't know. Some Nieroda trick. He cut a Toal down and . . . It was almost like the soul went out of *him*."

They approached friendly lines. A storm of arrows screened them from the pursuit. "Get him up to Covingont," the Mindak ordered. "I'll be there as soon as we turn them back."

Nieroda's whole army came up behind her raiders. They attacked all along the Ventimiglian line.

Somehow, the news had traveled ahead. Loida and several of Ahlert's best demonologists were waiting at Covingont's gate. "What happened?" the girl demanded.

Rogala ignored her. He cursed and gestured and bullied the fortress's garrison into lifting the youth off his mount and onto a stretcher. He used his own blade to cut the ropes binding Gathrid to the horse's back. "Come on. Come on," he snarled. "Let's get him out of this weather. He'll die of pneumonia."

Loida kept asking questions. Everyone kept ignoring her. The demonologists stayed close to the stretcher, trying to detect the presence of an attacking spirit. Rogala told them about the youth's Toal-haunt and expressed the opinion that that was not the cause of the present difficulty.

"It may not be the cause," one replied, "but it'll certainly take advantage if it can. We'd better prepare for it."

"Right. Right. Girl, what are you doing?"

Loida had managed to elbow her way through the crowd. She was holding Gathrid's hand as the stretcher moved along. She ignored Rogala.

Inside, Gathrid began to come out of shock. He began to explore this bizarre new soul that had, for a time, nearly displaced his own.

He knew he was lucky. Had Tureck Aarant had the habits of the creature that had possessed him, he could have taken control during the period of shock. But this Aarant was not the aggressive Aarant of legend. Indeed, he was a rather gentle being. But he had the impact of all the souls he had taken in his own time.

He shared some truths about the Brothers' War. They shattered the myths that had been handed down the ages. The Immortal Twins ceased being such ivory exemplars of righteousness for Gathrid. The great champions of the brothers developed mean, small-minded dimensions. All those heroic names developed their human sides.

The Dark People of Ansorge had perished, but not without leaving a legacy. The last act of the last of their elders had been to make certain that Tureck Aarant became one of the Toal. They had foreseen enough of the future to know that the Toal would battle the next Swordbearer. In their efforts to break the rhythm and cycle holding the world in thrall they had bet on Aarant coming to blows with his successor.

How had Mead put it? Do what you can for those who are yet to live?

The last of Gathrid's innocence fled when he met Tureck Aarant.

Nieroda had known he was one of her Toal. She had brought them together, knowing Gathrid would be stunned.

The youth realized she had not known the whole truth, had not understood the Dark People's motives. She would

164

not have faced the risks had she done so. Yet her ploy came within a whisker of success. Gathrid was in no shape for wrestling his haunt.

The stretcher-bearers carried him to a warm room deep inside Covingont. Loida, Rogala and the Mindak's people crowded in. "Build up the fire," someone ordered. One of the weary stretcher-bearers began chucking logs into the fireplace.

Loida kept on with the frightened questions.

Rogala snapped, "Girl, if you want to stay, get on round the other side there and keep quiet. The questions will answer themselves." He was surprisingly gentle. He turned, asked, "Has it started?"

The senior of the four wizards assigned to the youth replied, "Not yet. He seems to be in shock right now."

Rogala felt Gathrid's pulse, watched his breathing, considered the color of his skin. Shock, all right. He had seen it on a thousand battlefields. But no one had touched the youth. Why, then?

Gathrid suddenly arched his back and made a terrible sound deep in his throat. He began thrashing. Foam appeared on his lips.

"That's it," said the senior wizard. "Hold him," he told the stretcher-bearers. "Let's get him into some sort of restraints. Rogala, see that he doesn't swallow his tongue. Put something between his teeth. He could bite it and drown in his own blood."

The dwarf seized a piece of kindling.

The wizards chanted, then listened with an inner ear, then chanted some more. The senior finally observed, "It's a strong one, this devil."

"One of the Toal spirits," Rogala replied.

"This's going to be hard work, then. If it knows how to install itself with outside help."

The wizards practiced their craft. Two days would pass before they dared relax, before they saw themselves safely through the crisis. The Toal haunt was stubborn and determined.

For a time the Gathrid inside, so weakly anchored to his flesh, did not realize who or what he was. He knew only that he was fighting for his existence. And in the beginning he did not have much motive for winning.

He seemed to be in a different world, an imaginary world. He formed an army of one, and upon an unseen plain he met another such host, a formless shadow that seemed to be mostly hunger. It leapt at him, and bore him down, and seemed about to devour him. . . . Then they were back where they started, facing one another again. It leapt at him, and bore him, down, and seemed about to devour him. . . .

Gathrid was baffled. Over and over, the same thing happened. And each time something broke the chain before the moment of disaster.

Then he felt Tureck Aarant in there with him. Tureck Aarant, who could have taken him, fighting to save him. And then there were other forces, things unseen, from outside the dream, which put constraints upon the shadow, and weakened it while he grew stronger.

There was no feel of time in there. Nor did Gathrid care, till caring returned and he began to fight more from desire than reflex. The battle turned the instant he rediscovered his will to survive.

"That's it," Aarant whispered. "That's it. We have it on the run now. Come. Let's destroy it." And in an instant they were in pursuit, flying across the unseen plain.

The youth's eyes opened. He needed several seconds to get his bearings. He found Loida holding his hand, looking exhausted and worried. "Hi!" he croaked, grinning a rictus of a grin.

"Gathrid!"

"I'm back."

She threw herself at him, hugging him. Then she shouted, "He's awake! He came out of it."

Rogala and several Ventimiglians charged into the room. "How you doing, son?" the dwarf demanded.

Weakly, Gathrid replied, "I think the worst is over."

"What happened?"

"Careful," Aarant whispered inside him.

"I was going to ask you. The Toal thing, I think."

"That's what we figured. Ooh, that Nieroda was crafty."

Gathrid tried to lever himself into a sitting position. Loida had to help him. "How long was I out?"

"Two days. And she used every second." Rogala told the tale.

Nieroda's forces had ripped and torn at the army blocking the Karato. A finger of one assault had high-watered in the snows below fortress Covingont. The Mindak was still trying to drive that thrust back. The old scars on the walls of the pass had been obliterated by new ones.

Gathrid smiled. "What good would winning do her? Winter will hold the pass better than any army."

Rogala shrugged. "The seasons turn."

Gathrid tried to get to his feet. "I've got to get down there and help."

The Mindak entered. He examined the youth. "You aren't going anywhere for a few days."

"But . . ."

"You're too weak. To be honest, I don't want you going out there and losing the Sword."

Rogala agreed. "You just stay put. Take it easy. Girl, keep an eye on him. Yell if he gets too frisky."

They forced him back down on the cot. And once down, he found he did not mind having Loida fuss over him.

In his shy way he was fond of her. He did not yet know her well, but he did feel good when she was around. He was tempted to stretch his convalescence.

Loida was first to sense the changes in the Swordbearer. He had returned to the world possessed of an altered perspective, a new determination, a new hardness, a new hunger for the destruction of the forces toying with mankind. She found this new Gathrid frightening. She liked the old one better.

Chapter Thirteen
Gudermuth Again

That Nieroda was an inspired commander became ever more obvious. Rogala's prophecy of defeat seemed likely to come true despite a defense that he had guaranteed to be a sure thing. The dwarf began to doubt it himself.

Then, after having subjected the Ventimiglian host to seven days of savagery, Nieroda decamped and raced westward. Ahlert's people were too weak and weary to do anything but thank their gods that they had survived.

Nieroda told no one her intentions. The Mindak's man Belfiglio could tell his master nothing. The Eye could not look into the minds of Nieroda or the Toal.

Nieroda had a week's lead before Ahlert became organized enough to follow.

Now Rogala's scheme revealed its weakness. There were not enough draft animals to draw the supply train. Ahlert stumbled westward, losing ground every day.

Nieroda reached Gudermuth while winter still gripped the little kingdom. Her army was tired and cold and hungry, but confident.

In her absence Count Cuneo had managed to restore

much of the Alliance's shaky fighting spirit. Morale had risen when his vigorous campaign broke through the brigades holding the Beklavac narrows. In an effort to solidify the Alliance further, he marched on eastward and relieved the capital of Gudermuth, adding his own Imperial troops to those of Honsa Eldracher and Katich's native defenders. He believed further successes there would seal the remaining vacillators into the pact.

Nieroda challenged Hildreth and Eldracher as soon as she reached Gudermuth.''

"They've seen a hell of a fight," Eldracher observed. He was a tall, lean, weathered man of middle years. In manner and bearing he resembled his friend, Yedon Hildreth. He and the Count were of a class that had become inbred. "What do you think?" he asked Hildreth.

Nieroda's vanguard did look ragged and panicky, as if in a hurry to escape. Her main force, a hill farther away, seemed to swirl and surge, as if hurrying along in disarray.

"The rumor is true." Hildreth scowled ferociously. "The boy made big talk, but he's gone over to the Mindak. He's no better than Aarant was."

"Stopping Nieroda seems a sound enough reason."

Hildreth's scowl deepened. He was a black or white man, this Count. His viewpoint held little room for compromise. "They'll hit the city," he guessed. "They'll want our food stores. It's just possible they don't know I'm here. I'll go out and hit them first. See if your spook pushers can find out how close Ahlert is."

"Of course."

Neither Hildreth nor Eldracher was a man easily misled, yet each, attaching too much weight to Gathrid's shift of allegiance, leapt to the conclusion that Nieroda was fleeing in defeat.

Hildreth first suspected the truth three hours later. Nieroda's arrival and shift to combat order was too smoothly and confidently executed. Her renegade wizards came into play easily, with their strongest and subtlest spells prepared. He realized he had been sucked in. He would have refused battle had Nieroda come up in good order.

Easy disengagement was impossible. Nieroda and the Toal were applying pressure all along his line, which he had thrown across their path a mile from the city.

Eldracher became ever more puzzled as he searched for the Mindak. He could not locate the man. Nieroda appeared to be fleeing ghosts. He tried searching her far flanks.

"My god!" He called for his weapons and armor and bodyguard.

He had discovered the truth too late.

A mounted brigade had circled the city. It erupted from the hills southwest of Katich, thundered into Hildreth's rear. A strong, Toal-backed force attacked and screened the city gates. Hildreth then had nowhere to retreat.

Eldracher reached the wall in time to watch the disaster unfold.

Hildreth had brought half the Alliance's strength out of Bilgoraj. Already half that had fallen here. The survivors were being crushed against Katich's walls. They were fighting bravely, but would be dead before nightfall.

Three times Hildreth tried to clear the enemy away from the gate. Three times the Toal hurled him back. Eldracher did what he could from above, with covering fire, and hauling the wounded up by rope. His efforts were fruitless. Come midafternoon Hildreth himself ascended to confer.

"Nieroda's won this one," he said. "It's all over but the slaughter."

"I could sortie."

"That's what she wants. You'd lose the gate. And the city. I'm going to break out to the south. If I get through, I'll run for Bilgoraj."

Eldracher nodded. "All right." It was the only real hope for Hildreth's men. "I can hang on here."

"Did you find Ahlert?"

"No. He's nowhere near here."

"Wonder where he is. What do you think he's planning? I won't bring another column out just to get torn up."

"Maybe she finished him."

"He had the Swordbearer with him."

"The Nirgenaus are closed for the winter. Maybe he never left Ventimiglia."

"Maybe. If it looks that way, I'll relieve you again. Maybe we can get this settled before the season shifts. If we could smash Nieroda . . . that'd pull the Alliance together. They'd give me what I need to make sure Ahlert stays home. I'd best get back."

His absence had begun to tell. Some units were dissolving.

"Until we meet," Eldracher said. They clasped hands. They had been friends a long time, just as their masters were friends. Neither expected to meet the other again.

Eldracher supported Hildreth's breakout in every way possible. Count Cuneo managed to escape with two thousand men. Ten times as many did not win free. Eldracher salvaged those he could with his hoisting ropes.

Eldracher's group consisted entirely of Blue Brothers. None of the other Orders were represented.

That night a Red Brother visited Nevenka Nieroda.

The siege lasted four days. The first three involved exchanges of messengers. Eldracher feigned an interest in negotiating in order to buy time for Count Cuneo.

Nieroda lost patience. She attacked. Her thrust lacked intensity. It puzzled Eldracher.

The mystery cleared during the night.

Something wakened Eldracher from a deep sleep. He sat up, looked around, saw nothing but darkness. Then a man-shape rose over the foot of his bed.

He rolled, grabbed at his dagger.

The assassin struck with a sword that, hours before,

had been carried by a Toal. The sorceries upon it devoured those protecting Eldracher's life.

It was a long, slow death.

In the flash of conflicting wizardries Eldracher saw the face of his murderer. The assassin was one of his own Brothers, a man he had sometimes suspected of being a tool of Gerdes Mulenex.

Eldracher could not open his mouth to call for his guards. He expired with a moan so soft they never heard a sound. The assassin went out the window he had entered.

An hour later the Toal tramped through a gate won from within. The fighting was vicious. Neither the Blues nor Gudermuthers willingly surrendered.

Gerdes Mulenex stood at a window in his mansion in Sartain. He smiled gently. A document had arrived from the east. He held it to the light again.

"Stano," he said to a trusted servant, "tell our man in the Raftery that it's time. Tell our people round Elgar to be ready."

"At last, Lord?"

"At last." A great rumbling laugh shook Mulenex's heavy belly. "At last."

His plans were about to bear fruit. They were not taking the exact shape he had anticipated when he had insinuated his agents into the enemy camp. But close enough. Close enough.

He laughed long and hard after his man departed. It was a good joke, at the expense of Honsa Eldracher and the Fray Magister. He pictured their faces. The humor left him.

Well, they were out of the way at last.

"It's barely a shadow of its former might," the Mindak said of the Western army. It lay drawn up in order of battle near Kacalief, where the whole thing had begun for Gathrid. The Mindak, Gathrid, Rogala, and several

Ventimiglian staffers were studying Nieroda's dispositions from a rise on the Grevening side of the border.

Nieroda had been taking losses. Even with her western turncoats, she now had but a third of the Western army's original strength. What combat had not accomplished, desertion had. Morale had declined. Her troops had had little chance to enjoy the fruits of victory.

"The odds are in our favor," Ahlert observed. "Our men outnumber hers. Her wizards are almost all gone. Only seven Toal remain corporeal. It was a happy day when I decided not to teach her the binding spells."

"Yet she's offering battle," Rogala replied. He had healed with astonishing rapidity. He was the only man in the Mindak's army ever to have survived the kiss of a Toal blade. Now his fierce gaze darted over the Savard, seeking traps.

"All her people are here," Ahlert said. "Belfiglio can't detect any other force nearer than Hildreth's, in Bilgoraj. She means to win."

"Then she's confident of her sorcery. Or she's a step ahead of us again, and the outcome here doesn't matter."

One of the Mindak's generals said Nieroda's confidence had convinced him the encounter was a trap. He favored eschewing battle till later.

"We have the Sword," Ahlert replied. He glanced at Gathrid. Of late the youth had grown reticent. He was more interested in Loida Huthsing than in the coming battle.

She was supposed to have returned to Ventimiglia with the camp followers. Gathrid had refused to let her go. No one had called him to account.

Ahlert's gaze swept across his army. His brigades were in line of battle. They had recovered during their lazy march westward. Their morale had improved.

Still, they were not the engine of war he had hoped. Nieroda had made of them a sword with a dulled edge.

She might defeat him if she remained sufficiently stubborn.

That devil Doubt dogged him still.

"Down there," Gathrid told Loida. "That's where we caught the ducks that time." He indicated the marshy region beyond Nieroda's left flank. Her right she had anchored on the hill where Kacalief lay in ruin. Beyond Kacalief, to the north, lay the skeletal, winter-naked forests of the Savard Hills.

"And over there would be the vineyard where you and Anyeck tried to shave your brother's dog?"

"No. But that's close. Back there where Nieroda's camp is."

Ahlert listened with half an ear. He felt a certain compassion for the boy. To have been caught up in this so thoroughly, so young. . . . Should he pass along the latest from Magnolo, about events in Sartain? The news might keep the Sword with him after Nieroda's defeat.

Yet the boy could not forget what had happened here. That thirst for revenge would stay with him, like a tropical disease, and would keep shaping his behavior. . . .

Could that be why Nieroda had selected this site? For its impact on the Swordbearer?

Maybe there was something to Mead's viewpoint after all.

Gathrid, though, believed that he had banished his old pain. He was interested only in Loida. The journey west had changed her. And it had changed him, he admitted. They were growing up.

What would become of her after he was gone?

He remained convinced that his days were numbered.

He had to find some way to make sure she did not fall captive again. She had been hurt enough. A visit to the ruins of Rigdon had crushed her. The site of her childhood home had been a tangle of brambles and vines under which had lain blackened stone and bleached bones.

The Aarant soul told him to be careful with Loida. Suchara was a jealous mistress.

Tureck was the strongest of his secondary souls. He alone had managed to retain some individuation.

Gathrid still was not accustomed to its pressure. Aarant had brought him all the minds he had acquired as Swordbearer. It was weird, being able to remember things that had happened a thousand years before his birth.

"Swordbearer!" Rogala called.

Gathrid turned reluctantly. "What?"

"We're ready. The last battle is about to begin. You want to pay attention here?"

"This is no armageddon, Theis. It's just an episode on the road to the last battle. And you know it."

Rogala raised an eyebrow. The youth no longer sounded like Gathrid of Kacalief.

Gathrid added, "This isn't anything but a preliminary. An elimination to see who fights next round. The winner gets Ventimiglia."

Rogala nodded, but kept staring.

Gathrid's glance flicked to the Mindak. He thought of Mead. Her love was being devoured by Ahlert's pursuit of dreams more elusive than the wind.

The Mindak himself had declared all ambition self-delusion. Why didn't he abandon his fool's dreams?

Because they were Chuchain's. The Great Old One was dreaming him through his paces.

As Suchara was doing Gathrid.

A boy called Gathrid of Kacalief said good-bye to Loida Huthsing. The Swordbearer drew his blade. The breath of Suchara rolled across the world.

Nieroda's army braced itself.

Today the ancient sorceries were all in play. The Dark Champion had laid upon her followers a compulsion salvaged from the glory days of Sommerlath. They were as steadfast as the Toal. Not a soldier among them knew fear. Not a one conceded his own mortality. To a man the Western army would stand and win—or die.

Smokes materialized before Ahlert's host. Prancing

and screaming, a horde of Gacioch's cousins rushed out of them.

They were met by their like, summoned by Nieroda. They indulged in a shrieking combat that lasted only minutes.

Lightnings slashed here and there, always to be neutralized before they did any real harm.

Soul-devouring javelins and arrows that could not miss stormed through the winter sky, and slid away from their targets, or simply ceased to be.

Rains of poison and disease fell from no visible cloud, and never reached the earth.

Ahlert's infantry started forward.

A fissure opened between the armies. The earth thrashed like a broken-backed cat. The gap was deep, steep-sided and too wide to leap. Ahlert's soldiers dropped to the ground, clung for their lives. They stayed down while awaiting their commander's response.

A hail of stone blistered from the sky. It obscured the sun while it raced in from some land far away. It plunged into the gap with a vast hiss and rattle. It filled the chasm in minutes. The brigades took to their feet and tramped across.

Nieroda abandoned the more spectacular sorceries. The moment of mundane combat was at hand.

"She's holding the Toal back," Ahlert remarked as he walked his cavalry in the wake of his foot.

"And her horse," Rogala added.

Gathrid considered dismounting and joining the infantry. Daubendiek was impatient.

Heralds called for the Western army's surrender. A flight of arrows answered them.

The Mindak strove to overcome the sorcery which made near-Toal of the foe. He failed. The witchery of Sommerlath was beyond him.

"Recall," he ordered after a bitter hour. His men were making no headway. "We'll try breaking through with the horse."

"Through the middle," Rogala suggested. "You break through either flank, she'll hit yours when you turn to roll up her line. Just punch through and go for the she-devil herself. Try to get it over as fast as you can."

Ahlert nodded, but frowned a query.

Rogala continued, "This looks like she's set it up to kill people. On both sides. Like she wants both armies decimated."

"Why would she want that?"

The dwarf shook his head. "Beats me. But don't let her control it. If she does, this field is going to be knee-deep in blood. Get her and it'll end."

Gathrid glanced at the dwarf's back. Why would Rogala care how much blood got spilled? He was a puzzle, that runt. He refused to be consistent.

The Mindak smiled at Gathrid. "I understand," he said.

"What?"

The moment passed. Ahlert said, "You take Nieroda."

"Was there any question about that?" Nobody else dared try.

"I suppose not."

Gathrid peered at the enemy command post. He could not pick Nieroda out of the crowd. What surprises would he encounter this time? Despite Daubendiek's reassurances and growing blood-greed, the youth was apprehensive. Nieroda was too damned cunning.

"Now," Rogala told Ahlert. The infantry had disengaged. Their officers had received orders and were standing by.

The Ventimiglian cavalry advanced in two waves. The first was to open a hole through which the second could charge Nieroda. They were to give that hole over to the infantry, then join the assault on the enemy commander.

And so it went. To a point. Nieroda's infantry proved more stubborn than expected. They refused to let the one cavalry force follow the other. Ahlert's horsemen engaged Nieroda's at a severe disadvantage.

Gathrid rode at the shock point. Daubendiek wailed malevolently, downing enemy after enemy. Ahlert rode on his right quarter, dealing almost as much death with a captured Toal sword. But the numbers began to tell. Impetus vanished. The Mindak's men mingled with Nieroda's riders till all unit integrity vanished. Nieroda's locally superior numbers gradually overcame Ahlert's superior Power.

Once again, as during that skirmish before the Karato, the Toal closed in on the Swordbearer.

"Don't wait for them," said the ghost of Tureck Aarant. "Take the fight to them. Get them one at a time. Reduce the odds."

Gathrid spurred toward the nearest, chopping his way through a living wall. Ahlert tried to stay with him. Rogala clung to his wake.

Fear distorted the dwarf's features. His gaze darted from Toal to Toal. He called out for Suchara's aid. His cries were carried off by the thunder of battle.

The first Dead Captain tried fencing with Gathrid, stalling so the others could close in.

Gathrid glanced uphill. Less than a quarter mile away, behind his opponent and a thin screen of horsemen, Nieroda leaned on a huge black sword that might have been Daubendiek's twin. If he could break through. . . .

He sprang to the attack. With Aarant to show the way, he was able to guide the Sword. The Toal went down. It was as cold and evil a spirit as its brethren.

Another battled into his path. It, too, fenced, attempting delay. It, too, went down.

Aarant handled the spiritual input while Gathrid fought.

He was a hundred yards nearer Nieroda.

Now there were two Dead Captains. A third was trying to force its way past Ahlert.

Nieroda picked up a javelin. She bounced it in her hand

like an athlete getting its feel. She cast it too quickly to follow. Gathrid brought Daubendiek round to deflect it.

He was not its target. It slammed through his mount's breastplate. The animal dropped instantly. It never made a sound.

Nieroda relaxed against her sword. Gathrid cursed her as he disentangled himself from his mount while fending a blizzard of Toal swords. His armor hindered him. He cursed Rogala for having talked him into wearing it.

Loida was watching from Ahlert's one-time command post. She saw the javelin fly. She saw Gathrid go down. She squealed in dismay.

Rogala had left her Gacioch to babysit. The boxed devil remarked, "So it goes. They've got him now. The old witch has worked another trap."

"No." Loida did not know what impelled her. The will of Suchara, perhaps. Or that of Chuchain. Or something within herself. Whichever, she seized an imperial standard from its startled bearer, leapt onto a horse and raced toward the ruin of Kacalief. Gacioch whooped like the master of ceremonies at a devils' convention.

Some of the repulsed cavalry heard the demon, saw the standard, followed. One of the two reserve infantry brigades did the same. People were too confused to think.

Loida swung round Nieroda's right flank, trampling friend and foe alike. Gacioch hooted merrily and thundered orders that crashed over the rumble of battle. The effect was salutory. Loida and the horsemen passed through the lines unscathed.

The girl rose in her stirrups, searched for Gathrid. There he was. Alive still. Nieroda's creatures swarmed over him like maggots on a dead dog, but he was alive!

She then realized that she bore no weapon save the light spear from which Ahlert's banner flew.

She could not halt her wild career. Those behind her pushed her forward into the melee. The shock almost tumbled her from her saddle. Someone steadied her. She clung for her life. Swords flashed around her. A mace missed her face by a quarter inch. She went numb with fright.

But fate had a use for her.

The fighting swirled away. Her mount quickly lost interest, began cropping brown stubble churned up by thousands of hooves. Loida tried to regain her wits. She was shaking all over.

Something seemed determined to keep her from collecting herself.

Gathrid began to despair of his survival. Though Aarant whispered soothingly, bidding him remain calm, panic threatened. The storm of Toal swords drove him to one knee.

Then the reinforcements arrived.

The reserve brigade turned the enemy flank. The other brigade, scenting victory, rushed to the marsh end of Nieroda's line.

The shock wave of Loida's charge reached Gathrid. The death dance devolved into chaos. The youth staggered to his feet, conquered a Toal Rogala had unhorsed.

The pressure faded momentarily. He surveyed the situation. The victor would be little better off than the vanquished, whichever way it went. The issue remained in doubt. He had to get Nieroda.

Daubendiek agreed. Gathrid was surprised that it would ignore the easier blood around it.

The blade was an instrument of Suchara. Suchara had interests beyond simple bloodshed.

Gathrid hacked his way uphill. The going became easier as he went.

The Dark Champion waited impassively. As he neared her, she grew as she had that day on the Bilgoraji border. This time Gathrid definitely saw a grinning, malevolent, red-eyed face behind the umbra, waiting, as if sure of the outcome of the approaching combat.

Gathrid, too, grew. He felt half-a-mile tall. The brawling, screaming combatants dwindled till they appeared to be insects scurrying round the walls of a shallow bowl. The Mindak's troops were boxing their adversaries.

A hundred yards separated Gathrid and Nieroda, yet he felt he could reach out and touch her. And still she remained motionless. "Careful," Aarant warned. Daubendiek, too, became wary. The Dark Lady was too confident.

Gathrid swung the Sword in a mighty arc. It flickered through a dozen planes. The aquamarine nimbus around him became intense. He could see it himself.

For an instant he felt Suchara's touch on his shoulder, could sense her cold eyes staring over his head.

Nieroda blocked his stroke, responded with an attack of her own.

Gathrid understood instantly. She bore a newly forged blade. It had been invested with both new and ancient sorceries. It had been hammered on the anvils of Hell and tempered in the oils of evil. It was a potential match for Daubendiek.

Gathrid's Toal-haunt gurgled merrily, for a moment drowning the soothing voice of Tureck Aarant and the frightened susurrus of lesser souls. The devil distracted him. It had not bothered him in a long time.

"I'll handle it," Aarant whispered.

Daubendiek turned Nieroda's blade. It was startled by its enemy's power, yet it gained confidence as it recognized the other's immaturity. The new sword was Daubendiek's equal only in potential. It was not experienced enough to complete the task Nieroda demanded of it.

Viewed from afar, the struggle looked like a collision between towering thunderheads. One was black, the other the color of the sea. The infantry battle ground to a halt. The Toal kept the cavalry fighting, gradually turning the tide against the Mindak again. Ahlert tried to extricate his riders and consolidate them with his main force.

Loida observed the striving of giants from a deep mental fog.

Gathrid suddenly realized that, once again, he faced

an opponent trying to buy time. Nieroda knew she had little chance to defeat him. She had known from the start. Defeat had been calculated into her plan.

Why was she stalling? What was her game? He scanned the battle below. Was she giving her Toal time to slay more of his allies? Again, why?

He forced a bolder attack. She backed off a step, then a step farther. She fought with the cunning of ages, with the skill that had earned her the sobriquet Dark Champion. Every ploy and play sought his life. She was not dogging it. She would kill him if she could.

She did manage to delay till the westering sun neared the horizon.

Daubendiek studied the weaknesses of its adversary all that while. Now it took advantage. The flow shifted. Faster. Faster.

Tureck Aarant and the murmuring horde became ever more excited. But Gathrid's haunt kept laughing. . . .

Daubendiek pinked Nieroda-flesh at last. It was the lightest of touches. The end came minutes later.

Nieroda's umbra faded. Daubendiek lightninged through her guard. And there was nothing.

Nothing but symphonies of evil laughter. Once again she abandoned the flesh an instant too quickly.

Gathrid looked down at the thing that had been animated by the spirit of Nevenka Nieroda. It had been a woman once. . . . A voice within him screamed. It knew that flesh.

His voice. "Anyeck!" He had slain her again. . . .

She mortified before his eyes. His gorge rose.

Anyeck. How? He had buried her himself, way west of here. . . . What did Nieroda hope to gain by reminding him of past guilt? How many times could he slay his sister and still be morally stricken?

A hundred. Or a thousand. He felt her moving deep inside him, half-insane, hurting. . . . Never before had she been accessible.

He knelt, lifted a putrifying hand. It was cold with a

cold deeper than death's chill. But the body was free. He sensed no sorceries upon it.

So, he thought. He would bury her at home after all.

"Beware," Aarant warned. "The others don't know Nieroda survived."

The spells on the Dark Lady's followers had evaporated with her departure. The battleground had fallen into total confusion. Some rebels were trying to escape. Some were trying to surrender. Some fought on. The latter rallied round the Toal.

Ahlert became magnanimous immediately. He spared anyone willing to rejoin his army.

Gathrid frowned. That man was running against the wind, but he pursued his dream nevertheless.

Loida finally shook her fogginess. She saw Gathrid kneeling over Nieroda. She urged her mount toward him.

"Don't do it, girl," Gacioch croaked. His warning came too late. Gathrid heard the hooves.

Ahlert! he thought. This would be the moment for the Mindak to strike. And this was the moment to end the threat from the east. Nieroda could be hunted down later. She had become the lesser danger.

He let the hooves approach.

Aarant did warn him that Suchara was a jealous mistress.

It was all as inevitable as death itself.

Gathrid whirled. Daubendiek flicked like a serpent's tongue. The youth screamed. Screamed for Loida Huthsing, who could not scream for herself. The poor girl did not realize what was happening till it was over. . . .

Gathrid swore he heard Nieroda laughing in the distance.

Chapter Fourteen
Torun

Gathrid sat between the corpses of the women. The two long black swords flanked him. Hints of fire rippled along their blades. He rocked slowly and incessantly. His thoughts were so turned in upon themselves that even Tureck Aarant could not penetrate them.

How many more? he wondered. Anyone who would ever mean anything? Was there no way to stop this?

He went hunting the shadows, searching for Loida. He wanted to explain, to apologize, but he could not find her. Like Anyeck, she had burrowed deep and curled around herself like a grub in the earth. There was no sign of her.

He tried to find Anyeck. Surprisingly, he caught a trace here and there. Something had wakened her. When he did make a ghostly contact, she fled with a whimper. For an instant he had an image of her as she had been at Katich, only running away, a gown of moonstuff flying around her calves.

She was Anyeck still, still living in dreams.

"She was a beauty," Aarant murmured.

"Yes." Gathrid was becoming accustomed to these internal dialogs. He was becoming accustomed to Aarant, beginning to like the man. "But she wasn't a good person. Except to me."

"I'm sorry for you. I know how you feel. They made me kill my mother."

"I know. In a way, though . . . Anyeck earned what she got. She was looking for it."

"That doesn't make it right. There has to be an end to this cruelty."

Aarant had tried to broach the topic before. Gathrid had slipped away every time, though he did not know why. He agreed now. He had been thinking the same thing since Anyeck's death. "Look there." The sky had darkened in the east. "See the comet?"

"Yes. The same one foretold the fall of Anderle. It's almost gone. If it goes like before, this mess will turn real bloody once it disappears."

"It's not bloody now?"

"Bloody enough."

A hand touched the youth's shoulder gently. He glanced up into Rogala's eyes, surprised a tender moistness there. The dwarf did not look at all well. His face was not suited to a display of compassion.

"We've got to get out of here," Rogala said. "Before the Mindak has a brainstorm and realizes his future would be less complicated without a Swordbearer in it."

"We've only been allies a little while."

"Long enough. He needed you to beat Nieroda. She's gone. Now he's going to head west. He knows your first loyalty lies there. And that without you the Alliance won't stand much chance. The pragmatic course would be to eliminate you now. That's bound to strike him before long."

Gathrid had a feeling Rogala was telling but a part of the story, but was too distracted to pursue the matter. Ahlert would try, given a chance. That was his nature.

The sun was setting but there was enough light to show

prisoners being herded about the grisly field. The Toal and a few survivors were retreating to the southwest. Ahlert would come soon if he came.

Aarant agreed with Rogala. "Better move."

Aloud, Gathrid said, "I was sitting on this hill when Symen brought the news that Grevening had been invaded." He glanced at Rogala. The dwarf remained pained. "I never thought it would come to this."

"It does begin to grate. Come on. We've got to go."

"All right." Gathrid collected the swords. Rogala had brought horses and supplies. "Ever the efficient esquire, eh?"

Gently, the dwarf removed a silent Gacioch from beneath Loida's still form. "I try, son. I try." He said nothing more till, days later, they neared Katich. Gathrid had only Aarant for company.

"He's changed since before," Aarant observed at one point. Gathrid had been watching the dwarf's back. They were riding single file. "I can't believe he's the same man. The Brothers' War must have had a tremendous impact."

"How has he changed?"

"He's become unpredictable. And emotional. I don't think I ever saw him show anything but anger before."

"I think he's losing his faith. I don't know how he fits in, but I think he's gotten sick of his part."

"Probably right. It's bad not knowing what it's all about, but maybe it's worse knowing. Maybe there's no point at all and that's what's getting to him."

"I think he believed there was a point, and now he's begun to doubt."

The discussion went on all the while they crossed Gudermuth. Gathrid found himself liking Aarant more and more. They were much alike beneath the cruel armor of experience. He suspected they could become friends.

He wondered what it would be like to share his brain with his best friend.

They topped a rise and faced Katich.

"That was needless," Rogala said. For a moment Gathrid thought he meant the destruction of the city. But the dwarf had turned in his saddle and was looking eastward.

"Thank you, Theis." It was the best he would get from the man. Perhaps the best anyone ever had gotten. Aarant again mentioned his astonishment at the changes in Rogala.

Over campfires and during the boring rides across wasted countryside Gathrid often studied the sword he had taken from Nieroda. It had been defeated. It remained bruised and weak. But, like a living thing, it had a capacity for recovery. And it presented him with a moral dilemma.

Could the world endure the existence of another such blade? One seemed curse enough.

What could he do? He did not possess the Power to destroy it. He feared that no one did, not even its creatrix.

"Keep it," Aarant urged. "I have a feeling about it."

Gathrid, too, felt something. He thought a day might come when he would be glad to have the blade available. On the plus side, it did not have Daubendiek's insatiable hunger. Though hammered on the forges of evil, it was not of itself insane and black of heart. Unlike Daubendiek, it remained a controllable tool.

It was an infant still. It could become a Daubendiek had it the tutelage of a Suchara.

When Gathrid's thoughts did turn outward he had to face what had happened to Gudermuth. The little kingdom was a state no more. It had become a vast desolation. The native survivors seemed to have become brigands who existed by preying upon one another. Plague and famine had taken up where war had left off. Gathrid wondered if the stolid endurance of the peasant would suffice him during this disaster.

"You think we'll face much trouble?" he asked as he and Rogala crossed the Bilgoraji border, following the

Torun road. Even the boundary marker had been destroyed. The waste went on.

Rogala shrugged. "We've yet to be challenged."

"Hildreth might attack us."

"I doubt it. He won't be pleased to see us, though."

A few miles beyond the border, at Pletka, they encountered a Gudermuther company which had attached itself to Yedon Hildreth's Guards Oldani. Their reception was cool, though Captain Sir Baris Kraljevac became warmer in private.

"Your return might help clarify the situation," he told them over a supper attended only by themselves and a Blue Brother who insisted on anonymity. "The political scene has gone strange lately."

"How so?" Gathrid asked. He listened with only half an ear. He was more interested in devouring his meal.

"At Sartain," the Blue replied. "Since Misplaer was murdered . . ."

"What?" This was the first Gathrid or Rogala had heard of events farther west.

"We thought you knew," Kraljevac said. "I would've mentioned it earlier if . . ."

"Then Mulenex . . ."

"He's trying to grab the Raftery. Naturally. Count Cuneo and the Emperor are using their moral force to resist his election. They think he had Misplaer and Eldracher killed. They think he was behind Katich's betrayal, too."

The Brother continued, "Mulenex denies everything. Naturally. And nobody can prove anything. There's an understandable scarcity of witnesses."

"Seems suspicion would suffice where Mulenex is concerned. I've never heard anybody say a good word about him."

"He has his friends," the captain said. "He'd be impotent if he didn't."

"These are troubled times," the Blue Brother observed. "Opportunists are crawling out of the weeds with an eye to the main chance. Mulenex isn't unique. The Orders are filled with his ilk. We seem to attract as many villains as idealists."

Gathrid told Rogala, "I should've killed him when I had the chance."

"You wouldn't have seen the logic then. Wouldn't have mattered anyway. Like the man says, there're always more Mulenexes waiting."

Gathrid rewarded the dwarf with a sour look. That perpetual kibbitzer, Gacioch, laughed and made snide remarks.

"How would my return change anything?" Gathrid asked the Blue.

"It'll scare people into jumping one way or the other. The Orders feud a lot, but we like to present a united front to the world. Hell, you coming back might even wake up the mundanes. Let's hope so. Right now Ahlert could walk to Sartain unmolested."

Kraljevac added, "The Empire is starting to amount to something again. The Emperor and Count Cuneo are doing a good job of getting people to see them as symbols of stability. The Alliance is a dead letter. Its members are all squabbling and trying to pass the blame. I'll make you a bet. Before the summer is over, somebody will sell out to the Mindak."

"Why?"

"There's a rumor going round, says there's a vice-regalty over the old Imperial Home Provinces going to the King or prince who joins Ahlert. That would tempt most of them. They're used to ruling less."

"It's really that bad?"

"Or worse."

"And at the moment when Ahlert is at his weakest," Gathrid muttered. When a western victory could be finalized with ease. If westerners would stand together. Curious how fate wriggled and turned. "Sounds to me like Mulenex is dragging everything down the road to Hell."

The captain said, "Some would agree, I think." He grinned.

The Blue Brother snapped, "His dreams aren't that much different from Elgar's. He wants a restoration of the Empire and a union between Imperium and Raftery. It's a dream popular on both Faron and Galen. It's just that some of us don't think Mulenex is the man to run things."

"Sounds like he's halfway there," Rogala growled.

The Brother nodded. "Misplaer and Eldracher are out of his way. If he's elected Fray Magister, Elgar and Count Cuneo won't have much of a life expectancy."

Gathrid prompted, "Yedon Hildreth is no fool."

"He can't fight Ventimiglia, root out treason amongst the Alliance Kings, and shield the Empire from Mulenex all at the same time. He'll have to compromise somewhere. He'll have to surrender something. He'll do it with his usual savage cunning, of course. He'll salvage what he can."

"Politics," Gathrid grumbled. "Always politics."

The Blue Brother offered a sad little smile. "Happens whenever you get three people within shouting distance. It's what separates us from the beasts."

"I find it repulsive."

"I expect you would. Life is simpler when you have the Power to impose your will."

Captain Kraljevac gave them passes which permitted their passage through the cold-eyed guardians of the Beklavac narrows. They rode on to Torun.

"Put your eyes back in," Rogala whispered.

Despite having seen Senturia, Gathrid gawked endlessly. Torun was less populous than Ventimiglia's capital, but its massive public works were more impressive. He saw buildings bigger than all of Kacalief.

Torun's people seemed to know them. Crowds came out. Each street showed its unique temper, ranging from friendly to hostile. Gathrid could detect no pattern of response.

A King's messenger intercepted them. He bore an offer of royal hospitality. Gathrid glanced at Rogala. The dwarf shook his head. Gathrid refused graciously.

"Don't ever put yourself in the hands of princes," Rogala told him. "That's a good way to get your throat cut. There's a likely looking inn."

The inn refused their custom. They asked in the streets, and were directed to another. The dwarf found it acceptable. Its landlord was willing to take them.

Gathrid walked back outside and looked up. The structure was four storeys tall. A private building. He was amazed.

He went back inside. Something seemed to bore in between his shoulderblades. It became an almost physical ache. He whirled, saw nothing.

"What's the matter?" Rogala demanded.

"I don't know. Just had a funny feeling."

Rogala scrutinized the common room narrowly. "I don't feel anything."

That spot on the youth's back still itched. He glanced round again. "False intuition, I guess. Your senses are better than mine."

"Not necessarily." Rogala kept a hand on his dagger.

That same pain wakened Gathrid in the middle of the night. He did not move immediately. Aarant made warning sounds inside him. Across the room, near the single candle, Rogala was dozing in his chair. Gacioch's box lay on the table, beside the candle. He and the dwarf had been talking when Gathrid had gone to bed. Now the demon was snoring.

There was something badly wrong.

"Sorcery," Aarant told him.

No doubt. Rogala did not sleep. He always took the night watches. Should Gathrid waken, he would be mumbling to himself or, lately, with Gacioch.

Moving slowly, he reached for the Sword.

"Use the other one," Aarant suggested. "They'll be listening for Daubendiek."

Quietly, Gathrid made his bed look occupied. Finished, he scanned the room. Nothing seemed to be happening. He went and crouched in a shadowed corner, leaving Rogala to his slumber.

Whence would they come? The door was locked and barred. The window was sealed against the winter's chill.

A section of wainscotting crept away from the wall.

Ah, he thought. This was why the landlord had insisted they have "the best room in the house."

He had intuited the best lurking place. The swinging wainscotting masked him.

A head popped out, glanced around. The whole man stole forth, reached back, helped another. The first then stalked Rogala with a garrote while the other went toward the bed. He carried a knife which burned a bright blue.

Gathrid took the strangler first.

The new sword was slower than Daubendiek, but devoured a soul as greedily.

The man's name was Fiebig Koziatek. He was a Torun assassin, a freelance. He had no idea who had paid him. His equally ignorant associate, Zais Baukla, died a moment later.

"Behind you," Aarant snarled.

A thin golden rod poked out of the hatchway. Gathrid jumped, evaded pale fire which sliced six inches into the wall behind him. He charged. His blade found flesh.

This was a man who had known something at one time. His mind had been cleansed of all but a command to kill. Even his name had been taken. Gathrid dragged him into the room. He neither wore nor bore anything condemning.

"Someone will be watching for them," Aarant suggested.

Rogala and Gacioch still slept. After checking them, Gathrid entered the hidden passageway. If no one else, he thought, the landlord would do some explaining. He had to be involved.

The passage reached many of the rooms. Gathrid checked each and found it innocent. The hidden way ended in a cellar accessible both from the kitchen and an alley. The horizontal, hatchlike alley door was a rough, weathered lumber with wide gaps between time-shrunken boards. Through these Gathrid spotted a watcher on a nearby rooftop, crouched beside a pot-topped chimney.

How to approach him? The detailed planning of the attack suggested that all exits would be watched.

There had to be a way to trace the principal. Mulenex? Nieroda? Ahlert? Hildreth, trying to frame Mulenex? Or some local entrepreneur trying to obtain Daubendiek for his own use? Torun had an underworld replete with famous names.

The watcher drifted away for a moment, pacing in boredom.

Silent as a weasel, Gathrid slid into the alley. He took cover in a shadow out of view of the roof. He listened for evidence of a trap.

"You're becoming another Rogala," Aarant chided good-naturedly. "It's safe. The sorcery was likely bought."

A dog with an odd bark spoke from the far side of the inn. A cat yowled above Gathrid. A moment later a rope dropped and the watcher clambered down. He kept glancing around and muttering to himself as he stole to the cellar door. He grabbed a nearby keg, knocked its bung out, started splashing liquid around.

Some sort of combustible, Gathrid realized. The assassins had been written off. The backup plan was to burn the inn with everyone inside. "That's getting a little carried away," he whispered. Aarant agreed.

Gathrid sprinted toward the arsonist. The man just had time to look surprised. . . . Another ignorant hireling.

Gathrid raced down the alley, into a side street, then round front, where he found another arsonist at work. A warning hooted from a rooftop. An arrow burred behind Gathrid's head and thunked into the inn wall.

So. Bowmen to prevent escapes through the windows. Very thorough.

The arsonist ran like all the imps of Hell were after him. Gathrid chased him a few hundred yards, then doubled back. He hoped to pick up the director of the team.

Luck ran with him. He crossed the trail of a vagrant who gave himself away by moving with too much speed and suspicion. He glared at every shadow. Gathrid narrowly avoided betraying himself.

The man led him to a small, neat house guarded by dogs. The animals fled from him without a whimper. He listened at the one window revealing a light.

The vagrant reported to an underworld chieftain whose name, Suftko, Gathrid had heard in faraway Kacalief. In Torun he was as powerful as any prince. Once the vagrant guaranteed his unnoted escape, he took the failure of his agents philosophically.

A short time later the crime baron took to the streets. Four bodyguards accompanied him. He led Gathrid to a large church. There he met briefly with another man. The bodyguards made it impossible for Gathrid to eavesdrop. The meeting ended. Gathrid had to make a choice of pursuits.

He chose the paymaster, reasoning that if another attack had been ordered it would find Rogala wakened and on guard.

His man went on to another church, a tiny chapel hugging the skirts of Torun's royal citadel. His stride was confident, his attitude bold. He was not concerned about being tailed.

In the chapel he met an early-rising monk.

Who was no monk. Gathrid recognized him instantly. He was Bilgoraj's King, Kimach Faulstich. The Kimach Faulstich he deemed responsible for Gudermuth's destruction. "How did it go?" this make-believe monk asked.

"Failed. The Swordbearer didn't respond to the sleep spell."

"Damn!"

"Suftko is willing to try again. For another fee."

"The man is greedy."

"He has his uses. He'll keep trying till he succeeds, till you go broke or there's a shortage of blades. He's got pride. But he won't risk his own people."

"Alfeld, there's gold in the sacristy. I'll send more down if it's necessary. Just get it finished before noon tomorrow. That's when we finalize the agreement."

"It went through, then?"

The King fiddled with a chalice. "It did. Don't ever forget. When Sartain is mine, Torun is yours."

"And the Contessa?"

"Of course. I have no other use for Hildreth's brat."

So, Gathrid thought. Kimach was plotting to usurp Emperor Elgar. Sartain was going to grow crowded with all the pretenders. And this cousin Alfeld was to receive the Bilgoraji crown for his part in the treachery. Meaning he had an eye on the Imperium himself. Elgar had no natural heir. He had declared Yedon Hildreth his successor. The Count's claim would descend through his daughter, the Contessa Cuneo, Fiona Hildreth.

"Is Suftko suspicious?"

"No." Alfeld snickered. "He's convinced we're working *against* Ahlert. He wouldn't have helped otherwise."

"Patriotic blindness has its uses, too. Pay him. And don't stint. Light a fire under him. I need those people dead."

Kimach turned to the altar, knelt. Alfeld fetched a sack from the sacristy, hurried into the night.

Kraljevac was dead on target, Gathrid thought. He eased out from under the pew where he had hidden. There was a sellout in the script. Though Ahlert probably had other prospects, a great treachery could be smothered in its cradle here. And Gudermuth's demise could be counterbalanced a caratweight.

Kimach glanced up from his prayers as the blade fell.

He died before he fully realized that he had placed his bet and lost.

How very vulnerable they become when they get sneaky, Gathrid thought. Had Kimach remained faithful he would have been surrounded by so many bodyguards even Daubendiek could not have reached him. To play foul he had to venture out on his own, baring his neck. . . .

Gathrid swallowed Bilgoraj's politics in one great, sticky, sour, disgusting lump.

There would be hell to pay in the morning. He wished there were some way to make the Red Order look responsible.

He ran into the street, toward the gangster's home. He overtook Alfeld four blocks from his destination. The royal cousin was strolling along whistling. The sack he bore had, mysteriously, lightened by half. Gathrid cut him down and took what was left.

Despite the cumulative gruesomeness of this night's work, he chuckled. It was a sound as fell as any ever to issue from the mouth of Theis Rogala. He was changing. There were moments when he enjoyed his role.

He was delighted with what he learned from the dead man. Neither Kimach nor Alfeld had been honest with his cohort. Kimach had used Alfeld so he would have a convenient scapegoat. He had had no intention of delivering the promised crown. Or the Contessa, whom he had earmarked for a favored son.

Alfeld had had his separate arrangement with Gerdes Mulenex. It had promised him kingdom and Contessa in exchange for the life of his cousin.

Gathrid's loathing of politics grew stronger.

There was Suftko yet. The gangster had tried murder, yet seemed clean by comparison. Maybe he could be manipulated.

Again the dogs did not challenge the youth. He eased to Suftko's door, gave the knock the pseudo-derelict had used.

The guard within sensed trouble. He opened the door a crack, then shouted.

Gathrid drove his blade through wood and flesh, withdrew it, hacked at the chain holding the door. As he entered, attacking in a whirlwind of steel, he realized that he had made a tactical blunder. The house was dark. He could not see his foes. They could see him silhouetted in the doorway.

His weapon knew where they were. In seconds it was over. Three lives had been devoured. Gathrid pushed on to a lighted room from which panic sounds came.

He found another three men. One was Suftko, another was a bodyguard. The third was a renegade Brother. Gathrid slew the bodyguard and was closing with Suftko when the magnitude of his peril struck Aarant. "Behind you!"

Once again he dodged the aim of a golden rod. A beam sliced furniture and scarred walls. Gathrid ducked and dove forward.

The sorcerer was nimble. His weapon was one the younger sword could not negate. It took all the youth's borrowed skill to survive the next minute.

The sorcerer died.

"A Blue!" Gathrid said. "And owned by Mulenex. . . ." But no more. He had fled, had enlisted with Suftko. A man in Suftko's business could find a thousand uses for a competent sorcerer.

The man was overdue for death, Gathrid reflected. He had murdered Honsa Eldracher and betrayed Katich. No punishment was adequate. . . .

Suftko had been hiding him from both Yedon Hildreth and Mulenex, each of whom wanted him desperately.

"Watch the other one," Aarant whispered.

Gathrid whirled. Suftko was opening the door as he had been fighting. "Stop right there! Or you'll die."

The gangster turned, raised his hands. He was a small, hard man. Gathrid guessed him to be as shrewd and pragmatic as Hildreth or Ahlert. No doubt he was aware of the dead wizard's entire history.

"There'll be hell to pay tomorrow. Unless somebody does one good cleanup job."

Suftko said nothing.

"You've got one chance to buy your life." Gathrid told the man the true story behind his hiring. "I want the trail covered. For both our sakes."

"All right. I don't have much choice, do I?"

"Not much. I'll be back if you don't deliver."

The hard little man nodded.

"Good luck, then." Gathrid went away admiring the gangster. The man had shown no fear.

He returned to the inn before dawn more than tainted the eastern sky. The scullery help were about, but did not notice him slipping into the cellar. The body in the alley was absent. The fish in the Blackstun would feed well today.

Rogala still snored. So did Gacioch. The corpses in their room had not been disturbed. Gathrid left them lie. He placed his weapon near Daubendiek and slipped into bed. The Sword moaned softly, evilly, jealously.

"Be careful," Aarant whispered.

"I plan to."

He was adrift on the twilight edge of sleep when he suddenly realized that he had been away from Daubendiek for hours, and by miles. Well might the Sword be jealous. His hand stole toward the new blade. He yanked it back. Suppose? . . .

There were always levels to Nieroda's schemes. This might be one to seduce him away from the blade he hated, then leave him powerless. He lay back. "Tureck, mull that one over."

"I am already."

Gathrid bolted up again, horrified.

He had slain no fewer than a dozen men that night, without qualm or question, and without being controlled.

He could not deny responsibility. . . . The Swordbearer's fate was closing in. He was becoming a man without remorse.

Sleep was a long time coming. He could not stop poking a stick into the hornet's nest of his conscience.

Chapter Fifteen

Sartain

Gathrid and Rogala hit the road again after just the one night in Torun. Kimach's disappearance had stirred too much excitement and speculation. None of it was pleasant.

The dwarf had less than usual to say. Gathrid tried to enjoy the passing countryside. He failed. He felt Rogala's veiled, curious eyes too strongly.

The youth had said nothing about his night's work except to admit that he had forestalled the assassins. The dwarf, though, had seen the innkeeper's terror that morning. He had heard the news, rumors, and speculations in the streets. He had done his sums.

And he was well aware that Daubendiek had done no slaying. He and the Great Sword were tools of Suchara. They knew one another well.

West of Torun Bilgoraj consisted of populous farm country inhabited by curious, reticent peasants. They had scores of questions for travelers, but few answers.

The farms eventually gave way to timber land. The Blackstun River, which had meandered north from the capital, now swung back to parallel the high road. It joined the Ondr where Bilgoraj butted against tiny Fiefenbruch. "This country is smaller than Gudermuth," Gathrid observed. "West of it lies the March of Armoneit, the easternmost of the principalities still liege to Anderle."

The dwarf grunted noncommittally. He was more interested in changes time had wrought since last he had passed this way.

It was in the March, in the hills overlooking the ferry town of Avenevoli, that Yedon Hildreth had won his celebrated victory. The enemies of then were allies now. The father of the King of Fiefenbruch and Kimach Faulstich's elder brother both had fallen on the Avenevoli slopes.

The Ondr, swollen by a hundred tributaries, eventually debouched in the long reach of the Secrease Sound. Sartain stood on a vast island, causeway-connected with the mainland, that countless generations had expanded into a canal-riddled, almost self-supporting city-state. The island nearly blocked the wide, shallow Sound, and stretched dozens of miles toward the sea. The original dromedary-backed island had become lost in the expansion. One of its two humps boasted the Raftery, the other the Imperial Palace.

"It's doubled in size," Rogala said. They were studying the sprawl from a promontory where once a mansion had stood. The dwarf had chased some memory to the scene and found it one with all his recollections of the former age. "Chrismer lived on Galen. That's the eastern peak. Karkainen lived on Faron, where the Imperium now crouches like a whipped cur. The harbor isn't what it used to be. Hundreds of ships came up from the sea every day, bearing treasures and emissaries from the world's ends. Those proud hulls seem to have been replaced by drab fishing trawlers."

Gathrid glanced at Rogala, puzzled. Once again his

companion had revealed an unexpected facet. He had never seemed the nostalgic sort.

"Let's go see what the barbarians have done with the Queen of the World. Raped her, belike."

Not so, they discovered. Not only Elgar, but the long parade of his predecessors, had been obsessed with preserving the shadow of the glory that had been. The carefully nurtured wealth of the diminuated Imperium had for centuries maintained and improved the Queen City.

It began on the mainland shore. There, sturdy, intimidating fortilices, brooding amidst grain fields, shielded the approaches to the Causeway. There were a score of them all told. Each was manned by Guards Oldani, veteran soldiers proud in their service. They were not the pampered, King-making, fight-avoiding praetorians one might expect squirming like maggots in the corpse of a decadent Empire. For them Anderle remained real.

The roads were paved, and scrupulously clean, as were the people upon them. But ghosts of worry occasionally slid across their scrubbed native faces. The grain fields flanking the roads were garden-perfect. The peasants working them were cheerful and friendly. The highborn did not scorn to answer their greetings, nor to pause to chat amiably.

"Pride," said Rogala. "That's what you see. Pride not only in what Anderle was, but in what she is and might be again. Every man has his contribution to make."

And a little later, Rogala observed, "The germ is here. If fate stays its hand. If a genius appears among the merely competent Emperors who keep the dream alive, they might achieve their goal. They might see their new Imperium, their new Golden Age." He sounded wistful.

Gathrid was impressed by the obvious health of the people. In Torun, and even more so in Senturia, ill-health had been common.

He was more impressed when they passed through the wide, tunnel-like portal of the Maurath. The Maurath was the last and greatest of the outer fortresses. It bestrode the head of the Causeway like a squatting colossus. It was not just a fortification. It contained all the Imperium's war offices, and the headquarters of Yedon Hildreth and his Guards Oldani, who formed the backbone of the Imperial army.

That one structure was half the size of the city of Katich. Twenty thousand men could quarter there comfortably in time of siege. The passage to the Causeway was a quarter mile long.

The Causeway itself was fifty yards wide and two miles long, stone, and divided into directional lanes which separated the various classes of traffic for flow efficiency. As Gathrid and Rogala were obviously foreigners, a polite soldier cut them out of traffic and explained a few of Sartain's ordinances. For example, they would be responsible for cleaning up after their animals. He pointed out orange containers, with tools racked beside them, which, he said, could be found everywhere.

A wagon piled with containers, empty, passed inbound. Then another appeared, bound outward, presumably to the farms.

"The cleaning crews are paid from fines levied on people who don't clean up after themselves," the soldier said. "Most of our block magistrates enjoy fining foreigners."

Rogala grumbled something uncomplimentary. After he and Gathrid asked a few questions, they moved on.

"There've been a lot of changes," the dwarf observed. "None of those fortresses were there before. Guess they built them because the Hattori and Oldani managed to force the Causeway back when. In the high days Sartain didn't need defenses. All the fighting took place so far away it took half a year to reach it. The Causeway wasn't half this wide, either."

"Looks like they're building another one." Several miles to their west a fleet of boats were busy around what looked like cofferdams. Huge dumps of stone and timber lay on either shore. On the mainland side workmen were laying the foundations of a second Maurath.

"They need it." The Causeway was crowded. Moreover, Sartain's expansion seemed to have been in the direction of the new construction. Reaching the mainland from those extremities would require a long journey through crowded streets. The straits were dotted with ferries providing shortcuts, especially for produce and goods.

Gathrid wished he could have come to Sartain as a tourist, not as Swordbearer. Already he had questions and curiosities enough to busy him for weeks, even without the worries and obligations of politics and war.

"Even the Immortal Twins would be impressed," Tureck Aarant observed. It was the first he had come forward since Gathrid and Theis had crossed the Ondr at Avenevoli. He had been locked away with his memories and his guilt.

"Blame Grellner, not yourself," Gathrid told him now.

Rogala looked at him queerly. "What did you say?"

"Uh? Oh. I was thinking about something." He had to be more careful. He had not told Theis about Aarant, and did not intend to. Aarant might provide a valuable edge later. "Doesn't seem to be much excitement about us," he said.

"I noticed. I guess we're early, what with us leaving Torun in such a rush. It isn't politeness that's kept us from being trampled by people from the Hills. And for sure Hildreth wouldn't let us wander around without keepers."

"Might be useful to stay anonymous while we can," Gathrid suggested.

"Absolutely. We both need a rest. But we tend to stand out."

They stood out not only because Rogala was a shaggy dwarf who carried a talking head, and because Gathrid wore bits of foreign armor and had two huge black swords

Xed across his back, but because they were going armed in a city where the only weapons to be seen were those carried by soldiers. Unlike the Alliance peoples of ruder kingdoms farther east, among whom even peasants felt naked without their dirks, the citizens of Sartain shunned personal arms. It was a matter of civic pride. More than one pair of eyes turned away as if embarrassed for them. Rogala suggested the attitude reflected Sartain's historical invincibility.

"A city this old, that's only ever been invaded once, gets a little smug. It stops really believing in the possibility of violence."

Gathrid frowned. "There's always personal violence."

"There is. I suppose they handle that sort of informally. With butcher knives. Or, in an old, almost decadent society like this, poison. They probably figure it's gauche to actually go stab somebody."

They found themselves a room in a quiet quarter where outlanders seemed to congregate and mellow one another's strangeness by their numbers. Rogala said, "Somebody's bound to realize who we are. Maybe we ought to change our appearance a little. Any suggestions?"

"I'll settle for changing mine with a good hot bath."

"A complete toilet will be a good start. Go see if the landlord has a pair of scissors."

An hour later Rogala had trimmed his vast black beard to a ghost of its former glory. Gathrid grinned, said, "Your tenants are going to have to find new quarters."

"Eh?"

"Old fairy tale. King Thrushbeard. He had a beard so gross birds nested in it."

"Oh. I know the motif." The dwarf grinned back. "I didn't realize you had a sense of humor, son."

"Haven't had much chance to exercise it, have I?"

"Yeah, well. For a while now. We'll just take it easy till they find us. You want the bath first? I warn you, when I get done with that water you'll be able to walk on it.''

After their baths they exchanged haircuts and donned new clothing purchased for them by the landlord's son. They sized one another up. Gathrid said, ''Whatever became of Theis Rogala? They might never find us.''

''What happened to that skinny kid who woke me up? You've turned into a man, son. They won't recognize either one of us.''

Their newfound anonymity lasted the day. During it Gathrid enjoyed a triumph over Daubendiek and Suchara. He managed to leave their room without arms.

''I think you're tempting fate too much,'' Rogala growled. They were loafing at a sidewalk cafe, watching traffic pass, occasionally exchanging a few words with citizens and other outlanders. Many of the latter were more bizarre than they.

Aarant had offered an argument similar to Rogala's when Gathrid had asked his help overcoming the Sword's control.

''If Mulenex's bullies stumble across us now, we're deader than a wedge, and not a damn thing we can do to stop it.''

''You don't look all that terrified.''

''Oh, I am. Petrified. I'm just a good actor.'' He signaled for a waiter.

''From what I've seen, I think I could be comfortable here,'' Gathrid observed. Dusk was closing in. A quaintly attired lamplighter was at work across the street. The afternoon had stolen away on them. ''Just laying around like this. It's been a hundred years since I've relaxed this way.''

''Uhm. Or a few thousand.'' Something wistful touched the dwarf's voice.

Aarant claimed that Rogala was more open and emotional than he had been during the Brothers' War. Even so, Gathrid knew next to nothing about the man's true age, his origins or his background. Or what had damned him to serve Suchara.

"It would never last, would it? Got to be rich to loaf here. We don't have the pocket money. Nor the temperament. Even Heaven would get dull for such as us."

"That might be true," Gathrid replied sourly. Much as he despised his fate, it was becoming part of him. He was becoming one with it. Being Swordbearer seemed less and less a cosmic imposition.

News from the east had not yet reached Sartain in reliable form. That there had been a big battle between Nieroda and the Mindak was common knowledge, but no two accounts agreed as to site, outcome, or the part the Great Sword had played. The battle at the Karato and that at Kacalief had become confused. And as to the disappearance of Kimach Faulstich, they had outdistanced that news entirely.

Sartain was little concerned with happenings in faraway places. It had excitement enough at home. The contest for the Fray Magistery had the whole city on tenterhooks.

Balloting had begun. Each tally shifted more and more in favor of Gerdes Mulenex. Bookmakers were giving odds that he would receive the requisite majority in the next poll.

The citizenry were not pleased, but neither were they afraid. While occupied by Klutho Misplaer the Raftery had impinged on their lives not at all. They could foresee no potential danger from any successor. Elgar had far more effect on everyday life.

His were the laws that ruled their days. His were the dreams that shaped the Queen City. His was the voice to which people listened.

"Much as I hate the idea," Rogala said, "we'd better announce ourselves tomorrow. We can't let Mulenex's play for the Raftery go unchallenged."

"Uhm." Gathrid felt he had enough evidence to abort

Mulenex's election. He need but present the details he had learned from the sorcerer in Torun.

"One more cup of wine, then a last sleep in freedom."

"One more," Gathrid agreed. When the wine arrived, he touched cups with his esquire.

Tomorrow he would become Chosen of Suchara once more. He did not look forward to resuming the role.

Hildreth's messengers located them while they tarried over breakfast, loathe to plunge into the cesspool of Brotherhood politics. The chief messenger was a man Gathrid remembered as having been among the Count's escort during their tête-à-tête in the Alliance camp. He delivered a terse letter. It asked them to accompany the officer to the Raftery, where Count Cuneo would meet them. It was signed with a squiggle Gathrid assumed to be Hildreth's personal chop.

"Give us a minute to collect our gear," Rogala said, after struggling through Old Petralian much changed since last he had had to read the language. "We don't own much more than what we're wearing, so what little we do have we like to keep with us." He hurried off.

The dwarf was gone five minutes. During four of those minutes the messenger looked like a man trying to make up his mind. Finally, he asked, "How can you be poor?"

The question so surprised Gathrid that he laughed. Then he became serious. It was a valid query. Why were he and Theis habitually short of funds? They could take whatever they wanted. How many men had he slain? He had not plundered a one but Alfeld, and his swag bag he had left at Suftko's. Seldom had he seen Rogala loot, and then only for small amounts. Just enough to get by. Curious.

"Lieutenant, I can't answer you. I never thought about it before. Theis," he said as the dwarf returned, "how come we're not rich?"

"Our employer doesn't pay very well. Let's get rolling."

Count Cuneo met them at the base of the Hundred Steps, among the Winged Victories of Chrismer, in the shadows of the pitted and tottering Pillars of Empire that at one time had honored Chrismer's share of the tributary principalities. It was there that Tureck Aarant had at last overcome Chrismer, after battling his way through an island-rocking storm of wizardry.

Daubendiek remembered the day. Aarant did too. The Sword hummed. Aarant radiated a diffuse unhappiness. Gathrid wondered if Hildreth had chosen the meeting place because he suspected what even Rogala did not, that Tureck Aarant had returned.

The Count had aged, but was as hard-willed as ever. "I'm afraid we're too late," he said, ignoring the amenities. "He must have heard you were here. He got the balloting moved up today. I'd really hoped you could do something to stop him."

"I could stop him cold," Gathrid replied. "I know things he doesn't believe anyone else alive knows. But I'm surprised either of you cares."

Hildreth shrugged. "I don't like what you are, and I don't like what you've done. But that business in the east did give us a respite. The pity is, we've wasted it. We've turned on one another. The Alliance is dead."

"Deader than you realize. Why don't we see what we can do? Maybe a few care who they elect." Gathrid began the climb to the Raftery. He was mildly surprised to discover that Count Cuneo no longer awed him.

"You've grown," Hildreth said. "Come of age, perhaps." The Count's years showed in his heavy breathing.

"Been tempered in the fires of Hell, I think, would be an appropriate observation." A few steps onward, Gathrid added, "You should meet the Mindak, Count. You'd make good friends if you weren't in one another's way."

"Could be. He looks more honorable than most of my so-called allies."

"But a bit mad. A bit mad."

"But you all are," Gacioch said.

"What the hell is that?" Hildreth demanded.

Gathrid had become so accustomed to the demon's ir-
reverence that he habitually ignored it. He had forgotten
the creature completely this morning.

Gacioch continued, "If you weren't all insane, you'd
be off somewhere with fishing poles, a jug of wine, or a
woman. You know damned well the world can go to hell
without you. It's good at that."

"What is it?" Hildreth asked again.

"A demon's head. I captured it in Ventimiglia. Theis
took a shine to it." He winced. Loida had been fond of
the head, too. They had spent many an hour fencing with
insults.

"Is it wise to have him around? He served your enemies."

"He's been more help than trouble. Usually he doesn't
get involved."

"You've got some new ghosts, haven't you?"

Hildreth was perceptive. "Too many. Way too many."
They reached a portico surrounding the Raftery, that once
had been the Palace of Chrismer. Surly men in red tried
to keep them from entering. Gathrid rested a hand on
the hilt of the Sword. They parted.

That's real power, he thought. But how much longer
would Daubendiek tolerate being used only as a threat?

Hildreth muttered, "I'd like to see those boys go
through the Brotherhood entry test again. The only power
they can handle is muscle power."

Delegates from the five Orders packed the Grand Fo-
rum of the Raftery, their robes forming rainbow stripes.
Gathrid saw just one empty seat. That was the throne of
the Fray Magister.

In days of yore it had been Chrismer's audience throne.

The waterfall roar of voices diminished as people recognized the Swordbearer. Gerdes Mulenex met Gathrid's

eye. His face became as red as his robe. He controlled himself, managed a half-mocking bow.

"I don't know what you can do," Hildreth whispered. "But try something. You're the last hope. For the Raftery and the Empire."

Gathrid descended the worn marble steps leading to the main floor. The delegates were seated on benches surrounding that, rising stadium fashion. The handful of men down on the circular floor appeared to be the leaders of factions, negotiating deals.

Gathrid walked across that floor and mounted the small, circular speaker's rostrum. Mulenex sputtered, but did not stop him. He turned slowly, surveyed the silent gathering.

Daubendiek moaned. The audience heard, but appeared more interested in the other blade. It whined as well, at a higher pitch.

Gathrid said, "On the spot where I stand, where the bloodstains remain to remind us of the cost of not questioning the follies we hear, the Winged Tempter perished at the hand of my predecessor." He pointed. "Blood. Blood. Blood. There's no end to the blood when the affairs of nations are managed by fools. There're a hundred tales told about the Great Sword, and the Swordbearer, and their roles in the Brothers' War. Most are but shadows of fact. Listen while I tell the true story of Tureck Aarant."

He closed his eyes and blanked his mind and yielded his mouth to his predecessor. Out poured words and warnings formulated by Tureck Aarant himself. "Then, as today, men were not the masters of their destinies. Only a handful knew the truth. They weren't allowed to tell it. But today I can. The eye of Suchara has wandered for the moment.

"The Immortal Twins, and all the great names of the Brothers' War, weren't fighting for their beliefs or ambitions. They were toys. They were pawns."

Theis Rogala went narrow-eyed and pale. Gathrid

knew things he should not. He related details of Aarant's life that only Tureck and his esquire could have known. Somehow, Suchara had erred. Something strange had happened.

The youth paused. He surveyed his audience. He saw puzzled looks, hostile looks, friendly looks. Hardly a face bore the stamp of disbelief. He suspected the Brothers had access to undoctored accounts of the war, where a glimmer of the truth would have shown through.

To a man the delegates were attentive.

"I am the Swordbearer," he thundered, smiting the rostrum with a fist. His audience jumped. "I am the Chosen! I am the Eater of Souls and Discoverer of Secrets. I have one of the latter to share. It belonged to Brother Sagis Gruhala of the Blue, whose true allegiance was Red, and whose doom overtook him in Torun.

"Brother Gruhala was a lucky man. The agents of the Imperium, of the Blue, and of the Red, all sought him. He eluded them all and found himself a place in Torun's underworld. Then chance or a jest of the Great Old Ones caused our paths to cross."

Gathrid studied Mulenex while he related details of the murder of Honsa Eldracher and the betrayal of Katich.

"And that, Brethren, is Truth. Tally these details against the facts you know. Then try to deny it."

The long silence died. The mood became dangerous. Blues charged onto the floor. Mulenex looked round like a trapped rat seeking an avenue of escape. The color fled his gross face.

Here and there, fists flew.

A grim, pale Count Cuneo joined Gathrid. "Well done, lad," he said. "But a count too late. They finished the balloting before we arrived. He was elected."

"They can't reverse themselves?"

"Only by hastening his elevation to a higher plane." The Count wheeled, waved. A trumpeter winded his instrument till order was restored. Hildreth assumed the rostrum.

"Gentlemen, an announcement of import. Let me get it in before the brawling begins. I've just received a communique from the Imperial Legate at Torun." He waved a letter. "It says the Mindak Ahlert, having concluded an Alliance with Bochantin, has brought his army through the Gastreich Pass in the Lowenguth Mountains. He's sweeping south out of Bochantin. Kimach of Bilgoraj has disappeared in mysterious circumstances. He didn't establish a regency or inform anyone of his whereabouts. There's no one in charge there. The Bilgoraji army is collapsing. The Alliance garrisons in the Beklavac narrows are cut off. Because you're here, there's no wizardry to neutralize Ahlert's Power. The Legate says Bilgoraj is done. His letter is eight days old."

The Brothers seemed bewildered. A few expressed outright disbelief.

Gathrid watched Mulenex. The Magister's response was interesting. The man became so outraged he was inarticulate. He looked ready for a fit of apoplexy.

Hildreth bellowed into the uproar. "Gentlemen! Our survival is at stake. Brotherhood and Imperium alike. It's time to set aside everything but desperation."

They let him speak, though the confusion did not subside. Not a man sat quietly. The animosity between Red and Blue became palpable.

Hildreth shouted, "Till now Bilgoraj has been a stone wall keeping the wolves out of our sheep cot. Now that barricade is gone. The predator is upon us. Only Malmberget can field a significant army.

"But! Brethren, but! Ahlert is weak. He spent his winter campaigning. He had a bitter time downing Nieroda's rebels. He may not be strong enough to follow up this triumph.

"Nevertheless, he'll try. He's seen the consequences of indecision. He may swing to the opposite extreme. If he does so, we can expect him at the gates of the Maurath within the month. If he comes, Malmberget won't have time to intercept him—assuming they're inclined to try.

"If Sartain goes, the west goes. Anderle isn't a great power these days, but it has emotional import. Ahlert knows that as well as anyone.

"The Swordbearer has been in the east. I haven't had time to ask about Ahlert's strengths and weaknesses. While I'm talking with him, I suggest you put aside your differences and turn your wits to helping Sartain survive. Your lives are on the line too. You'll be the first put to the sword.

"Let's save the squabbling till we can afford it."

Hildreth stepped down. He handed the Legate's message to Gerdes Mulenex. "Give it some honest thought, Gerdes." He turned to Gathrid. "Come with me." He strode to the exit stair.

Chapter Sixteen
The Maurath

"The man has his occasional flash of brilliance," Yedon Hildreth observed. He, Gathrid and Rogala were watching Ahlert's approach from the Maurath's roof. "But he's bet everything on one pass of the dice."

Even with the addition of western renegades and his allies from Bochantin, Ahlert had fewer troops than he had brought across the Karato.

"You should always hold something back," Hildreth said. "You've got to keep a surprise or two tucked away. And you should, by damn, have an exit in case things go sour."

Gathrid peered across the countryside. The Mindak's western friends were having a good time plundering the farm villages.

Count Cuneo continued to think aloud. "He can't starve us out. He'd have to close the lanes to the sea to do that. I don't see how he can take the Maurath and cross the Causeway, either. He's in a spot. He *has* to take Sartain before Malmberget arrives. If he doesn't, he's dead."

"He's got a plan," Rogala said.

"Of course he does. He wouldn't be here if he didn't. I'm just trying to figure out what the hell it is. Wish I'd beaten him to Avenevoli."

As soon as he had convinced himself that Ahlert was coming, Hildreth had taken the Guards east in hopes of repeating his famed victory. The Mindak, probably through the agency of Magnolo Belfiglio, had anticipated him. His cavalry had taken the ferries and the heights overlooking them. The Count had retired without offering battle.

"I doubt he's found anything to replace Nieroda and the Toal," Gathrid said. "And he knows the Sword is here. He's trying to bluff us. Or his dreams of conquest have driven him completely mad."

Rogala's permanent companion, Gacioch, chuckled wickedly. He refused to reveal what he found amusing. When the dwarf threatened to put chains through his ears and wear him as a necklace, he did remark, "The caverns of Ansorge contain more evils than you ever thought, Theis."

Gathrid could not fathom the remark. Rogala seemed aggravated by it.

Magnolo Belfiglio, by informing his master of Count Cuneo's thoughts, would allow Ahlert a tactical advantage, Gathrid thought. But that would not reduce the Maurath and its satellite sub-fortresses. They were too formidable for the host the Mindak had brought.

"He's not wasting time," Rogala remarked.

It was early. Ahlert had spent the night camped beyond the promontory from which Gathrid had first seen Sartain. His forces were dividing into units facing the outer line of fortresses. Some of them would have to be reduced before the Maurath could be approached. Their war engines had punishing, overlapping fields of fire.

Attacking those outer works would be expensive. Each boasted a garrison of six hundred seasoned Guards supported by a dozen skilled Brothers. The fortilices had been designed by the best military architects of recent centuries. Neither Rogala nor Hildreth believed Ahlert's manpower resources sufficient to reduce more than two or three.

Then there was the Maurath, the elephantine, wolverine fortress designed to withstand the efforts of a hundred thousand attackers.

The more he thought about the situation, the more nervous Gathrid became. The Mindak *had* to be armed with something really devastating.

Ahlert's forces moved with a swiftness and precision amazing for such a mixed bag of fighting men.

Men in dark armor, on dark horses, advanced under a flag of truce. Behind them, Ventimiglian quartermasters spread out across the abandoned fields, staking out campsites and erecting biers for the expected dead. They trampled the freshly planted crops. A company of peasant militiamen near Gathrid cursed and shook their fists.

"There's confidence for you," Rogala muttered. "He figures he'll be here long enough to properly care for his dead." No biers had been erected before the battle at Kacalief.

"At least he's still realist enough to expect casualties," Hildreth replied.

The parleying party stopped at a respectful distance. Only the Mindak and his standardbearer came closer.

"Don't look directly at him," Gathrid warned. "He's wearing the Ordrope Diadem."

"Grellner's toy?" Hildreth asked. "I wasn't sure he'd recovered it."

"Don't be surprised by anything. Ansorge is a cellar filled with black miracles."

"Let's go see what he's got to say."

Above the tunnel through the Maurath was an alcove-balcony for confrontations such as this. The tunnel itself had been sealed by massive stones forced up from road level by water pumped into chambers beneath them. The tunnel, in theory, would be harder to break through than the immensely thick wall of the Maurath itself.

"Gathrid. Theis." The Mindak wore what appeared to be a genuinely friendly smile. "Glad to see that you're still well. I'd feared for your health. These westerners are treacherous."

Aarant prodded Gathrid. "They are that. It hasn't been that long since I heard one of their Kings plotting to betray the rest to you."

"Ah. Poor Kimach. You see? He was a greedy man. And a fool. He was a flawed tool at best. He would have broken in heavy work. And he knew it. No doubt he's happier where he is now. The gentleman with you, I presume, is the renowned Count Cuneo?"

Hildreth bowed slightly. Because Ahlert had chosen to speak Old Petralian, the formalities had to be observed. "I'd hoped to meet you earlier, Sir."

"At Avenevoli? But I was there! I heard you were in the area. I'm sorry we missed each other."

"Such is luck. Such is luck. I suppose conditions weren't propitious for any early meeting."

"And Mead?" Gathrid interjected. "I trust she's well?"

Ahlert managed to look startled, wistful, and mildly annoyed. "Magnolo says she's as well as can be expected. She bore me a son two days ago." He glanced eastward for a fraction of a second, his dream momentarily interrupted by the anxieties of a husband. "Your lady, too, is resting well. I knew you would've wanted the right thing done. I took the liberty of having artisans prepare a suitable resting place. And another for your sister as well." He peered at Gathrid intently, as if trying to determine whether or not the youth were surprised. "May we all have the good fortune to revisit those places and people whence our heartroots spring."

Hildreth was puzzled by the personal exchange. He brought the conversation back to the present. "That's a big traveling party you've brought on your pilgrimage to pledge fealty to the Empire.''

"When one visits Sartain, I'm told, no display of pomp and power is too great."

"This one isn't great enough."

"Perhaps not. Yet we petition entry, and audience with the Emperor and Fray Magister. I note that the latter isn't represented in your party. That's curious.''

"He finds himself occupied elsewhere. No doubt he'll be heartbroken when he hears that you departed without making his acquaintance.''

Mulenex and the best minds of the Brotherhood were deep in the bowels of the Raftery. They were trying to discover the source of the Mindak's confidence. And some means of negating it.

"That would never do. I'll have to insist on paying him a visit."

"The Emperor has bid us tell all would-be visitors that the Causeway is closed. My apologies, Sir.''

Gathrid found the evasions and false politenesses amusing. Petralian was a language for diplomats. It seemed to have been specially shaped for men who wished to avoid being pinned down.

"That's final? Beyond compromise?''

"Unfortunately.''

"A pity, though not unanticipated. Gathrid, my best. Theis, the same to you. Have you heard from our friend from Sommerlath? She'd be interested in our reunion, I think.''

So, Gathrid thought. He knows Nieroda survived. And he doesn't consider her a danger at the moment.

"No. Nothing," he replied. Probing with little hope of illumination, "You wouldn't know where she is, would you?"

The Mindak smiled a tired, wary smile. "She's where she always is when you don't see her. Looking over your shoulder. I suppose there's nothing more to be said. Count?''

Hildreth's frown suggested he was puzzled by the exchange. "That's all."

"So be it, then. So be it." Ahlert returned to his party. As he went, he thrust an arm toward the east, making a come hither gesture.

Hildreth asked, "What's that about?"

Gathrid shrugged. "I don't know him that well."

"We'll find out the hard way," Rogala said. "Let's get back upstairs."

When they reached the battlements they saw that a low, dense blackness now masked the eastern skyline. Occasional clouds surged up, collapsed back into the onrushing wave.

"A storm?" Hildreth wondered. "Out of the east? Signalmen. Pass the final alert."

Men with wigwag flags and mirrors communicated with Sartain and the satellite fortresses, bringing them to maximum readiness.

The Mindak reshuffled his forces but did not attack.

Gathrid stared eastward. The darkness drew closer. In places great banks of blackness rose to obscure the morning sun. His nervousness grew, though there was nothing to do but wait. There were no more preparations to make.

"Those are birds or something," he gasped. "Big ones, too."

Hildreth swore. "We should have nets."

"Too late," Rogala said.

The Count signaled the island anyway. "We'll strip the fishing fleet. For the next attack."

Gacioch laughed. "That's what I like. A man with a positive outlook."

"Shut up!" Rogala snarled.

It grew dark. Gathrid muttered, "I hope this place is as invincible as everyone claims." He had his doubts now.

The things were terrier-sized. They had long leathery wings and jaws like crocodiles. Hundreds of thousands descended on the Maurath. Their stench was overpowering. Gathrid felt as though he had fallen into a bat cave as big as the world. He swung Daubendiek in a murderous blur.

The things had no flavor. There was no evil in them, nor even the rage of attack. Their little animal souls were bland. Hunger was all they knew.

They had been created in a time more eld than Nieroda's Sommerlath, as tools for just this sort of attack. Like knives, they cared not how they were wielded. Their only imperative was to increase their numbers against their next employment.

The Dark People of Ansorge had removed them from the earth and sealed them in stasis in caverns far beneath their city. Ahlert's investigators had stumbled onto readable instructions for controlling them.

Gathrid suspected a twitch of the hand of Chuchain.

Daubendiek howled with joy. It preferred drinking the blood of men, but was happy enough with this.

The Guards Oldani, Imperial army and Sartain's militia merely howled. The attackers had no more self-concern than army ants. They drove through a storm of arrows and flung themselves against upraised blades. They plunged past the massed defenses of the Brotherhood, and ripped spellcasters to pieces.

The only defense was cover.

Ahlert began his advance. The winged things did not harry his people. His allies, in forces a thousand strong, assaulted each of the satellite fortresses. The defenders managed a few wild shots from their engines, but were so preoccupied with flyers that they could not reload.

It seemed a hundred flyers replaced every dozen downed. The attacking cloud grew more and more dense. Bodies piled a yard deep atop the Maurath.

A larger cloud swarmed over Sartain. Gathrid hoped the civilians would bar their doors and windows and wait the storm out.

It did not break. It did not let up. The winged things forced the Guards to retreat to the interiors of the smaller fortresses. Ahlert's troops threw up ladders and climbing ropes. Arrows shot from embrasures too narrow for the flyers took their toll, but the point had been won. The defenders would be overcome inside their citadels.

The embittered Ventimiglian veterans began advancing on the Maurath.

Hildreth, Gathrid, and Rogala fought as a team. While the taller men stood back to back, keeping the air around them clear, the dwarf finished wounded flyers and pitched carcasses off the wall.

It was rough work for everyone but Gathrid, who received energy from the Sword. Hildreth was first to confess exhaustion. "Got to get under cover and rest," he gasped. "This way." They were the last to leave the roof.

Gathrid examined the Ventimiglians as he shielded Hildreth's effort to open a door. It had become so dark the easterners had to carry torches. They were advancing with drillground precision.

The Maurath, unlike the outer works, had towers and turrets. The Ventimiglians encountered heavy arrow fire and a rain of burning pitch balls spewed by an engine of Hildreth's invention. The latter caused more confusion than damage.

The masonry shuddered.

"What was that?" Hildreth demanded. The Count had collapsed the moment they were safely inside. Now he clawed at Rogala, trying to regain his feet.

Calls of "Count Cuneo! Count Cuneo!" echoed up from the lower levels. Gathrid and Rogala trailed Hildreth round and round a circular stair, back down to the level where they had spoken with Ahlert. A Guards officer directed the Count to an observation port opening on the tunnel through the fortress.

Ahlert's thaumaturges had begun pulverizing the blocking stones. "That'll take them forever," the Count said, unworried. "I need a messenger."

"Here, Sir."

"Go up top and round me up four Blues. Bring them here."

"Yes, Sir."

The Brothers were still trying to decimate the flyers. Their task appeared hopeless. The roof of the Maurath was buried four feet deep in bodies. Blood flooded the scuppers meant to drain the roof. It was backing up. In places it leaked through, clogging the Maurath's upper levels with its smell.

Gathrid found the magnitude of the assault stupefying.

Four shaky Blues reported. At Cuneo's direction they began exchanging sorceries with the Ventimiglians in the tunnel.

Gathrid peeped through an aperture into the gloom outside. Bochantin's banners now flew over several satellite fortresses, though fighting apparently continued within them. "What time is it getting to be, Theis?"

The dwarf growled something.

"Been going on only an hour? Seems like all day already."

More lead-footed hours slogged past. Hildreth's men fought stubbornly, but the Ventimiglians established a foothold on the ramparts. They began expanding it, bringing up men for an attack into the Maurath's interior.

"It's going to be long and bloody," Hildreth predicted. He remained undaunted. "Despite his numbers, he can't capture the Maurath. It'll be a different story when his men have to come inside." He checked the tunnel. A stubborn enemy persisted in his efforts to clear it. "That's his main thrust there. Trying to break through to the Causeway."

"I could go after Ahlert," Gathrid suggested.

Hildreth laughed.

"With a million flyers to swarm you?" Rogala snorted derisively. "There you go getting romantic again. Listen, son. Don't start getting the idea you're invincible. Bet there's nothing Ahlert would like better than to have you come after him."

Aarant concurred. "Be patient. The confrontation will come when both Suchara and Chuchain think it's to their advantage."

"You just don't want to risk getting killed."

"Damned right I don't. This isn't exactly living, but it's damned well better than being dead."

"Then so was being run by a Toal."

Aarant became very cold and vacant. "No. Death would be better than that."

Gathrid reflected on the Mindak and grew cold. Ahlert was as much Chosen as he. They were pawns of the Great Old Ones. Soon one of them would have to die. . . . The inevitability of it made him want to scream. He checked the smaller fortresses. "Hey. Looks like he's breaking off out there."

Hildreth edged him aside. "You're right. Figures he's done enough damage, and the flyers will keep them neutralized."

The Count sounded deflated. Aarant suggested, "He's in over his head and can't admit it."

"You're right. Sartain doesn't have anybody else to turn to. The responsibility is getting to him."

Count Cuneo had faced no sorcery at Avenevoli, and at the Beklavac narrows control responsibility had rested on other shoulders. When it fell entirely upon him, he could not make quick decisions. He did not know what to do. He was wasting his men of Power by deploying them as he would ordinary soldiers. The Brothers were his most valuable tools, and he was frittering them away because he understood neither their strengths nor limitations.

Gathrid prowled his backbrain, trying to locate the memories of Sagis Gruhala. Aarant saw his thrust. He contributed the memories of witchmen he had slain. Many were the great ones, the old ones, whose names still rang in legend.

What Gathrid wanted was not to be found in any of their minds. "Messenger," he said to one of the youngsters who dogged the Count. "I want you to assemble me a list of all the Brothers assigned to the Maurath. Find out where they're stationed and what their specialties are." He hoped something in writing would jar his mind into yielding what he needed.

"What're you doing?" Hildreth demanded.

"We can't do much about the flyers, right? So why don't we address ourselves to something we *can* handle? And I think we've been taking too defensive a stance."

Historically, Hildreth had been at his best on the defensive. As a young mercenary he had won his reputation defending small lords from the predations of their more powerful neighbors. It was that skill which had brought him to Elgar's attention. The real miracle of Avenevoli was not that Hildreth had won there, but that he had done so with essentially offensive maneuvers. The results at Katich were more characteristic of his few offensive attempts.

After the one challenge Cuneo seemed content to permit Gathrid his way.

Rogala whispered, "The man's had his head under the axe so long that he'll jump at any chance to share the responsibility."

"Won't matter who's responsible," Gathrid replied. "Unless we can scrounge up a miracle."

"Folks would get in line to claim credit in that case. But don't be so pessimistic, son. Ahlert has his limits. Like no reserves. He's losing his momentum now."

"Excuse me a minute." Gathrid took twenty. He spent them chatting with Guardsmen, soldiers and militiamen. He found them less beaten than he had supposed. To a man they still believed in Daubendiek, the possibility of victory, and in Count Cuneo.

Gathrid told Rogala.

"You want to see morale rise, stick around." Amidst everything else, Hildreth had been organizing a counterattack against the Ventimiglians on the ramparts. It was now near jumpoff time.

"How so?"

Glen Cook

"The old fox was holding back. On everybody but Elgar and a few engineers. Apparently even the Mindak's mindreader missed it."

"What?"

"That there are tunnels connecting the Maurath with the outer fortresses. They're designed collapsible. And completely secret, so the men stationed out there wouldn't get lax knowing they had an easy out."

Gathrid felt he had to re-evaluate Hildreth once again. As long as Ahlert had been willing to spend lives to take the satellites, Hildreth had been willing to defend them. He was a hard commander.

Gathrid glanced outside. Belfiglio knew about the tunnels now. He had informed his master. Troops were racing back to the fortresses, hoping to seize the passages before they were destroyed.

"They're too late," Rogala observed.

Sections of grainfield were falling in. From the dungeons of the Maurath came the clatter of the garrisons arriving.

"We'd better move now," Gathrid said. "While they're disorganized and we're in good spirits." The counterattack was ready. Redistributed according to their talents, he hoped the Brothers would make possible a counterstroke unhindered by flyers.

The key was a noxious gas. He had found a White Brother using it to protect a remote tower.

Hildreth could not climb back to the higher levels. Gathrid took over for him. He assembled the men in a hall below the Maurath's roof, told the White Brother to explain.

The man indicated several big copper kettles and a mound of rags. "Tear off strips of cloth and soak them in this brine. Tie them around your faces, covering your mouths and noses. As long as you breathe through the rags, the spells on this brine will protect you from the gas. Take an extra cloth to wipe your eyes and use if you lose what you're wearing. If you do find yourself breath-

226

ing the gas direct, get below as fast as you can. Prolonged exposure will make you quite miserable. Sir?''

Gathrid went first, and allowed the White Brother to adjust the rag bandana he fixed across his face. "How long will this last?" he asked.

"There's enough oil in the mixture to make it good for an hour," the Brother said. "If the mask starts feeling dry and salty, you might want to duck back down and get a fresh one. That's a point. Don't use the same one over again. . . ." He went on till Gathrid lost patience.

"Let's get with it," the youth snapped. "You men, line up. Brother, get up there and start your gas."

Fifteen minutes later the youth gave the signal. Men yanked the bolts holding the heavy doors. Gathrid charged besiegers amidst a rolling cloud. Ventimiglians coughed and gagged around him, heaving up their breakfasts and clawing their eyes. They went down under Daubendiek's furious blows. The flyers, blinded, began colliding. Gathrid kept pausing to wipe the sting from his eyes with a rag he carried in his left hand.

He felt terrible, even protected. How much worse the enemy felt he did not care to imagine.

The counterattack spread like oil on water, groups from different sallyports joining forces. Brothers came out behind the soldiers. They hurled their Powers against the flyers.

Gathrid ripped through Ventimiglian platoons like a scythe through wheat. He searched for enemy captains.

The most important were obvious. They were men of Power, standing in small islands of sanity, trying to disperse the gas. Spells Aarant recognized as wind-callings rumbled across their lips.

It was a slaughter till one Ventimiglian did manage to summon a breeze. Daubendiek stole so many lives Gathrid became lost in their complexities. Aarant was supposed to integrate them, but could not handle the flood.

Some of the enemy trampled their brethren in their haste to escape.

Gradually, the gas did disperse. And then the flyers could not be turned back. The counterstroke collapsed.

"Valiant effort, lad," Count Cuneo said after Gathrid abandoned the action. He had come within minutes and yards of clearing the ramparts. "It bought time. It'll be dark before they regain their strength. Let's hope they wait till morning to break in. Meantime, I need your help down here."

Gathrid was staggering. "I need some rest."

"One of the tunnels didn't collapse the way it should have," Hildreth explained. "They managed to get some people through. We've got to push them out before we can demolish the passage."

Ahlert kept Gathrid rushing hither and yon all night, stemming threat after threat. And all the while the Ventimiglian wizards and engineers kept grinding away at the tunnel to the Causeway.

Dawn came. It brought Rogala with news. "The flyers have left us."

"What?" The youth was too tired to concentrate.

"They're all attacking the island now. Folks over there are showing a little ingenuity. They're rigging nets over the Causeway. Under the nets, carpenters are boxing in a wooden passage."

"What good does that do?"

"We're cut off till they get here. We couldn't get out if it turned bad. Meantime, Hildreth wants to hit Ahlert's tunnel crew. Sartain is done for if they break through."

Sighing, Gathrid took up the Sword once more. Soon he found himself astride a horse, about to lead a hundred men in a charge from a hidden sallyport.

Fearful sorceries met the surprise attack. Brothers in the Maurath replied with sorceries of their own.

Gathrid hacked and slashed in fighting so close the dead remained upright in their saddles. The Ventimiglians concentrated on him. In those brief intervals when he won a respite, he stood in his stirrups and searched for the Mindak.

The man was nowhere to be seen.

But he was out there, employing archers and slingers with a callous disregard for the allegiances of the men being hit by his missiles.

There was little Daubendiek could do to shield Gathrid from a random arrow. "Back inside!" he ordered. "We've done all we can." He covered his companions' withdrawal.

As Rogala removed Gathrid's helmet, the youth sensed bad news. Count Cuneo's eyes were distant. His face was rigid with despair. "What happened?"

Hildreth opened his mouth. Nothing came out but a croaky gobble.

"We've been suckered," Rogala replied. "We've been thoroughly swindled."

"How?"

"This whole attack was a diversion. The Count finally managed to contact the island."

"And?"

"The Imperial Brigade landed near Galen during the night."

"What? How did they manage that?"

"With boats. A lot of boats. Seems Ahlert commandeered every boat and barge while coming down from Torun. He cleared the Blackstun and the Ondr. He assembled them behind the promontory there. Last night they slipped out and made a landing on the island. The Count's best men are out here. Nothing but militia in Sartain."

Gathrid handed his horse to a groom. He sat on the floor, rested his back against a wall. "And we can't send help because of the flyers."

"Right. Even if we could afford to break the men loose."

"There's a million people on the island," Gathrid muttered. "Can't they hold off one brigade themselves?"

He realized he had slipped into Suchara-thinking. Damn the casualties! He was disgusted with himself. "How bad is it, Theis?"

Rogala shrugged. "Who can tell? They're holding out. They're covering the Causeway. But Ahlert put in his best. Only time will tell."

Time had nothing to reveal before sundown. Though weariness depressed the tempo of the fighting, it continued. News from Sartain remained sketchy. A quarter of the vast city appeared to have been captured. The Imperial Brigade had bogged down for lack of strength to exploit its coup. It appeared to have trapped the Fray Magister in the Raftery.

That night Gathrid found time to sleep. And for the first time in months his Toal-haunt plagued him.

He was dreaming confused dreams, his brain laboring at the Augean task of integrating the souls Daubendiek had devoured, when it began. Sudden, vicious, determined, it hit him. It was a cold evil intent on making him its own. There was no warning. One moment there was nothing, the next a reverberating shock as it smashed in, driving tentacles into his soul. The sleepy semiawareness that was Gathrid of Kacalief almost succumbed.

Tureck Aarant never slept. He was like Rogala in that respect. He fought the Toal. He gave Gathrid time to assume control, to begin resisting.

They seemed lost in another universe, the youth and his enemy.

Gathrid interpreted the struggle in symbols he could understand. While aware that his body lay on a rude barracks cot, foaming at the mouth and speaking in tongues, he lived a savage unarmed combat with a faceless foe whose muscles were iron, who whispered of devouring him. Back and forth across a cold, featureless plain they battled, beneath moons and stars that might have been the faces of mocking gods. The chill evil of the Toal filtered deep into his being, to the dark recesses where his worst fears and blackest desires lay hidden, straining at their chains.

Rogala, Hildreth, and a dozen Brothers and physicians stood by, unable to help, unsure, even, that this was the attack of Covingont being repeated. At first the dwarf thought Gathrid's mind had snapped under the assault of too many new personalities.

In that inside place Gathrid realized that he was losing. His opponent knew neither fear nor fatigue, and had nothing to lose. It could maintain the assault indefinitely. Panic lashed the youth.

In a moment of inspiration, Rogala placed the Sword in his hands.

Another apparition materialized on Gathrid's subjective plain. Tureck Aarant looked down on the struggle. He radiated an infinite sadness. He was his own master no more. His ancient mistress had reclaimed him.

He waded in with the chill fearlessness of the Aarant of legend. Suchara's will drove him. Hatred marred his features, curses distended his mouth. There was no escaping the mistress.

His was a hopeless mission. His ages enslaved to a Toal had left him vulnerable. As it had promised Gathrid it would do him, the Toal-monster did Tureck Aarant.

Others of Gathrid's stolen souls bombarded him with unwanted advice. They feared for him. He was their immortality.

He did accept the advice of an assassin from Torun. He got behind the Toal and tried strangling it with a forearm. . . .

Those were his perceptions. The reality was a pure battle of wills.

Aarant's will was not strong enough. As the Toal twitched in Gathrid's arms, before spinning away into the plane of Hell whence it had been summoned in ages past, it took a last killing bite.

The saga of Tureck Aarant ended at last. His personality faded. Only his memories remained. Gathrid felt hollow, incomplete, as if some critical organ had been ripped from his chest.

He had lost his best friend.

He sat and wept. For a while he shook uncontrollably. Great moaning sobs racked his body.

The body in the Maurath responded in the same fashion. Rogala gaped.

And outside the Maurath the battle continued. The attempt to connect island and fortress beneath a wooden canopy collapsed. The Ventimiglian penetration of the fortress highwatered and began to fade. But Ahlert's wizards had the great tunnel two-thirds cleared.

All through the night Ahlert's boats ferried troops to Sartain. A dark stain spread on the map of the island. Anderle's diminutive navy intercepted many of the Mindak's boats. The Imperial Brigade proved unable to take the Raftery.

Ahlert had lost his momentum.

Gathrid regained his self-control. He covered his embarrassment with a show of business. "It's been two days. Any news from Malmberget?" His companions shook their heads. Hildreth, looking ashen, did not respond at all. "What's wrong with the Count?" the youth asked.

"Had a go at their gate-clearing party," Rogala replied. "Took an arrow. Stubborn old coot hid it. Nobody noticed till he was ready to keel over from loss of blood."

"He do any good?"

"Not enough. I figure they'll break through in another hour. We'll cut them up some while they make the passage, but there's no way to stop them all."

"Thought this place was supposed to be able to hold out forever. Katich did better without our resources."

"Katich didn't have to deal with those flyers. Even so, you've got a point. The engineers should've given more thought to the fact that the defenders might have to face sorcery."

Gathrid reflected. The gantlet would be expensive for the men passing through. Each one who fell in the tunnel would make the journey more difficult for others. The Mindak might waste half his army before succeeding.

Gathrid was sure Ahlert would try. His obsession would compel him. "Theis, better think about what we'll do if Sartain falls."

A messenger rushed in. He tried to report to Count Cuneo. "The flyers are back! They're driving them inside."

"Inside the Maurath?" Gathrid asked.

"Yes, Sir. They're all over the upper level."

The youth dragged himself upright. "Help me with my armor, Theis. We should've expected this."

"There're a lot of things we should have expected," Rogala said. "Only we didn't."

"They won't have room. . . ." Hildreth protested weakly. He seemed to be coming back.

"They don't need any," Gathrid retorted. "They just have to keep us distracted till Ahlert breaks through." He addressed the Brothers present. "Block the stairwells and barricade the doorways. Keep them off the tunnel levels."

"What's Ahlert going to do with Sartain once he gets it?" Rogala asked. "He hasn't taken the Maurath. He'd have to fight his way out again."

Gathrid could not answer that. Only the Mindak knew why he wanted the Queen City so badly.

He considered allowing a reversal of roles. For an instant only. There were a million people on the island. He and these soldiers were here to protect those people, not to defeat Ahlert. The Mindak would show them little mercy.

Rogala would say so what. Let Ahlert through. The people of Sartain would fight. They would hurt their conquerors. Malmberget could clean up what remained.

The dwarf's focus was a little narrow sometimes.

"Theis, I wouldn't be surprised if he didn't know why he wants Sartain himself. I don't think he's thought about it. It's a move in Chuchain's game. It's an end in itself."

"Dumb."

"Not so tight with that lace. I want both arms loose.

And you don't have room to criticize, Servant of Suchara.''

Rogala yanked the lace tight. "Sartain is symbolic to the Power Ahlert serves," he admitted. "Chuchain will score a few points if his champion captures the city."

Gacioch whooped crazily. Rogala glared at the demon. "That was a howler, eh?''

Gathrid listened carefully. That was one of the demon's augury laughs. They always presaged some special unpleasantness. As usual, Gacioch refused to elucidate.

"Theis, that critter is starting to irritate me." His latest bout with his Toal-haunt had left everything to do with higher and lower planes, demonology and Power, irking him tremendously. He had lost his only friend. . . . Why, of all times, had it chosen to strike now? In what way had Nieroda profited? "I think I'll stuff him in a sack with fifty pounds of rock and drop him into the Sound.''

Gacioch hooted merrily. "Not today, son. Not today. You're going to be busier than a one-legged sword dancer.''

Gathrid gathered his weapons.

"What're you doing?" Rogala demanded. He did not like the Nieroda-blade.

"What I should have done a long time ago. I'm going after Ahlert. Make sure the tunnel control areas are sealed. Especially at the Causeway end. And bring enough Brothers to neutralize anything his wizards throw around. Find me a couple of carpenters. . . .''

Chapter Seventeen
The Raftery

The Maurath's engineers allowed the last stones to slide back into their shafts. The passage through was open save for a lumber barrier across the Sound-side mouth. Flyers chewed and clawed at those timbers.

Inside the barrier, Gathrid stood with his palms on the pommels of his swords, waiting. A mob of Ventimiglians swept toward him. He glared into their startled faces.

The twin blades whined and slew. Daubendiek protested having to share. Gathrid smiled grimly. The blade could not refuse to perform. If it would not respond to his will, it must to that of Suchara.

She was there with him. He felt her displeasure. She was being compelled to serve the will of a servant. But Aarant, lamented Aarant, had shown him the ways. She had to support him or abandon all hope of success in her own enterprise.

Gathrid heaped bodies before him. The Ventimiglians lost their momentum. They fell back, tried sorcery.

Sea-green light blazed. It blinded them. They charged again. Again they failed to best the Swords.

It may have taken minutes or hours. Time had little meaning when Gathrid had Daubendiek in hand. Finally, he sensed the Mindak approaching.

The man was reluctant. There was a feel of panic about him. He did not want this meeting. But both Chuchain and his own obsessions drove him to it.

Mead's ethereal beauty ghosted through Gathrid's thoughts. He wished there were another way.

The flyers stopped assaulting the Maurath. The constant clangor of combat faded as an uneasy truce developed. Gathrid smote the timbers blocking the tunnel and stepped outside, onto the head of the Causeway. He would have more room there.

He waited.

A silhouette appeared in the tunnel's mouth. It bore nothing save a tall staff.

Ahlert seemed to walk a mile, so slowly did he approach. He stopped ten feet away.

He wore no armor. He had shed all weapons save a ceremonial dagger. He had robed himself as High Thaumaturge of Senturia, one of his many titles. His face was sad. His eyes were remote.

"I'd hoped we could avoid this, Gathrid. I felt like an older brother toward you. But the Great Old Ones are indifferent to friendships."

"How well I know." Get out of my heart, Tureck, he snapped at himself. Though Kacalief remained in the back of his mind, he added, "I'd hoped to avoid it too. I keep thinking of Mead. Can't you go home? Can't we end this any other way?"

"Ask your Sword, Gathrid. Ask your Mistress. If I dared defy Chuchain, if I dared turn away, what would happen?"

Gathrid pictured it. Daubendiek would leap into Ahlert's back. He would not be able to stop the blade. "There must be a way."

"Not for us. For us it's too late. Only if They were conquered. . . . There's no end to the Game, Gathrid. I learned that much in Ansorge. And we have to play. However it comes out, I'm sorry."

"So am I. For you, for me, for everyone who's died and for all of us yet to die. What are you after, anyway? Why are you here? What do you have to gain by overcoming me?"

Daubendiek whined impatiently.

Ahlert shrugged. "I don't know. Do you know why you're here? What's Sartain to you, that its fate should matter enough to risk death?"

"As you say. We have to play. Even when we think we're free, we're being manipulated. You've come unarmed. Do you really expect to win past me? Or are you going to defy Chuchain by committing suicide?"

"Not likely." Ahlert smiled. But his eyes hardened.

Gathrid never really saw the move, so swift did the Mindak swing his staff. Daubendiek lightninged up, absorbed most of the blow's force. But the staff's tip caressed his temple.

His ears rang. His knees wobbled. His head began to ache.

"The Staff of Chuchain," Ahlert explained. "You didn't see it in the Brothers' War. . . . Aarant? Are you still there? The Great Old One showed me where the people of Ansorge had hidden it."

He struck again. The Staff slid over and along Daubendiek to prod Gathrid's stomach. Agony exploded at the touch, like all the cramps in the world. The Sword's counterstroke rang like thunder as Ahlert turned it. "You don't have Aarant to help you anymore, do you? And I have at last come into the fullness of my Power as the Chosen of Chuchain."

Daubendiek wove a deadly pattern. Ahlert retreated a few steps into the tunnel. Its confines seemed to expand around Gathrid as he experienced the feeling of growth. All things mundane became beneath notice. Rogala, who chattered advice from an observation port, was no more worthy of attention than a chattering monkey. Count Cuñeo, leaning out a sally port, was of even less account.

Daubendiek turned Ahlert's third blow. Gathrid had a feeling of a universe sagging past on rusty wings as the Staff's tip rocketed away from his face.

The Sword had encountered this weapon before, in ages past. It remembered. As it did, so did Gathrid.

Daubendiek had been defeated in their last encounter.

That battle had lasted two entire days. Then, as now, the fates of Empires had swung on its outcome.

Daubendiek had learned from that defeat. It applied its lessons now. But the Staff had learned, too. The two rang upon one another like demon hammers in the forges of Hell.

In Gathrid's weaker moments Suchara shielded him with her umbra. Chuchain did the same for his servant. Ahlert fought in light that danced between shades of gold and scarlet. The face of his master appeared behind him, filling the tunnel, glaring past Gathrid.

The youth knew another such face blocked the passage behind him. He wished he could see Suchara's material image. It would tell a lot about what she thought of herself.

He began to recover. He was able, occasionally, to unleash an offensive flurry.

Wits recovered, he could see that his situation was not as desperate as he had feared. The Staff was a mighty talisman, but was limited by the limitations of its wielder. Ahlert remained handicapped by the injury he had sustained before the gates of Ansorge. Evidently Chuchain could not overcome the bite of a Toal as easily as Suchara could the old gnawing of polio.

Daubendiek spotted the weakness. It began probing to Ahlert's left, driving deeper and deeper into his guard. Soon the Sword was slicing air scant inches from the Mindak's withered arm.

Seeing the tide shifting, Ahlert abandoned attack. Hope faded from his eyes.

Applying his will and Aarant's teachings, Gathrid forced Daubendiek down.

Suchara projected rage. Gathrid ignored her. "Will you go now?" he asked.

The Mindak leaned on the Staff, panting. He said nothing for a long time. Then, "I can't."

"Don't be stubborn. I don't want to do this."

"I'm not. I really can't. I don't have the will to break his spell." He readied the Staff.

"Damn!" Gathrid raised the Sword.

The pressure from Daubendiek and Suchara became intolerable. He gave them their head. Ahlert ducked and weaved, keeping his left covered while trying to trap Gathrid with his only hope, the Ordrope Diadem. The youth evaded with an almost instinctual ease. His one previous exposure had burned a lesson deep into his brain.

There was no doubt. This time Ahlert would perish. Even Chuchain, who drove his servant to mad extremes in a vain effort to nurse victory from the teat of fate, realized that. The Mindak could not overcome Daubendiek using one hand.

But Gathrid could control the manner of the man's demise. He could allow Ahlert to perish with dignity intact.

He let the Sword think it had control. He encouraged its attack to Ahlert's left. He pushed till he and the Mindak had danced through a half-circle.

He finished it with the long quiescent blade in his left hand. The surprise was complete. It took in not only Ahlert but Daubendiek and Suchara.

The Mindak staggered to the tunnel wall, good hand pressed to his wound. Blood darkened his fingers. Scarlet trickled along the Staff.

The younger sword groaned in triumph.

Daubendiek lashed like the tail of an angry tiger.

Ahlert sank till he rested on his knees, back against

the wall. He beckoned Gathrid. The youth stepped closer, placed a foot on the Staff.

"Tell Mead," Ahlert gasped. "Tell her I'm sorry. I couldn't. Be what she wanted."

"I will," Gathrid lied.

"And trust no one. The Dark Woman. Is among you. I feel her. Very near." He grimaced, ground his fist against his stomach. Only the Power of the Staff kept him going. "It hurts. More than I thought it would. The Sword would have been. More merciful. More to your benefit. Finish it now."

Gathrid refused. He still nurtured some pale, pathetic hope that the Great Old Ones would relent.

Daubendiek lanced out. Gathrid tasted its spite.

The mind that had been the Mindak Ahlert was as strong as Tureck Aarant's had been. It was as disorienting as it had been in that brief glimpse through the Ordrope Diadem. Gathrid staggered under its impact.

He returned to reality to find someone bending over Ahlert, trying to pry the Staff from his bloody fingers.

Daubendiek lashed out again.

Gathrid reeled as the stiff, stubborn personality of Yedon Hildreth hit him. He screamed. As he seemed to have done so many times before.

For two furious minutes he smashed Daubendiek against the stone of the Maurath. His rage was so overpowering the blade could not stay him.

Then a cold rationality returned. He bent over Ahlert himself. The Ordrope Diadem he shifted to his own head. He tucked the Staff under his arm. Someday, he thought, Staff, Diadem and both swords would accompany him on a long sea voyage. He could consign them to the deeps. . . .

A shadow fell across the mouth of the tunnel. A feeling of threat tainted the air. Gathrid left off his silent apologies. His gaze met that of a Toal.

It was like none he had encountered before. This was a man in the flesh and armor of an Imperial Legate. The

body still lived. But Gathrid recognized its spiritual
stench. He knew those cold, dead eyes. He knew the
Hell-stallion it rode, that only a Toal could master. No
mortal animal would permit such a devil to bestride it.

So. Nieroda had found her way around Ahlert's refusal
to reveal how to introduce a Toal into new flesh. She had
begun installing her fallen Dead Captains in live bodies.
The bodies of Imperials.

She's close, Ahlert had said. . . .

This monster was a fit object for his wrath.

The youth hurtled out of the tunnel, oblivious to the
possibility that the flyers might have returned. The Toal's
mount reared, screamed.

Daubendiek protested Gathrid's action. The youth had
seized total control. His will was behind his decisions.
The soul, the stubbornness of Yedon Hildreth had tilted
the balance away from Suchara. At that moment Gathrid
was completely confident of his ability to master the
Great Sword and defy Suchara.

Daubendiek whined in fright. Gathrid bid it slay the
Dead Captain.

Suchara fought him. Fought him for no better reason
than because this was what he wanted to do. Had he not
wanted to slay the Toal, She would have driven him.

"Kill it!" he thought at the Sword. Reluctantly, the
blade went for the Toal.

The false Legate tried to flee.

Gathrid slew its mount with the younger sword. He
allowed the Toal itself no chance to gain its footing. He
drove Daubendiek through its breastplate.

Deep inside Gathrid, the half-forgotten soul of Mohrhard Horgrebe cackled evilly, spitefully, feeling its former possessor suffering.

Gathrid did not let the Toal flee with the smoke rising
from the corpse of Legate Cervenka. On a subjective
level, with his newfound will and a year of anger, he
seized the fell spirit. They struggled for a moment,
crashing around that nowhere place where he had de-

stroyed his own haunt. He took that demon by the throat and shook it the way a terrier shakes a rat.

It ended quickly.

Gathrid bent, recovered a glowing Toal-sword. He tossed it to Theis Rogala, who had pursued him onto the Causeway. "Hang onto that."

The dwarf gulped, bobbed his head. He was pale and frightened. He could not believe what he was seeing, what he had heard when Ahlert had spoken to Tureck Aarant.

Gathrid smiled at him, his eyes narrow. "Greetings from Tureck, Theis." Rogala flinched. He would do some heavy thinking before using his dagger to complete this cycle of the Sword's history.

No need to worry yet, Gathrid thought. Suchara would not order him murdered while Nieroda yet remained in the game.

Or would she? Would she be that frightened?

He shrugged. Rogala was too disturbed to try anything soon.

He stared at Sartain. The Dark Champion was there somewhere. The Toal had proved Ahlert's statement. He reached inside and read Legate Cervenka. Sometime after Hildreth and the army had moved into the Maurath, Nieroda had descended on the Raftery. Now she was subverting the Imperial Palace.

The youth smiled, though he was not amused. Gerdes Mulenex had made a pact with a devil at Katich. The devil had come to collect.

That was what the Mindak had meant by saying she was looking over their shoulders.

The youth examined his surroundings. The flyers had vanished. Ahlert's wizards had packed up their witcheries. Easterners lined the ramparts of the Maurath. In their faces he saw awe, fear and dismay. Their officers were trying to get them to withdraw.

They knew what had happened to their Emperor. The

hopes that had brought them west had died with him. Despair had fallen on them like a deadly cloud.

Gathrid thought of Mead again. Belfiglio, too, would know. The task of informing the Mindak's wife would fall to the old slave. Gathrid did not envy him his mission.

Hildreth's senior officers began gathering in the tunnel. "Let them depart in peace," Gathrid said, pointing upward with the younger sword. "Muster your battalions. We have work on the island. Nieroda is there."

He was sure they would revolt. Someone must have seen him fell Hildreth.

His previous usurpations had accustomed them to accepting his authority. There were no witnesses to Hildreth's murder, apparently. They began forming their units.

Gathrid gazed down at Count Cuneo. He indulged in a moment of self-loathing. Suchara and Daubendiek had surprised him again. He swore it would be their undoing.

Being free of self-doubt was a new experience. It pleased him.

He went roaming through the soul of Legate Cervenka, his quarry knowledge of Nieroda and the Toal. The Legate knew very little. He had been seized during the night, by Red Brothers, while directing a militia regiment in counterattack against Ahlert's Imperial Brigade. He had been spirited into the Raftery. He had been unconscious, so did not know how he had been taken through the Ventimiglian lines. He had wakened possessed by the demon. Nieroda had handed him a Toal sword. The lights had gone out again. He had wakened back at his command post, under instructions to break the siege of the Raftery.

That siege seemed to bother Nieroda. She had revealed herself in order to press the counterattack.

The imminence of conflict between Ahlert and the Swordbearer had caused her to rush Toal Cervenka to the

Mindak's aid, judging him to be the weaker man. The Toal had arrived too late.

Two thousand weary survivors of the battle for the Maurath assembled on the Causeway. The rest Gathrid left to oversee the Ventimiglian withdrawal.

A Colonel Bliebel, who had been an intimate of Count Cuneo, protested the force's weakness and exhaustion.

"I just want you to keep order, Sir. I'll handle Nieroda and her devils myself. Theis. My horse."

Ever efficient, Rogala had the animal ready.

Gathrid mounted, started toward Sartain. He searched the sky, wondering what had become of the flyers. Only their dead remained.

It won't be long before Theis draws his dagger, he thought. The dwarf had developed a sudden slyness, an evasiveness, which suggested thoughts he did not want to reveal. Might Suchara be ready to concede this round to Bachesta? She might fear losing the Sword more than she disliked losing the Game.

He surveyed Rogala from the edge of his vision. The dwarf was watching him intently, nervously.

Should he disarm the man?

No. That would make him more dangerous. Suchara would provide another blade, in an inconspicuous time and place. And Rogala himself would become less predictable.

A committee from the Imperial Palace met them at the Causeway's end. They bore instructions from Elgar, who wanted the Raftery relieved. Despite the efforts of the Brotherhood and Anderle's militia, Ahlert's Imperial Brigade remained solidly entrenched.

The easterners were aware of their Mindak's demise. But their commander, Tracka, felt obligated to fulfill his final charge. He had abandoned all his other operations to concentrate on rooting out Nieroda and the Dead Captains.

Gathrid glared at the messengers suspiciously. He did not have to be schooled in the treacherous ways of the Great Old Ones to see that, on at least two levels, it was in Elgar's interest to let the Ventimiglians reduce the Raftery. They would settle a personal score with Gerdes Mulenex *and* rid Anderle of the long-standing problem of the Brotherhood. An eastern victory would devour the leaders of the Orders.

He merely nodded to the messengers, then led the surviving Guards Oldani toward Galen.

"Peace," he told the first Ventimiglian patrol to cross his path. He waved his followers back out of earshot. "Please inform Thaumaturge-General Tracka that the Swordbearer would like to confer."

He was, it developed, not unexpected. Tracka arrived within fifteen minutes.

Gathrid had met the brigadier but had seldom spoken to him. Their paths had crossed at both the Karato and Kacalief. Tracka respected the Power Gathrid represented, but did not fear him. Ahlert had been known to remark that his leading commander had only one weakness. He feared nothing at all.

"You fought well here, General," Gathrid said. "I'd say brilliantly, considering your resources. We've been both enemies and allies. I want to suggest an armistice now, while there's yet something to be saved."

Tracka, like many men of his class, physically resembled Ahlert. Gathrid had little *déjà vu* flutters while speaking with him.

Tracka frowned. He was the most taciturn of the eastern commanders. He communicated more by gesture and expression than by the spoken word.

"I know your orders, General. I commend you for trying to execute them. But I think it's time you passed this task on. The Western Army is headed home. The wives of the men of the Imperial Brigade await them just beyond Covingont."

"Vermin infest the Raftery."

"Is that your opinion, or just the Mindak's?"

Tracka's face became as lifeless as that of a corpse.

"Mine, Swordbearer. The place must be scourged and scoured."

"I'll go along with that. The point I want to make is, your people don't have to do it. I'll handle it. I owe the Mindak that much."

Tracka shrugged. "I haven't been relieved of my obligation."

Gathrid felt Ahlert fuming inside him. "Damn all stubborn men!" he growled. "Can't you compromise? To save the lives of good soldiers?"

The intransigent general stared at Gathrid for more than a minute. His gaze moved over the youth's swords, neatly avoided the trap of the Ordrope Diadem. "Perhaps," he said at last. "If you can convince me that the traitors will be destroyed."

"Tell me about their defenses."

Tracka peered again. His right cheek twitched nervously. He scratched at it, shrugged. "The usual. And the Toal. We've handled them with massed ballistae fire. They keep finding new flesh, though."

"You gain with every Brother slain."

"Exactly. They have to run out of bodies sometime."

"What about Nieroda?"

"She's most evidenced by her absence. She hasn't involved herself in the fighting."

"Why would she be so determined to hold the Raftery?"

Tracka shrugged.

"The same reason the Mindak wanted it?"

"His Lordship didn't confide in me."

Gathrid leaned toward the general, whispered, "I think we'll become allies again. I'll join your next assault. Will you go afterward, win or lose?"

Tracka did his peering. He had flat, narrow eyes. He was intimidating. Gathrid wondered if there were something wrong with his eyesight. "If your effort satisfies me."

Gathrid returned to Bleibel, who immediately protested the arrangement. Gathrid ordered him to clear the streets for the Brigade's evacuation. "We won't spill any more blood if we don't have to, Colonel. While you're at it, assemble some boats in case they have to go off that way."

"Sir. . . ."

"I'll get them off the hill," Gathrid promised. "But without us paying for it in blood." He allowed his hand to drift suggestively near Daubendiek.

Bleibel accepted the orders.

Gathrid returned to Tracka. "How soon can we begin? Some of my officers have a taste for blood. I've put them to work. I'd like to finish before they get back."

Tracka smiled. "I'll start it now. You'll have Toal to face in a minute."

Gathrid glanced at Rogala. The dwarf had fallen into one of his dark, brooding moods. He could not stop thinking about Ahlert having called out to Aarant. The possibility that Gathrid had shared his predecessor's soul had shaken him deeply.

Tracka did not exaggerate his timetable. By the time Gathrid had climbed to the Winged Victories four Toal were leading a counterattack. Small witcheries had set the slopes of Galen aglow. Another two Toal had taken station halfway up the Hundred Steps. No Ventimiglian would battle past them.

"You'll have to guard me for a while after I make each kill," Gathrid told Tracka. "I'll be making real kills, not just separating them from the flesh. I have to leave my body to manage it."

The Thaumaturge-General nodded.

The first two Toal were easy. They were not expecting the fate he brought them. The next two fought more desperately, with more cunning. They consumed more of his strength. They were vicious. They did not mind having their bodies killed, but wanted no part of being done for themselves.

Six more, Gathrid thought when he finished the fourth.

His knees were wobbly. He leaned against the plinth of a Victory. That last one had been tough. He glanced round. The Brothers were losing ground fast now that they had no Toal to give them backbone.

He pushed off the column, allowed Daubendiek free rein amongst the Raftery's mortal defenders. He and the Sword devoured their energies. That no longer seemed such a wicked thing to do.

Reds and Mulenex street bullies, the defenders began scurrying amongst the Victories and Pillars in vain flight. A mob surged up the Hundred Steps, only to be turned back by unsympathetic Toal. Daubendiek feasted till they scattered.

Gathrid went for the Toal. The first was almost too easy.

The second proved to be a master bladesman. He was a genius both at surviving and delaying.

Gathrid began to wonder why the thing insisted on holding its ground. It had no long-term hope.

He saw why soon enough.

On the narrow veranda surrounding the Raftery the remaining Toal were assembling ballistae and training them down the Hundred Steps. One salvo would end the threat of the Swordbearer. He might deflect a shaft or two, but not an entire flight.

He retreated a dozen steps, sheathed his weapons, vaulted from the Steps to the steep, rocky slope of Galen. He felt neither trepidation nor lack of self-confidence as he scrambled across and up the hillside. The knowledge and skills of mountaineers came to his mind and muscles freely. He reached the veranda before the Toal could realign their weapons.

He had, he thought, achieved his potential as Swordbearer. This was the state to which every would-be possessor of the blade aspired.

Two more Toal perished before his ferocity.

He staggered to a wall. The last had taken him to his

limit. His heart was determined and his will demanding, but his flesh could be pushed no farther.

And three Toal remained. One held the Steps. One blocked the Raftery door. The third was among the ballistae, the strings of which Gathrid had slashed. It was closing in on him, sensing his weakness. Its sword swayed like a cobra about to strike.

Tracka engaged the Toal on the Steps. He used a blade plundered from one of the thing's comrades. Rogala scampered back and forth behind the general, looking for a chance to plant his knife. Down among the Pillars and Victories Ventimiglian artillerymen were setting up engines with which to support the assault. The last defenders there had surrendered.

Gathrid knew the artillery would not save him. It could not be brought to bear in time.

He tottered away from the Toal, scattering mortals, slaying several. Each gave him a bit more strength.

He stalked them in moments when he was not beating back some thrust by the Toal.

His bad leg began to bother him. His conscience called him vampire.

He went on, ignoring that pitiful little voice. They were just cattle. He would use or slay them as he saw fit. . . .

With the fulfillment of the Swordbearer's potential came Nieroda-thinking, Suchara-Chuchain-Bachesta-Ulalia thinking. He did not realize he was becoming more and more like the things he hated.

It was ever thus. The more mighty, evil and implacable the foe, the more like him one had to become to overturn him. Then, lo! There was a new power risen, scarcely distinguishable from that which had fallen.

So it went. The Lords of Darkness are crafty.

There were not enough Reds to give Gathrid the strength he needed to face several Toal. And the Toal guarding the Raftery entrance was spiriting the few available inside.

Glen Cook

Gathrid glanced down the Steps. Tracka continued his duel. The Toal appeared on his way to victory. The general did not possess the tireless energy of a Dead Captain.

He caught Rogala's attention, beckoned him.

Now, he thought, we'll find out where Suchara stands.

She was not yet ready to write him off. But she was tempted. Nearly a minute passed before Rogala plunged off the stairs. He scrambled up the slopes like some hairy rock ape.

Gathrid's antagonist pushed him hard, driving him to an edge of the veranda overhanging a precipice.

Rogala charged the Toal from behind. He hit as the Toal spun to face him.

Gathrid drove Daubendiek into the thing's side.

This time he avoided meeting the Toal on the nether plane. Having driven it from flesh sufficed. He could regain strength for a killing match while the thing sought a new body.

He pushed through oily smoke to survey the course of the battle.

Heavy bloodshed had not been avoided.

Tracka was weakening. But now the ballistae below were ready. That would be the Brigade's final victory.

A human wave had hit Ventimiglian positions along the line where rubble met housing the besiegers had not razed. Nieroda had ordered Bleibel back from the waterfront.

Gathrid turned to the Toal blocking the doorway.

There would be no passing the creature. It stood deep inside an entranceway too narrow for effective swordplay. It had discarded its own blade in favor of a fire-headed lance.

"Keep it busy," Rogala growled. "I'll fix it."

A roar drew Gathrid to the head of the Steps. Halfway down them smoke boiled up from a corpse porcupined with ballistae shafts. The Ventimiglians had disposed of Tracka's Toal.

The Thaumaturge-General staggered onto the veranda, looked at the doorway. "So close. So damned close."

The remnants of his Brigade were being battered by a mob. Gathrid supposed Nieroda had begun assembling them even before his departure from the Maurath.

She always seemed aware of his movements.

Rogala barely had time to complete his task, securing the Staff of Chuchain from Gathrid's horse as Bleibel's first armed breaker arrived. He had wasted time rescuing his boxed intimate, Gacioch. He barely outhustled the surge, which washed against the Pillars before receding. To Gathrid's eye it looked like every adult male in Sartain had come to relieve the Raftery.

The dwarf collapsed on his behind, gasping, after galloping up to the veranda. Attempts at speech gurgled through his foam-flecked lips. Retreating Ventimiglians cursed him as they tripped over him. Weakly, he offered Tracka the Staff. He communicated his idea by gesture.

Tracka caught on. He barked orders. Soldiers dragged a ballista around. They restrung and cocked it. Tracka tumbled the Staff into its trough. "Move!" the general growled at Gathrid.

The Toal saw what was coming, but had its orders. It could do nothing but try to turn the Staff with its lance.

It failed.

The Staff lightninged into its chest, smashing armor and bone. The Toal hurtled backward, clacking as it tumbled into the deeps of the council chamber. A wail of dismay rose inside the Raftery.

Gathrid whipped inside.

Down on the main floor the Toal thrashed like a cat with a broken back. The Brothers were fighting one another to get through exits to lower levels.

"Inside! Inside!" Tracka growled. A stream of Ventimiglians poured in. Bleibel had reached the Steps. The once strongest and proudest of Ventimiglian brigades had been reduced to a handful over two hundred men. More were fighting below, but they were doomed.

"Clear them out!" Tracka ordered, indicating the Brothers. His troops went after them. They were too panicky to use their sorcerous skills. Tracka told Gathrid, "Hell of a mess, isn't it? Now *they* get a shot at kicking the door in."

"Uhm." Gathrid stepped back outside.

Rogala, with Gacioch hooting him on, was tottering toward the doorway. Bleibel's face appeared over the marble horizon of the veranda. Combat clamor continued among the Pillars and Victories.

The lower slopes of Galen were carpeted with citizen corpses. The mounds of dead were only lightly freckled with bodies in Brigade uniform. Sartain would have much to mourn.

"You lied to me!" Bleibel panted.

"When? I didn't say I'd save the Raftery. I told you I'd get the Brigade to leave without fighting the Guards. But you wouldn't let me."

"Why did you do this?"

"Because Nevenka Nieroda is running this place."

"The Emperor sent orders to seize you. You have to answer for treason and the murder of Count Cuneo."

Gacioch guffawed. He made rude remarks concerning the intelligence of a prince who expected Daubendiek to swear fealty.

Gathrid smiled at the Colonel. "Did he tell you how you were going to arrest me?"

"Unfortunately, no."

"But, being as stubborn as everyone else, you're determined to get yourself killed trying."

"Who knows?"

"You're too late to rescue the Raftery. Tracka is cleaning it out. Tell Elgar that."

"I'm supposed to take Tracka in too. He's Ahlert's most likely successor. He'll have to answer for Ventimiglia's crimes."

Toal-sword in hand, Tracka tried to push past Gathrid.

"Easy, General. Colonel, did your orders come from Elgar himself? In person?"

"His messengers brought them."

"That's not the same. Doesn't tell me what I need to know. Tell you what. Give us fifteen minutes. Then we'll come with you."

Tracka protested.

Bleibel muttered, "I don't know. . . ."

"It's better than getting yourself killed, isn't it? All I want is a chance to find out why someone is so desperate to keep us away from here."

Bleibel surprised Gathrid. "It may mean my head. You've got fifteen minutes. No longer. I'll do what I have to when they're up."

Thirteen of Gathrid's minutes swifted past without result. He and Tracka swept through chamber after corpse-choked chamber on level after bloody level. There were a stunning number of rooms secreted beneath Galen. They contained nothing but the mundane. Tapping the walls turned up nothing but solid stone.

"I'm beginning to think you outguessed yourself," Tracka growled. "Or were misled. That's the woman's style."

"No. There's something here. She doesn't want it found. I'm positive."

The lowest level was a small, dank chamber footing a long, jagged stair. "This's got to be it," Gathrid said. "It can't just be a dead end. Look close."

Had the entrance not been left open by Brothers fleeing Tracka's soldiers, the downstair's itself might have gone undetected.

Tracka found the concealed doorway when he noted scrapes in the slime on the floor. Rogala then located a trigger mechanism hidden beneath a wrought bronze sconce.

"We're cutting it fine," Gathrid observed. "Just a minute left."

"You won't get back to Bleibel in time," Rogala grumbled.

A great slab of a door stuttered open. Its rusty hinges howled like a chorus of singing dragons. Light exploded from the other side.

Gathrid flung Daubendiek ahead of him and charged.

The sole occupant of the chamber was Gerdes Mulenex. The fat Fray Magister lay on his back on a stone bench, breathing shallowly. His bloated face was pale and without character.

"Let me," Rogala said, gesturing them back. He approached the fat man. After prodding Mulenex with a blunt finger, peeling back eyelids and smelling Mulenex's breath, he announced, "A Toal. With the demon on vacation."

"That explains a few things," Gathrid said. "And I think I know where the demon is. Hold it!" Tracka was about to use his blade. The youth pushed it aside. "She'll know what's happened if you do. We can't let her. Not yet." Slowly, like a sleepwalker, he eased round Mulenex and stalked toward the source of the brilliant light.

"Theis, look at this."

Rogala grunted. "No wonder Count Cuneo was pushing us about betraying Anderle."

Gathrid probed the glow with his left hand. "He knew this was here."

"Undoubtedly. Yes. No wonder."

Gacioch had grown strangely silent. Till now he had been providing a barrage of unsolicited suggestions. Gathrid frowned. Gacioch silent was more an attention-grabber than Gacioch with his normal logorrhea.

"Misplaer would have known," Gathrid reasoned. "And Eldracher, Elgar and Ahlert. This was why the Mindak wanted Sartain so bad. Mulenex probably didn't know till the end." The youth's fingertips brushed what felt like solid, polished iron. "The Shield of Driebrant."

He found the Shield's handgrip and armstraps. Laying Daubendiek aside, he fixed the Shield on his left arm. The Sword protested. Gathrid said, "We'd better hurry if we want to get to Bleibel in time."

Tracka nodded. The Thaumaturge-General's face remained expressionless. It seemed nothing fazed the man.

"Theis, stay here. If Mulenex starts to come round, kill him. Give it half an hour. Then do it anyway."

The dwarf protested, but found himself talking to the Swordbearer's back. Gathrid last heard Gacioch trying to convince Rogala that this was the best strategy.

Bleibel met them in the council chamber, ten minutes past deadline. Tracka's soldiers had managed to stall him without further bloodshed.

The Colonel stared for a long time. Finally, "You'll come with me now?"

"Yes," Gathrid said. "I wouldn't miss it."

"Yes," said Tracka, distracted. He was lost in the nuances of sorceries he might need to survive this day. Gathrid had shared his suspicions during their climb from the Shield Chamber.

"Your weapons, then."

"Don't be silly."

Tracka's hand went to his hilt. "I know only one way to give a weapon, Colonel."

"We're going with you," Gathrid said. "But don't expect us to put ourselves at your mercy. The grandest fool wouldn't do that after all that's happened."

The right side of Bleibel's face twitched. His sword hand strayed weaponward. He thought better of it, spun, stamped up the stairs. Gathrid followed. Tracka assembled his men, followed too. Near the door, at Gathrid's gesture, he recovered the Staff of Chuchain.

Lines of ragged Guards Oldani formed to their flanks once they descended the Hundred Steps. Glancing back, Gathrid reflected that this tattered, limping parade was a microcosmic cross-section of the continent west of the

Nirgenaus. It had been a bitter, demanding, devouring series of wars. A lot that was good had been destroyed.

To what purpose?

It was not finished yet. He might find an answer.

He hoped it would be acceptable, and feared that it would not be.

Chapter Eighteen
Imperial Palace

The palace was more impressive than the Raftery. Like the Queen City itself, it had grown with the centuries. Its vast maze rolled down Faron's flanks like melted wax down the sides of a candle. In places it had begun insinuating fingers into the surrounding city.

The Raftery, externally, had remained little changed since the reign of the Immortal Twins. The Frays Magister, when unable to resist the desire to expand, had added new chambers underground. Not so the Emperors. They had insisted that their works be on public display. Many had built to overawe the memories of their predecessors.

Plain vanity was the *raison d'être* for most of the vast stonework crowning Faron. The palace had become a city within the Queen City.

Gathrid had no time to sightsee. He was busy learning the ways of the Shield. By concentrating he could compel it to remain quiescent. When not shining it looked like just another battered instrument of war.

The thing was as slippery as Daubendiek. He had to stay with it every second.

The route they followed was so jagged Gathrid stopped the guide they had collected at the palace gate. "Straight on from here, fellow. No more stalling. Unless you'd prefer the Kiss of Suchara to that of your wife."

The man gulped. Internal conflict revealed itself in stance and expression. "Yes, Lord." Two minutes later he opened a door on a vast hall with a floor of jade.

Daubendiek quivered, hummed softly. It remembered this place. There, near that alabaster throne, looming so huge despite distance, Tureck Aarant had slain Karkainen. The floor remained scarletly alive where the Immortal Twin's lifeblood had poured out.

Guards tramped, stamped. They formed a precise line shielding the preposterously bloated specimen ensconced on Anderle's throne. They were quick and dangerous, the cream of the Guards Oldani.

Gathrid advanced cautiously. He sensed the presence of Nevenka Nieroda.

She was in that disgusting man-mountain called Elgar!

In this hour when Anderle's dream waxed strongest, when circumstance had made the Empire the one force capable of reuniting the west, its soul had been vampirized. The last dreamer had been dragged down. Nieroda had cut them out one by one and had brought their fancies to an end.

I'm the last one left, Gathrid thought. And anything I do is futile. She's murdered the dream. In that sense she can no longer lose.

The loss of Anderle angered him as much as the loss of Loida or Anyeck. The Empire was the last of the realities of his boyhood.

A gravelly voice deep within him rumbled, demanding attention. The Empire was not dead, it insisted.

Yedon Hildreth remained a stubborn man.

Gathrid thought the chance too remote, too improbable, too dependent on the unknown quality of the Contessa Cuneo. She was just an Oldani girl, a soldier's brat, thinly lacquered with civilization. What could she do, battling the subtle rigors of imperium?

She is my flesh, Cuneo insisted.

Gathrid had not met her. He admitted he could not know. If she *were* her father's daughter . . . But what value will and stubbornness against such as Nevenka Nieroda?

Irritably, Gathrid brushed off an attack by the Guards.

Bleibel went berserk. He screamed. Hordes of Sartainians swept in. They hurled themselves on the bewildered Ventimiglians.

Gathrid felt removed from it all. He seemed to be an observer watching killing machines at work. The attackers kept coming. Their corpses piled in drifts. Their blood gathered in lakes on the vast jade floor.

He felt no sense of time. It just seemed that, finally, they stopped coming. He stood alone except for grim, pale Tracka.

He felt stronger than ever. Daubendiek had fed on countless lives. He felt no connection with place or event. He was the Instrument of Suchara. . . .

He began speaking the words she wanted said.

Something inside him monitored and adjusted them. "Now, Nieroda. Now we settle the accounts. Finally. Forever." He thought he used a tight-throated whisper. Why were the walls shaking? "For all that you've done, and been, this time you die the death from which there can be no resurrection."

That great mass of flesh twitched a finger.

From behind the throne came the surviving Toal. They bore Gerdes Mulenex. They dragged Rogala, chained, collared and stumbling.

"You've blinded him!"

A monstrous cackle filled the hall. Gathrid saw that one of the Dead Captains was not a Toal at all, but the demon Gacioch restored to a whole body. He held Rogala's lead chain, and mocked the dwarf with every step.

Outmaneuvered again, Gathrid thought. But not beaten. Far from beaten. As he would teach Nieroda.

Gacioch had been deceiving them. Crafty demon. He had done his spying well.

Gathrid felt no pity for Rogala. Perhaps Suchara's indifference to the welfare of her tools was leaking over.

He sprang at the Toal, destroying one before it could defend itself. The second took but a moment longer.

Tracka handled the demon. He attacked with that savagery unique to masters betrayed by slaves. Gacioch let out one great long wail of surprise and dismay. He cursed Nieroda as he faded.

Gathrid laughed, a peal like a long roll of thunder. The demon had not foreseen his own fate. The Dark Champion had tricked him. "Roast forever," he called after Gacioch. "May it be a solitary Hell."

Gathrid turned to the throne. The thing that had been Gerdes Mulenex began to twitch. The gross corpulence of the Emperor began to snore.

The youth moved toward the two.

"Watch out!" the blind dwarf shrieked. "Trap!"

A storm of poisoned darts hurtled from a thousand hidden recesses. Their numbers darkened the chamber.

The Shield came alive. Missiles pattered off it like hail off a tin roof. Gathrid sighed. Its protection enveloped him completely.

Tracka was less fortunate. Gasping, one hand extended eastward as if he meant to yank himself home, he died. He was the last Ventimiglian.

He left a legacy. With his final breath he mounted a final, violent incantation. His body became a standing bolt of lightning. Jade melted beneath his feet. The blinding fire of him dissipated, becoming a foul, oily cloud. Something burst from its deeps.

It was a tentacular clump of nightmare a dozen feet tall. It had legs like a man. There the resemblance to humanity ended.

It leapt on Elgar. A mouth Gathrid could not see ripped

bloody gobbets from the Emperor. The youth muttered, "Wrong one, idiot!" He kicked a passage through the darts mounded around him. Nieroda-Mulenex responded uncertainly.

Tracka-monster realized its error. It whipped off Elgar and threw itself at the Red Brother. Nieroda barely evaded it. She seemed puzzled.

Wailing daggers hurtled out of nowhere. They pounded the Shield and Tracka's demon. The latter squealed and leapt at Nieroda again. Gathrid leaned into the storm of blades. He wanted to reach her before she eliminated the distraction.

Slithering like a snake, Rogala removed himself from danger. Though blind, he seemed to know exactly what was happening.

The jade opened between Gathrid and Nieroda. All Faron shifted, shaking like a dog coming out of water. Screams sounded throughout the palace. The hill groaned as whole wings collapsed.

Gathrid looked inside himself, hunting the spells Ahlert had used to bring in fill from afar. He could not find them. The Mindak had become as elusive as his sister and Loida. He sprinted along the abyss in search of a place narrow enough to jump.

Smoke ghosts drifted in through high, vaulted windows. Their frames were taking on an orange tinge.

Nieroda lacked confidence. She was trying to avoid a one-on-one. Gathrid grinned wickedly.

She was not retreating. Why?

At the moment she was preoccupied with the gift Tracka had left her. It froze. A struggle took place within it. It swayed, made a surprisingly kittenish sound. And turned on Gathrid.

The youth seized the Staff from where Tracka had dropped it. He used it as an old man uses a cane to discipline a belligerent dog.

The demon darted hither and thither, trying to get past

the youth's guard. Gathrid kept poking till, with a howl, it fled the palace.

"Now you've unleashed a Prince of Darkness on an innocent people."

Startled, Gathrid whirled. This was the first Nieroda had spoken. That sarcasm could not have come from Gerdes Mulenex.

"Better he than Hell's Queen." He prowled the edge of the abyss. It was pointless trying to anger her into doing something stupid. She did not act on emotion. He wondered if she had any feelings at all.

He had none at the moment.

Suddenly, surprising him, the Mindak was with him. "The Staff," whispered the voice from within. The feel was little different from what it had been with Aarant. "Speak the words I give you."

"All right." Gathrid locked gazes with Nieroda. Her Mulenex face settled into permanent bewilderment. Gathrid parroted the words Ahlert gave him, hurled the Staff at the abyss.

Thunder and smoke. For a moment there was a bridge. He danced over before Nieroda reacted. He went wondering if it were too easy. She'd always had something up her sleeve before.

Could she be running short, growing resigned in the face of repeated failure?

Facing an apparently unarmed enemy across jade stained by the blood of Karkainen, searching for the trap, he demanded, "Why?" A single thread connected all her actions: destruction. In success or failure, she destroyed. "What do you want from the world? Do you have to flog it like a teamster flogs a dying horse?"

A specter of longing tainted her Mulenex face.

She was ancient. She'd had time to brand her immortality upon the face of the world. Yet less was known of her than of Theis Rogala and Tureck Aarant. The records had been destroyed, probably with her connivance. Only names remained: Sommerlath, Spillenkothen, Wistma

Povich. And speculations about a forgotten Swordbearer, and Dreibrant and Grellner. Elusive, Gathrid thought. He wondered if Rogala remembered.

"Is it death?" he asked. "Will you lash the world till, in a rage, it ends you? Are you trying to escape your immortality?"

While he spoke he moved his head back and forth, trying to capture her gaze with the Diadem. She withdrew toward the alabaster throne, step-pause-step.

Going to her next move?

"What are Bachesta and the others? Why do they toy with our lives?" He could almost hear Rogala growling, *Kill when you have to. Don't talk.*

Intuition told him she had to be permitted the next move. She would turn any initiative against him.

She seemed as willing to wait as was he.

He suggested, "Suppose we just sit down and let the world get on with it? Let them seal us in and forget us. The Great Old Ones won't start anything new while they're waiting for us to finish."

Talk, talk, talk, he thought. When would she respond? Anything would give him an insight into her thinking. Why that one moment of sarcasm, then nothing?

He glanced out a window. Dense smoke masked the sun. Fires bloodied the billows. The temblors continued. The Queen City was dying. Contessa Cuneo's patrimony would consist of rubble and ash.

Nieroda changed during his moment of inattention. "It must yield," she declared. "It's stubborn. So stubborn. There's always one more barrier. . . . Someday it has to give in."

"What do you mean?"

Ahlert made a guess. Terrible and powerful as she was, Nieroda was a failure. The short-term tasks she set herself, even when they appeared to work out, invariably culminated in disaster.

She's immortal, Gathrid countered.

That, too, will end, Ahlert replied.

"Death," the youth said aloud. "I bring you death, Dark Lady."

She had won the war of waiting. He would make the first move. Suchara was impatient. He pushed through a dozen defenses the like of the darts and daggers. Nieroda backed away.

When first he spied the smoke he thought it just an especially thick arm drifting in from the burning city. Then it coalesced in his path. One end took the semblance of a cobra's head. More sorcery. He called on Ahlert.

The Mindak could not help him. This was beyond his knowledge.

It *was* a serpent. It became a smoke creature fifty yards long and as thick as a man's chest. It coiled round Nieroda, shielding her. Gathrid probed with the Sword.

Nothing happened. Daubendiek denied the thing's existence.

Red eyes glared into Gathrid's own. He saw a malevolent humor there. He backed away to consider.

It struck. Neither Sword nor Shield reacted. The youth survived solely on his own quick response.

Immune to the Sword. Able to penetrate the Shield. What was this thing? Nervously, he backed a few more steps away. One foot encountered the Staff, twisted beneath him treacherously. He regained his balance, dodged another strike.

The Staff, too, proved useless. So did the blade he had captured at Kacalief. He felt a growing uneasiness. He'd had an advantage. It was quicksilver in his fingers. She had gotten round the might of the great weapons.

"Death," said Nieroda. A wicked smile captured her fat Mulenex lips. "I bring you death, Swordbearer."

Gathrid saw it in those wicked red eyes as the serpent rocked to and fro, considering its next strike. He moved Daubendiek in time to the serpent's sway. Its gaze locked on the weapon, watching for his move.

Slowly, slowly, he drew the serpent's gaze upward, into contact with the jewel in the Ordrope Diadem.

Nothing. His mind opened on an emptiness so complete it could exist only as some philosopher's fantasy. He nearly fell in.

"Beware!" Ahlert snapped from the back of his mind. "It's another trap."

Gathrid surfaced. Nieroda was charging. Her serpent had vanished. She had acquired a weapon.

Its blade was wholly invisible. Daubendiek turned its first thrust uncertainly. The Shield absorbed a glancing blow. Nieroda danced away, moving lightly despite the gross Mulenex body.

She tossed, or pretended to toss, her weapon from hand to hand till Gathrid was no longer sure which wielded it.

Levels and levels, deceits and deceits, he thought. Was there no limit to her cunning? He maneuvered to where the Staff lay, kicked it at her.

She refused the bait. She dodged instead of blocking with her weapon. The Staff's passage across the jade produced an endless drumroll sound. It toppled into the abyss.

The gap closed instantly.

One point to the Dark Champion, Gathrid thought. He had lost a resource.

He struggled to retain his balance. The floor heaved and rolled like a strong sea. Trying to outwit the woman was going to scramble his brain.

He moved in, Sword and Shield high, ready to block a stroke from either hand. He ignored that part of the Shield's protection not backed by its physical embodiment. He had to push her, to deny her time for tricks. He edged closer, till he was inside her reach.

She could not resist.

He blocked with Daubendiek, locked blades and in the same instant hurled the Shield away. It danced a fiery tarantella across the jade. He seized Nieroda's hair, pulled her closer. He forced Daubendiek toward her throat. . . .

The high sorcery ceased to have meaning. The moment became a contest of strength. He was winning, forcing her to lean backward, dragging her gaze toward the Ordrope Diadem.

She could dispel a thousand mysteries.

Gerdes Mulenex had been a lazy wastrel. There was no strength in him at all.

Darkness.

Gathrid and his antagonist were in another place, another palace. They were locked in one another's arms upon another vast floor. Topless walls resembling human faces surrounded them. Three stirred memories for the youth. That snoring silver one he had seen looming over Anyeck's shoulders. The crimson, which wore an expression resembling that of a disappointed old man just nodding off, had floated behind the Mindak during their confrontation in the tunnel through the Maurath. The black face he had seen many times, supporting Nevenka Nieroda.

The black and an aquamarine face were very much awake. Each projected fear, excitement and hope. Each betrayed a vast displeasure with its Chosen.

Gathrid foresaw a struggle like those with the Toal on the endless plain. And he suspected that, for the vanquished, defeat would be final and forever.

He broke away from Nieroda. He and she, bereft of weapons, material trappings and stolen body, glared at one another.

Gathrid backed away. He now faced a woman, rather attractive and disarmingly unclothed.

He tried to cull his stolen memories, nearly panicked when there was no response. They were gone. He was Gathrid of Kacalief once more, with all that boy-child's frailties. His eye drooped. His leg hurt. He had no resources but himself to support him. A bitter year's growth

and experience were all that separated him from the terrified boy who had fled Kacalief's ruins.

She, then, would again be Wistma Povich of Spillenkothen in Sommerlath, perhaps as she had been before
becoming Sommerlath's Queen.

"Toys!" he spat. "That's all we are."

"That's all we ever were."

"Would that they were vulnerable."

"Yes." Her face looked haunted. "To be able to destroy them, as they've destroyed me by forcing me to
destroy. . . ." Her hatred became palpable. It surged
around her. The air crackled.

"Can there be games when the gladiators won't fight?"
It was a silly thing to say. The wannest of hopes. Too
much blood and pain knotted them into this death-dance.

Their eyes locked. She relaxed slowly. He did so himself, carefully, ever watchful for the Nieroda trap. Cautiously, he examined his surroundings more thoroughly.

It was a new subjective reality. It was both like and
unlike the plane-plain where the Toal had died.

Could these Great Old Ones die? Could they be slain?

Mead entered his thoughts. It had been she who had
put that name into his head. Where was she now? Had
she heard from Belfiglio?

Suchara's eyes burned like the flames of Hell. Her face
was an ever-changing landscape of emotion. Every expression was evil.

Gathrid was the focus. He had shared soul with Tureck
Aarant. Together they had conspired to deny her her will.
The ties were under strain. Yet, he suspected, he and she
could never sever them entirely. Nor could Nieroda separate herself from Bachesta.

The effort, ultimately, underlay all the frenzy and ir-
rationality of her earthly activities. Not lust for power.
Not love of destruction. Not even hunger for death. Just
a simple desire for freedom. She was engaged in a secret
war, the battles of which she sometimes lost and sometimes won.

Suchara's will beat upon him like storm breakers upon a rocky headland, insisting that he slaughter the woman before him.

The harder Suchara pushed, the more stubbornly defiant Gathrid became.

He stared into the eyes of Wistma-Nevenka. She had left the initiative in his hands. She would follow his lead. She would resume fighting if he yielded to Suchara.

Impulse.

He pulled her toward him, kissed her ancient lips.

Suchara and Bachesta gave vent to furies of deific magnitude.

Nieroda glanced at her mistress. Her eyes were merry. She seized Gathrid and kissed him back. She took his hand, faced the demigod walls.

This weak, scarcely genuine gesture of love between foes was arsenic to those connoisseurs of hatred and evil. Love was the one human attribute they could neither comprehend nor control, nor often bend to their advantage. They loathed and feared it.

In that context, Gathrid reflected, their Games almost made sense. Human love could take ten thousand forms. These devils shattered every sort when allowed to run their course. In their grinding mills the Chosen of the Great Old Ones destroyed what men loved, leaving them only things to hate.

How much hating had he done himself, as the Instrument of Suchara? Too much. Far too much.

And Nieroda? She was, he suspected, herself the thing she hated most.

He reached down inside for memories of the Mindak. Ahlert had not been directly possessed by hatred. His demon had been a warped, obsessive love that had generated hatred wherever it touched.

Anyeck had been possessed of a towering hatred for things-as-they-are.

And Rogala? What of Theis? The dwarf remained a mystery. The puzzle box of eternity. Gathrid now doubted the dwarf was human. Since Ansorge he had suspected that Theis might be the last of the Night People.

He doubted that Rogala would ever be solved.

He whispered, "I think we've found a way to fight back." He laughed. The sound caught in his throat. He remained unsure. A kiss seemed so little in the face of cruel, implacable powers like these.

"What we've found is damnation," Nieroda replied. "Willingly or unwillingly, we're in their web. They won't let us escape. I've been trying for ages." She despaired, but kept holding his hand. He drew a strange, almost motherly support from her.

"Once more," he whispered. "For their apoplexy."

She did not resist. Strange, he thought as he drew away. Nevenka Nieroda was as old as the hinges of time, yet was as unskilled as he.

As the thunders tramped and darkness marched like iron legions unleashed, he remembered Loida Huthsing. Sometimes it was not hard to hate.

Chapter Nineteen
Endgame

Gathrid reassumed physical reality. The Great Old Ones had spit him out like a sour plum. He found himself back in the remains of the Imperial Palace. The blood of Karkainen surrounded his soles. Daubendiek hung loosely in his right hand. Gerdes Mulenex sagged against his left arm. He staggered, went down.

Night had engulfed smoke-shrouded Sartain. It had brought no darkness, no relief for the eye. The great fires burned on.

He did not see a sign of Nieroda. She had not returned. Had he erred? Would she rise somewhere else now, and be lashed into another frenzy of destruction? He hoped not. He hoped she had seen the glimmer of hope, too.

But the Game was rigged. Of course. Even in defeat, the Great Old Ones had their way.

He waited an hour, till he was certain Nieroda would not return to the Mulenex clay. Satisfied, he finally strode from the wreckage of the great hall. The lone weapon he took was the blade he had obtained from Nieroda. He believed it free of any taint of control. The others, Sword and Shield, he left for whomever wanted them.

He did wish there were a way of disposing of them permanently. That was impossible. Even were they dumped into the ocean's deeps, the Great Old Ones would find ways to bring them back to willing hands.

He hefted the Nieroda blade. It was an almost-Daubendick. It might be of use to the Lady Mead. Or to the Contessa in her struggle to salvage the corpse of Anderle.

Could he bring the two women together? To scavenge a new, happier reality from the ruins of the old?

It seemed a goal worthy of his new life and blade. Perhaps, when faced by a champion as feared and deadly as he, the greedy, power-hungry Mulenexes could be cowed into building a world immune to such as Suchara.

Gathrid did not begin wondering about Theis Rogala till almost two months had passed. He was in Gudermuth, bound for Ventimiglia. Kacalief was not far away. He planned to stop and see what the Mindak had done for Loida and his sister. Curiosity began plaguing him when he passed the place where he and the dwarf had emerged from the caverns.

He strode to the nearest hilltop, slowly surveyed the naked landscape. He saw nothing. But the very fact that the dwarf had not entered his mind for so long seemed suggestive.

Was Suchara toying with him still? Was her agent stalking him with a hungry blade? Had he thought of the dwarf only because her attention had lapsed momentarily?

He finally shrugged, walked on. It did not matter. If the encounter was to come, it would come. He would not evade it. He would be prepared.

He went over the details with Ahlert, Count Cuneo and other wise and captive souls. A Theis so brazen as to bring the traditional dagger would be one surprised and short-lived dwarf.

Only a handful of the strongest minds had survived the passage through the realm of the Great Old Ones. He missed the others. His interior world had been his refuge from loneliness. As they had been for Tureck Aarant so long ago.

Funny. The best friend he had ever had was a man who had been dead a thousand years. A man who had died twice. He missed Tureck dearly.

The missing souls had left him much of their accumulated experience. He had learned to draw upon it as though it were his own. He had the knowledge to become an Ahlert or Eldracher had he the wish.

He felt as old as the time-worn hills of the Savard.

His birthday was approaching. He had overlooked his seventeenth in the chaos of the previous autumn. His eighteenth now approached more swiftly than seemed possible.

He had grown physically as well as mentally. He had confidence in himself. Reassurances would be pleasant, but he no longer needed outside support or direction. He could be his own creature and survive. In a few years he might fit the popular image of a hero.

He had been an introvert all his life. He remained one, but the impact of his adventures had shattered his fear of the world. He felt better about Gathrid of Kacalief. His shift in feelings about himself he saw clearly cast on the inside landscape of himself.

He had become a man.

His changes in attitude toward externals were more elusive and less satisfying. Mainly, he cared less.

The world's agonies no longer pained him. He had little sympathy for its self-torment. It had become an irritation.

Yet his idealism had not vanished. He just seemed unable to apply it in any direct, specific fashion.

Grass and brambles infested Kacalief's remains. Bones still lay heaped in monumental piles round the castle hill.

Rusty weapons and armor could be found everywhere in the weedy fields.

A handful of stubborn, enterprising peasants had begun reclaiming the land. It was blood-enriched earth where plows more often turned on broken swords than stones. The peasants were collecting the iron in hopes of someday selling it.

Gathrid abandoned his eastward journey for a time. Some of the peasants remembered him from his youth. They were not thrilled with his return. They knew too much of his tale.

For days he prowled the ruins or sat staring at the mausoleum on the flank of the hill. He tried to wish back the dead.

They were gone from his mind as well as his world. He could find them only in his heart, in faint, sad echoes of feelings that once had been.

Sometimes he considered searching for Loida's people. They would want to know what had become of her. He never got around to going.

He was sitting in the tall green grass, sword across his lap, sucking a sweet stalk and staring at the mausoleum, when he heard the soft brush of grass against stealthy legs. He listened carefully as the sound crept up behind him.

"Come on up and take a seat, Theis."

He had not turned. The sound died. Nothing happened for several seconds. Then the dwarf moved up briskly and settled himself. "You're learning."

"Yes. I am." The dwarf had healed as quickly as ever, except for his eyes. He remained blind. "And I've been expecting you."

They stared at the gray stone mausoleum for a long while. The Mindak's artisans had told the story of each girl in skillful bas-relief.

"Why?" Rogala asked.

"The dagger. It was time."

"Suchara has lost you already."

"I left, Theis. She didn't let me go. No more, I think,

than she'd ever let you go. Her pride will compel her to try something.''

''You think she still rules me? I'm free, Gathrid.''

''I don't hear your conviction, Theis. If you're free, what're you doing here with me?''

''Where else have I got to go? What else, whom else, do I know? They left me no options when they took my eyes. It's go with you or become a beggar. The Esquire has his pride too.''

''Uhm.'' That sounded as though it contained a grain of truth. Long life was a curse upon Rogala. It made him a time traveler marooned far from home. He had nothing in this world but his fragile association with the youth he was supposed to kill once Suchara had tired of him.

Was there anyone else with a use for the blind dwarf?

Perhaps someone who would use him as Ahlert had used the Toal.

''How did it begin, Theis? What are the Great Old Ones? Where did they come from?''

''I don't know.''

''Really, Theis? Pardon me if I have trouble believing you. You've always known more than you were willing to tell.''

''Gathrid, I'm a tired old man. Rehashing the past, and my ignorance, won't do any of us any good.''

''I want to understand, Theis. I've been a part of something. On a grand scale. I want to know what. I want to know what it means. And on a smaller scale, I'd like to unravel the mystery called Theis Rogala. You puzzle me more than the Great Old Ones.''

Rogala's sightless eyes scanned the ruined land. He did not say a word.

''Who are you, Theis? What are you? Why do you live on and on? Even Nieroda has to change flesh. Where were you born? When? Were you born at all? What's your real connection with Suchara?''

''That's all long ago and far away, Gathrid. None of it matters anymore.''

"It matters to me. Tell me about Suchara. Is she real? Is she a goddess? Why does she torment humanity so?"

"Peace, I say!"

"No, Theis. Not anymore. Peace is dead. I've lost everything I value. I've had my life shaped and warped in a direction I would've rejected had I been able. I've seen my whole world destroyed. I want to know *why*!"

"It can't be changed."

"Tell me."

"Damnit! Aarant was stubborn and nosy, but he wasn't half the pest you are. Let it lie, I say."

"Start with Suchara."

Rogala sighed. "You win. Yes. She's real. She does exist. She was a human woman once. One member of a family which delved deeper than even Nieroda. Farther and deeper than Nieroda could imagine, even as Queen of Sommerlath. And they went too far. They tempted fate too much. They outlasted most researchers, but they finally stumbled into the trap that takes them all. Now they lie caught in an endless sleep, hidden away somewhere. Sometimes they dream the shaping dreams. They touch the world with their minds. The world responds. They don't know that what they touch is real. They think they're playing on a game board with the scale of a world. After all, it isn't the world in which they fell asleep."

"I saw them awake, Theis."

"No. They only dreamed. Only dreamed."

"But . . ."

"Were Suchara here, Gathrid, you'd see nothing but a woman. A plain woman who clothes herself in gauzes of aquamarine to distract the eye from her homeliness. She uses perfumes that smell of the sea. She has eyes of green and, perhaps, a strand of seaweed threaded into her coppery hair. Her voice would be modulated to contain undertones reminding you of the whisper of the waves. She's a dramatic, and a talent, but she's just a woman."

Gathrid watched the man while he talked, startled. This was his terse, insensitive companion, Theis Rogala?

"It sounds like you knew her. Like you were maybe in love with her."

"Perhaps."

"And the others?"

"Chuchain. Her husband. Bachesta and Ulalia are daughter and son. Bachesta was a dark one. An evil one. The sleep may have been her doing. She wasn't a patient woman. Ulalia was her antithesis. Pure, if you like. And slow, lazy, and easily fooled."

Softly, Gathrid said, "I see why he attracted my sister. This family. Is their fighting for real? Are they just whiling the time?"

"It's real. Endlessly, agonizingly real. They knew, as the sleep took them, that only one of them would ever come back out. Three must perish that one may waken. Or be wakened. It'll take an outsider nearly as great as they. And in that aspect, they may unconsciously know what they're doing to the world. They may be trying to create their deliverer."

"Ahlert. . . ."

"He might have revived Chuchain. He came near succeeding without realizing what he was doing. For a while he had control of the dream, rather than the dream of him. The people of Ansorge had done most of the work for him. Had he found Daubendiek before Suchara quickened, and taken it to a certain place . . ." The dwarf shuddered.

"And what about Daubendiek? What *is* Daubendiek?"

"A sword. A trap. The Hell wherein Suchara's soul is tormented. In those days it was the practice to hide part of one's soul in some object. So with the Staff."

"And the Shield?"

"Like your blade there, just a creation of Nieroda's. No. Not 'just.' Bachesta nurtured Nieroda for ages. And, as she did with Ahlert, she turned on her master. She became capable of matching Bachesta evil for evil, on this plane."

"She seemed more lonely and unhappy than evil." Gathrid related his experiences before the Great Old Ones.

"What is evil but misery and loneliness?" Rogala muttered. "The child of those parents, surely."

Gathrid frowned. Theis had taken quite a philosophical turn.

"Even Nieroda is human, Gathrid. Dead and immortal, but human. Loneliness is the price of power. Even Gerdes Mulenex had his good side. You saw that side in your sister so strongly you couldn't see any other. So it goes. You should have learned that lesson by being Swordbearer. You tasted a lot of souls."

"There was love in Anyeck, Theis. There was even a spark of it left in Nieroda."

"That's what I said."

"There was no love in that place we went. Only hatred."

"Hatred born of jealousy. Or envy. Or inability to handle love. Love makes a family. And love destroyed that one, yet binds them in their dreams. They don't understand."

"I'm not sure I do, either."

"To be unable to comprehend love is human too, Gathrid. They still have love without knowing it. Only Bachesta has lost it entirely. Ulalia has lost care. His only desire is a peaceful, dreamless sleep."

"And Theis Rogala? What is he in all of that?"

"Once upon a time there was a man named Theis Rogala who was Suchara's lover. He was a whole man. . . . Now he guards the blade where a jealous Chuchain chained her soul. He brings it forth to do battle when he must. To protect its existence. To help Suchara defend herself. But what's left of that man has grown weary of the whole mess. I owe, but must I pay forever?"

The dwarf seemed to be thinking aloud rather than speaking to his companion.

"Why slay the Swordbearers?"

"They become too enamored of their roles. They enjoy their might. And they grow too strong. And she grows fond of them, thinking they might set her free. She gives them knowledge and power they might wield against her. I can't permit that. It has to be me. But I dare not use the blade myself. I'd become enslaved. She knows me too well, and her desperation is too great. So I wait till she chooses, and hope that someday all the right things happen at all the right times. But despair gnaws at me like the worms of the earth. I have so little left to give—unless I do take up the blade."

Evening was coming on. Peasant women were at their cookfires. The aroma of woodsmoke teased Gathrid's nose. Soon his stomach would compel him to go down and exchange another bit of Imperial silver for another bowl of burned stew. He would remain marginally acceptable as long as his money lasted.

He had become an outsider in his homeland.

"Finally, why did you follow me here?"

The dwarf did not respond.

"Theis?"

"To collect Daubendiek."

"I left the Great Sword in Sartain, Theis. I put it aside. I bear only the blade born in Nieroda's forge."

"You left metal. Not the attachment. There'll be a day when your path swings back to Sartain, whether you will it or not. She won't let you scorn her."

"It may have to be that only one of us will leave this hill, then, Theis."

"Could be."

"I wouldn't like that. And, Theis? I don't think I'd be the one staying. You're fast, but I don't think you're fast enough."

Rogala shrugged. "I'm getting older. Because I don't care as much as I once did. And being blind won't help, will it?"

"Does it always have to be this way?"

"I don't know what else to do."

Gathrid sighed. Silence stretched till it became oppressive.

Rogala coughed. "I like you, Gathrid. You've become like a son. I don't want to. . . . Show the blind old man another way. I taught you the art of killing. Teach me the art of living."

Gathrid could find no words. The silence stretched again. Finally, he tried, "You know the secrets of the greats and near-greats of a hundred ages, Theis."

"You've looked into more souls than either of us can count, lad. I've seen them only from the outside."

"There must be something in all that," the youth agreed. Rogala was trying.

Every path led to the same destination. A death. More blood on this hill that had seen too much already. The limits seemed inflexible, the end assured.

The sun had declined almost to the horizon, growing bloated and red as it touched the distant earth. The night would be here soon, and with it, perhaps, a longer night. Rogala would sense the gathering darkness. He would move when the sight advantage had disappeared.

Gathrid thought, I should kill him now. Quick as he is, he can't outdance this sword.

He could not cut the man down. Had the victim been anyone else . . . He just did not have Rogala's murder in him.

Was Suchara staying his hand?

He let his senses range. . . . Was that a calling, way over there, hovering on the edge of perception?

"Don't do it, Theis. You're dead if it clears its scabbard."

"I've taught too well."

"Maybe. I see two choices, Theis. We can join forces. We can find your Suchara and waken her. Or one of us can die here. Maybe both. You don't seem capable of letting it go."

"You know I can't."

"What happens if she returns?"

"The others perish."

"I know that. I mean, what would happen to you and me? And my world?"

"I don't know. I don't care about the world. It's not mine anymore. She's what interests me."

"Theis, turn to your right thirty degrees. Good. Out there about a half mile are some cookfires. Feel them? Around them are all the people left in this part of Gudermuth. Winter will be here soon."

"So?"

"Those people have survived the Mindak, Nieroda, and a winter of famine already. And they did nothing to earn any of that. How much more must they endure?"

Rogala shrugged, his face a mask of indifference.

"Once you said they'd endured too much already. I've heard you say this thing has gone too far." The youth nodded toward the mausoleum where his sister and Loida lay.

"She's a jealous woman, Gathrid. And insane by your way of looking at things. Don't forget. She dreams. Are we responsible for her nightmares? Her power is godlike. She doesn't realize that she shapes reality. A moment of pique gives us pain, but she doesn't know she's hurt anyone real." Thoughtfully, he added, "She may have lost track of the line between reality and fantasy even before the trap took her."

"I owe her, Theis. For my sister. For Loida. For Count Cuneo and the Mindak. She's taken a lot from me, Theis."

"But you want to waken her?"

"Maybe so I don't have to kill anymore. I really don't want to. Especially not tonight."

"What the dream has raped away the dreamer might restore."

"What?" Gathrid spoke so sharply, so suddenly, that Rogala exploded like a startled quail. He came to a halt ten feet away. His knife was in his hand.

"Calm down, Theis. I was startled. What did you mean? She could bring back the dead?"

"I think so. No guarantees. I can't pretend to speak for her. But she has the souls of all those Daubendiek has slain. They went into you, but also into the blade. You lost them, but they're not lost. If you see what I mean."

"Theis, I don't really trust you. But I'll try to make you a deal. I'll give you your life and Suchara's awakening. If . . . *If* you can get her to give me back what I've lost."

Rogala shifted tack. "No one can turn back the sands."

"I want my dead. You want your dreamer. Help me and I'll help you. Could it be simpler?"

Rogala continued facing him from a fighting crouch, his head turning slowly back and forth as he listened for movement. He waited. And waited. Finally, "All right." He sheathed his dagger. "Unless she changes my mind."

Gathrid laughed nervously. "Let's go get supper." He approached the dwarf carefully, rested a gentle hand on the man's shoulder. "Partner."

Halfway down the hill, Rogala said, "You ever hear the tale of Lundt Kharmine?"

"No."

"It's old. Probably lost now. Lundt Kharmine went down into Hell to rescue his lost love."

"Sounds like the story of Whylas Rus. So?"

"You may wish you'd killed me after all."

"Theis, I've been to Hell already. Nothing terrifies me anymore."

The distant campfires all flared at once. For a moment they illuminated Rogala's face. He wore his wicked, knowing smile.

Gathrid shuddered, forced it out of mind.

THE BEST IN FANTASY

☐ 53954-0 SPIRAL OF FIRE by Deborah Turner Harris $3.95
53955-9 Canada $4.95

☐ 53401-8 NEMESIS by Louise Cooper (U.S. only) $3.95

☐ 53382-8 SHADOW GAMES by Glen Cook $3.95
53381-X Canada $4.95

☐ 53815-5 CASTING FORTUNE by John M. Ford $3.95
53826-1 Canada $4.95

☐ 53351-8 HART'S HOPE by Orson Scott Card $3.95
53352-6 Canada $4.95

☐ 53397-6 MIRAGE by Louise Cooper (U.S. only) $3.95

☐ 53671-1 THE DOOR INTO FIRE by Diane Duane $2.95
53672-X Canada $3.50

☐ 54902-3 A GATHERING OF GARGOYLES by Meredith Ann Pierce $2.95
54903-1 Canada $3.50

☐ 55614-3 JINIAN STAR-EYE by Sheri S. Tepper $2.95
55615-1 Canada $3.75

Buy them at your local bookstore or use this handy coupon:
Clip and mail this page with your order.

Publishers Book and Audio Mailing Service
P.O. Box 120159, Staten Island, NY 10312-0004

Please send me the book(s) I have checked above. I am enclosing $_____
(please add $1.25 for the first book, and $.25 for each additional book to
cover postage and handling. Send check or money order only—no CODs.)

Name _____

Address _____

City _____ State/Zip _____

Please allow six weeks for delivery. Prices subject to change without notice.

GLEN COOK

☐ 53379-9 AN ILL FATE MARSHALLING
$3.50
Canada $4.50

☐ 53376-3 REAP THE EAST WIND
$2.95
Canada $3.95

☐ 50307-4 THE SWORDBEARER
$3.95
Canada $4.95

☐ 50389-9 THE BLACK COMPANY
$3.95
Canada $4.95

☐ 50842-4 SHADOWS LINGER
$3.95
Canada $4.95

☐ 50844-0 THE WHITE ROSE
$3.95
Canada $4.95

☐ 53382-8 SHADOW GAMES
$3.95
Canada $4.95

☐ 50220-5 THE SILVER SPIKE
$3.95
Canada $4.95

☐ 50210-8 DREAMS OF STEEL
$3.95
Canada $4.95

THE BEST IN SCIENCE FICTION